"What is going on?"
Danna asked the little girl.

"Sorry, Marshal," the girl responded. Marshal? A sick feeling began to steal over Chas.

"My brothers *stole* my dolly and I thought—" her lips quivered as she looked up at Danna "—I thought you might put them in jail. Or help me get her back."

Chas looked at her, too. Looked at the woman he'd spent the past twelve or so hours with. Really looked at her.

And was astonished he hadn't seen it before. The gun belt slung low on her shapely hips. The trousers and man's shirt. The flash of sunlight from a *badge* pinned to her shoulder, just visible inside the lapel of her jacket.

She was the marshal?

He glared at him and he realized he must've spoken out loud.

"Why don't you see if..." Danna advised th...

He watched her, wea...
...ouldn't decipher...

He couldn't conta... ...ally ...onger. "You're a m...

LACY WILLIAMS

is a wife and mom from Oklahoma. Her first novel won ACFW's Genesis award while it was still unpublished. She has loved romance books and movies from a young age and promises readers *happy endings guaranteed* in all her stories. Lacy combines her love of dogs with her passion for literacy by volunteering with her therapy dog, Mr. Bingley, in a local Kids Reading to Dogs program.

Lacy loves to hear from readers. You can email her at lacyjwilliams@gmail.com. She also posts short stories and does giveaways at her website, www.lacywilliams.net, and you can follow her on social media at www.facebook.com/lacywilliamsbooks or twitter.com/lacy_williams.

LACY WILLIAMS

Marrying Miss Marshal

Love Inspired

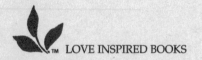

™ LOVE INSPIRED BOOKS

ISBN-13: 978-0-373-82881-4

MARRYING MISS MARSHAL

www.LoveInspiredBooks.com

Printed in U.S.A.

Many are the plans in a person's heart,
but it is the Lord's purpose that prevails.
—*Proverbs* 19:21

This book is dedicated to Luke and Laney
for their endless patience. Love you two.

Acknowledgments

To the God who gave me everything needed to
make this book a reality—all praise.

To those who have pushed me:
my beloved Luke, Denice Stewart,
Margaret Daley, Vickie McDonough—
thanks for not giving up on me.

To those who have encouraged me:
Mom and Dad, Haley, Sean & Megan
(and all my family), Janet Barton,
Linda Goodnight, Darlene Franklin & the rest of
OCFW and WIN—thanks for believing in me.

To those who have made this book better through
critique, brainstorming and more: Megan Yager,
Mary Brookman, Haley Yager, Denice Stewart,
Mischelle Creager—thank you for pushing me
to make this a better story.

To my agent, Sandra Bishop,
and my editor, Emily Rodmell:
thank you for taking a chance on a new writer.

Chapter One

Wyoming Territory, September 1889

The report of a rifle echoed through the red-walled canyon, ringing in Marshal Danna Carpenter's chest. A second report sounded close after the first.

She reined in her mount and pushed back her Stetson, instantly alert and scanning the area for trouble.

The shots could've been someone hunting game— although there wasn't much of it to be found in these washed-out ravines southwest of town—or it could've been someone discharging their weapon for a more nefarious purpose. As town marshal, she had to be prepared for both possibilities.

Danna's horse shifted beneath her, its movements telling her it sensed something wrong, as well. But what?

Then she saw him, in the last rays of sunlight slipping over the canyon's edge. A man staggering along the canyon floor, booted feet dragging in the sandy soil. He carried some kind of luggage over his shoulder. From this distance, she couldn't see a rifle....

Too far away to determine his identity, Danna guessed she didn't know him. His clothes were too fine for these parts—dark pants, vest, jacket and a bright white shirt. Most folks around here wore woolen trousers or denims, and plain cotton shirts.

What was he doing so far from town? And on foot? Any halfway-intelligent person knew you didn't traipse around the unforgiving Wyoming landscape without a horse, or a mule at the very least.

Before she could decide whether to waste the last of the sunlight to check on the stranger, or to head out of the canyon toward home, her horse's ears flicked back and his shoulder quivered beneath her gloved hand. The ground trembled.

From around a natural bend in the canyon, a cloud of dust rose like steam from a kettle and sent fear skittering down Danna's spine.

And the terrible sound she was hearing began to make sense: hundreds of pounding hooves, getting closer every second.

Stampede.

She couldn't leave an injured man to be trampled to death. Danna kicked King's flank and gave a shouted "Hiyah!" The horse rocketed toward the figure still too far away.

Peripherally aware of the canyon walls racing by, Danna watched the greenhorn pause and looked up toward the sky. What was he doing?

A few hundred yards behind him, cattle began to round a bend in the canyon. The beasts bellowed, and that must've jarred the tenderfoot from his stupor, for he turned and faced the approaching wall of horns and hooves.

He froze, the item he carried sliding to the ground.

Words rose in Danna's throat but she had no breath to call out, not when all her concentration centered on reaching him in time. He wouldn't be able to hear anyway.

As the cattle closed in, the man's sense of self-preservation seemed to kick in, for he turned to flee, caught sight of Danna and began to run in her direction.

Danna fisted her mount's mane with both hands, leaning forward until her torso rested against his foam-flecked neck as she pushed the animal even faster.

The man looked up and, for a moment, time seemed to suspend itself. His eyes—a bright, clear blue—met Danna's, and she saw his fear and surprise.

A solid wall of cattle closed in behind the man. Too close.

Clinging to the saddle horn with her right hand, gripping with her knees, she caught hold of the tenderfoot under one arm, and used her horse's forward momentum to sweep him up behind her.

"Hold on!" she cried.

The man's arm slung tight around her waist, Danna pulled the horse into a tight turn and fought to keep the stallion from unseating them both. She knew the fear of death in that moment, her twenty-four years playing out before her eyes, so many mistakes made…mistakes she desperately wanted a chance to rectify.

They weren't going to make it.

A squeeze of Danna's legs sent the horse into a smooth canter, but it was too late. Several cattle overtook them, one bumping the horse's flank. The animal stumbled, but somehow managed to keep its feet.

Fear stealing her breath, gasping, Danna clung to the

horse's neck as it sped forward, quickly outrunning the cattle and their thundering hooves.

Thank God.

What had the fool man been thinking?

"Do you have a death wish?" the woman—woman!—who'd saved Chas O'Grady's hide shouted over her shoulder. He barely heard the words over the din of the cattle still surging around them.

Her glossy black braid flopped over one shoulder and thwapped him in the chin. "Didn't you hear the stampede?"

Chas sucked in breath after breath of wonderful, fresh air before he could force any words—like *I thought the racket was distant thunder*—out of his frozen jaw. "You're a woman!"

His arms still around her, he felt her stiffen infinitesimally. But the pounding adrenaline and building anger in his system kept his words flowing. "Are you entirely out of your head? You could have been killed riding straight into a stampede!"

"Perhaps you'd rather I *hadn't* rescued you? Because you *would've* been killed—trampled—if I hadn't scooped you up out of there." He felt her inhale deeply, then she blasted him again. "And I certainly didn't see any *men* around to do the job *properly*."

The woman's fiery retort stymied him for the moment, because it was true. There hadn't been anyone else in the canyon, and he would never have been able to outrun the cattle.

The thought of what she'd risked—her life—brought bitter memories to the surface. Chas blinked away the images of another woman falling, her blood spilling.

This woman, whose name he didn't even know, wasn't dead. Even though she'd put herself in danger for him.

Memories and self-loathing churned in his gut until his rescuer turned her horse up the canyon wall, nearly unseating him with the sudden movement. Chas clung to the woman's waist, eliciting a huff from her.

Her faded denims and wide-brimmed hat had caused him to assume she was a man from a distance, but with his arms wrapped around the curve of her waist, there was no mistaking his rescuer was pure female.

He couldn't get a good look at her features from behind her, but she must be nearly as tall as his six-foot stature; the brim of her hat rested only inches in front of his nose. Several dark strands of hair escaped from her braid and curled along the nape of her long, slender neck. Her head was in constant motion, darting left to right, and it gave Chas fleeting glimpses of her cheekbones, the soft bow of her lips, the dark sweep of her lashes. She was beautiful. And she guided the horse as if she and the animal were one.

In any other circumstance, she would have turned his head, trousers notwithstanding.

Instead, with his detective's nose for curiosity already piqued, his mind swirled with questions. Why was she riding alone in this rough part of the country? And dressed as a man? Could she possibly work for one of the ranching outfits in the area? What rancher or foreman would hire a *woman* to work on their range?

"What are you doing out here alone, anyway?" he demanded, trying to force back his darker emotions. "It's dangerous."

"I could ask you the same," she returned sharply. "You're obviously from a big city, and this isn't a populated area. These arroyos are subject to occasional flooding. You're on foot. What happened to your horse? Have you gone astray from your destination?"

Her questions implied he couldn't take care of himself, and they sparked his irritation.

"I'm not lost." That statement was a bit of an untruth, but Chas wasn't about to admit that his sense of direction had been compromised by the winding canyon. He'd been operating as a private detective for several years. Being a little out of place was not the worst situation he'd ever managed to escape from. He would've found shelter eventually, if this female cowpoke hadn't come along. Probably.

"And if you must know, I *had* a horse. I bought her in Cheyenne, but…well, let's say the man who sold her to me may have exaggerated her condition."

He thought he heard a small noise of amusement from his unusual companion, but he couldn't be sure. His curiosity got the better of him and he couldn't resist asking, "Tell me, do all women in the Wyoming Territory dress the way you do? Or are you attempting to pass yourself off as a young man?"

"No" came the sharp retort.

"No to which question?"

She didn't answer, but he felt her draw back on the reins, and the horse slowed.

"Are we stopping?" he asked. "Why?" They hadn't even attained the canyon's rim yet. He'd hoped to make it to the small town of Calvin before evening set in.

"It's getting hard to see." The woman's voice was soft and melodic, but her words were clipped and terse. "I won't risk my horse or our lives trying to climb this shale in the dark."

Chas glanced at the purpling sky, realizing how long the shadows had gotten along the canyon walls. He was no outdoorsman, but even he could tell it would be full dark in minutes.

"We can't just stop, can we?" Chas brought to mind the hotel room he'd hoped to find tonight. With a bed. A chance to wash away the trail grime he'd accumulated since leaving Cheyenne.

"It looks like there's a level patch up ahead." She nodded, though he couldn't see what she was talking about. It all looked the same to him—an uphill climb. "We'll stop until the moon comes up."

"Are you sure it wouldn't be better to keep going?" Chas persisted, not ready to give up on the idea of that bed.

She ignored him.

As the last of the sunlight faded into pitch-black, the woman pulled up her horse on a somewhat flat piece of land.

If they were going to spend the next few hours trapped together in the dark, perhaps he should apologize to his companion. Certainly, it wasn't her fault her actions had touched on a sensitive memory he spent most of his time trying to suppress.

Best get it out of the way quickly. "Miss, I'm sorry—"

She interrupted him by pulling out of his loose grasp and sliding off the horse's back.

A bit miffed at her dismissal, he followed—and misjudged her closeness, thanks to the darkness. His momentum nearly knocked both of them to the ground, but he steadied her with hands on her forearms.

Her breath fanned his chin, her warmth tangible as the night cooled around them. Chas's heart thundered in his chest, much like those hooves that had been so close to taking his life. This time for a different reason.

"Miss, I meant no offense by my earlier words. I was..." He paused, looking for the right thing to say, knowing he couldn't tell her about Julia's death. "I was simply expressing my surprise to find my rescuer a woman."

She pulled away, but he still sensed her nearness. Her movements in the dark—getting something from the saddle?—seemed jerky and stiff. It was clear she'd rejected his apology.

He went on. "I *am* grateful for your fancy riding. I'd rather not meet my Maker today, and I've no doubt those beasts would've stomped all over me if not for you."

"I would've done it for anyone."

Her voice sounded muffled, and he wished for a candle or a beam of moonlight, so he might see her face.

"Stay here."

She disappeared into the darkness. Only the muted sounds of boots scraping against stone told him she was still nearby.

Stay here. He mimicked her curt words silently. What did she think? He would wander off in the dark and get lost? She'd already made it clear what she thought of his abilities traversing this very canyon. Agitation and impatience made him restless, and he paced away from her horse.

And stepped right off the edge into nothing.

Danna heard an indistinct shout, the scrabble of falling rocks, and then silence.

"Hello?" she called, not bothering to disguise her annoyance.

She kept after the small stand of bushes she'd spotted

as darkness fell. If she had to wait until the moon came up, she wanted to be able to see the man she was stuck with. She tried again. "Mister?"

He'd flustered her with his nearness after he'd landed on top of her while attempting to dismount the horse. She hadn't been so close to a man since her husband's death. And even during their brief courtship and the early days of their marriage, Fred Carpenter hadn't caused turmoil in her gut like the warmth from this man's hands did. What was wrong with her? Fred had only been gone a few months! And she didn't even know the stranger's name.

Irritated with herself, she spoke once more. "Tenderfoot?"

No answer.

Her extended boot met some resistance and she knelt to gather the dry undergrowth from the bushes. Using the flint and steel she'd retrieved from her saddlebags, she had a small fire burning quickly. She turned toward her horse, standing right where she'd left it, but the man was nowhere to be seen. She resisted the urge to groan.

Making sure the fire had enough fuel to burn for a few minutes unattended, she returned to where she'd left the tenderfoot just moments before.

Past her placid mount, the rocks on the edge of the slope had been disturbed. She frowned and walked over, noting this area had a bit of a dropoff, instead of a gentle slope. It was hard to see in the dark, away from the fire, but by leaning out over the edge and squinting into the darkness, Danna was able to catch sight of the tenderfoot several yards away. He lay still, with one shoulder cocked in an awkward position.

"Oh, no," she breathed. Louder, she called out to him, "Mister, can you hear me?"

A soft moan erupted from his lips, but he didn't move, other than to roll his head toward her.

Forcing calm she didn't feel, Danna retrieved her rope from its tie behind the saddle and looped it around the saddle horn before tossing the length to where her unlikely companion lay.

"Mister? Can you reach the rope?"

She didn't expect a reply, so she wasn't too surprised when none came. Keeping one hand on the rope, she scrambled down the steep incline as best she could. She slipped twice, and rocks bit into her palms as she fought to keep from joining the tenderfoot in a tumble. She wouldn't do him any good if she injured herself, too.

When she reached him, Danna knelt at his head and studied the man.

His hat had slipped to one side, and his sweat-matted hair was dark next to his fair skin. "Mister, you've sure got a way of getting into some pretty good scrapes," she muttered. She probed his scalp and neck gently with her fingertips, searching for injury. Though obscured by a few days' growth stubble, he had a strong jawline.

He gasped when her palm brushed his right shoulder. Keeping her touch as light as she could, Danna ran her fingers over the arm and shoulder, and he moaned again. "Hurts."

"I know. Looks like you've knocked it out of place." She prodded his torso and legs, but found no additional trauma. She did find a gun belt and weapon at his hip, but ignored it for now. "I can reset it for you. But we need to get you up the hill so I can see what I'm doing."

"I'll try," he said, and clenched his teeth as he rolled onto his good side.

She helped him to his hands and knees, but he shook

his head and collapsed onto the rocky soil. "I can't..." he wheezed "...make it."

"All right." She smoothed a hand over his forehead, as if she was comforting her almost-niece, Ellie. "Tell me your name."

"Chas." A breath. "O'Grady."

She filed the name away. O'Grady sounded Irish. She nodded absently and murmured, "I'm Danna Carpenter," as she considered the best way to get his shoulder back into the socket. "What brings you to Wyoming?"

"Job."

"Not cattle."

One corner of his mouth quirked upward. "How'd you know?"

"Lawyer?"

He snorted a laugh, then grimaced as if the movement pained him.

"Railroad surveyor?" she guessed, and gave a mighty tug.

O'Grady's upper arm and the shoulder slid into place with an audible click. She was impressed when he didn't cry out, just rolled his head and *looked* at her with those blue eyes.

"Thanks. You're a doll."

Then he passed out.

Danna sat next to his unconscious form in the darkness, willing away the blush that had flamed across her cheeks at his words. Stunned.

Something had happened inside her when he'd looked at her, when she'd heard the endearment he'd spoken.

Something inside her opened, like a flower unfurling. Attraction? Whatever it was, it was decidedly uncomfortable.

Chapter Two

Chas sat quietly near the small fire his rescuer had built. With nightfall a chill had fallen, and he was thankful for the warmth the crackling fire generated.

"How's your pain?" His companion asked as she propped herself against a medium-size boulder and removed her hat, loosing a spill of dark hair that had come out of its braid. She stretched her trouser-clad legs out in front of her, eyes on her boots, though her question had sounded curious. Was that a blush on her cheeks? It was hard to tell in the dim, flickering light from the fire.

He rotated the shoulder, wincing a little. "Bearable. Better than before, thanks to you." He didn't want to think about what would have happened to him if he'd been left on his own in a haze of pain, shoulder dislocated.

He was grateful to Danna for her part in saving his hide—twice—but embarrassment was the primary emotion that registered.

He'd never had this much trouble with a case before, and he hadn't even made it to the town where he was supposed to scare up a group of cattle rustlers. It didn't matter that his cases usually took him to large cities like Chicago, St. Louis, or Austin; he'd been a private detective long enough that he shouldn't have required help.

And, his shoulder still ached, though not with the piercing pain he'd felt before she'd knocked it back into its socket. The pain was enough that he sat back while Danna Carpenter had spent several minutes scouting for more firewood. His mother would have had a conniption if she'd seen him allowing a lady to perform such a task without offering to do it himself. His mother had subjected him to extensive training during his youth, preparing him for a life as the second son of one of Boston's prominent Irish families. A life he would never live, not after the disaster he'd made of his life.

"Do you live near here?" he asked, because he needed to keep his thoughts away from Boston and everything he'd lost.

"In town."

"Really? Hmm. How far?"

She grinned softly at his question. "Calvin is a few miles still. North, if you were wondering."

Her smile did funny things to his insides, left him feeling like he'd fallen off the edge of the cliff a second time.

"What's your business in Calvin? Are you visiting family?" she asked after a moment of quiet not long enough for Chas to gain his composure.

"You're a nosy one, aren't ya?" His irritation with himself made the words sharper than they might normally be.

Her eyebrows pinched and she looked away from

him, one side of her face falling into shadow. "Comes with the territory."

What did she mean?

Chas didn't have time to consider the meaning behind her cryptic words, for she looked back at him with unabashed curiosity, obviously waiting for his answer.

He used the general answer he'd prepared. "No, I don't have family here. I'm a businessman."

Her eyebrows pinched briefly before her face cleared. "What were you carrying with you? It looked like luggage."

He groaned. "A pair of saddlebags." With his letter of introduction for the local lawman inside. Passing his good hand over his face, he huffed a breath. "I don't suppose there's any way we could go back for them..."

Then another thought occurred. "Do you think they could have survived being trampled?" How much more misfortune could befall him?

"I don't know if they'll still be intact. But to be honest, I wasn't too keen on climbing this hill in the dark." She motioned behind her. "Even after the moon comes up. We can wait until morning and try to find them."

"Thank you."

She got up and went to her horse, untied something from behind the saddle and tossed it to him. A dugan— a bedroll, he'd heard them called.

"Sure you don't need this?" he asked as she pulled another object off the horse.

"I'm sure." She shook out a slicker, a large one that could have belonged to a man, or at least someone taller and broader than Danna. It made Chas wonder if *she* belonged to someone else. Was she married?

Returning to her seat against the taller rock, she swung the coat around her shoulders and tucked it underneath her chin. Her dark eyes met his and he felt a spark sizzle between them before she looked away into the fire.

What was this? He'd never felt this…connection with anyone else, not even with—

He spoke quickly to keep the thought from its finish. "Will your husband be out looking for you? I'd hate to fall asleep and wake with a gun in my back."

Something flickered across her face, and the smile lingering at the corners of her lips disappeared. "No."

"A father? Brother? Uncle?"

Now her mouth flattened into a grim line. She tossed the twig she'd been playing with into the fire and dusted her hands together. "No. No husband, no father. Not anymore."

Her words hinted she might've been married at one point, but her clenched jaw and closed expression told him it would be best not to continue that line of inquiry.

Suddenly, she straightened her shoulders and met his gaze head-on. "Where are you from? Back East?"

"My accent?" he asked with a rueful smile.

She nodded. "You're Irish?"

Intrigued, he leaned forward, resting his elbow on his bent knee. "How did you know?"

"A good guess." She shrugged, and he followed the motion of her hands as she folded them over one knee. "And I believe your hair is red, as well, although I didn't get a good look because it was dark."

"It is."

Another silence fell, this one charged with tension, almost palatable. Chas watched her fidget. Now she fiddled with one of the cuffs of her shirt.

He wanted to keep talking to her, wanted to know why she dressed as she did, why she was alone out here.

But he also wanted to protect himself from this tenuous tie they seemed to share. He who always pried for every piece of information from any person he came into contact with—knowing that every detail helped him do his job better—feigned a yawn and rolled himself in the dugan she'd tossed to him earlier.

"Thank you again, and good night."

"Mister."

The sound of gunshots rang in his ears, blood covered his hands. Pain speared his right shoulder. Had he been hit?

"Tenderfoot."

A boot nudged his ankle and drew Chas out of the nightmare. Memory.

He blinked, trying to dispel the images of the woman he'd loved dying under his hands. He rolled off his injured shoulder—that's what caused the throbbing pain—and shook his head to clear it, taking in his surroundings.

Muted gray light threw Danna Carpenter into silhouette as she knelt over the embers of what had been their fire last night. The sight of her calmly going about her business quieted the raging maelstrom of emotion and memories bombarding him.

At least she had her back turned so he could shake off the trembles his nightmare always left behind.

He couldn't help groaning as he pushed himself to his elbow. It took Danna's help to get him sitting upright on the hard, cold earth, the dugan still covering his legs.

"Here, this should help with the stiffness in your shoulder."

Before he realized what she was doing, she'd opened his coat and unbuttoned the first two buttons on his shirt, exposing his injured shoulder. She hesitated— must've seen his gunshot scar—but then a welcome heat began seeping through his skin. She'd warmed a folded square of wet cloth to make a compress.

Her eyes met and held his as she pressed the hot bundle against his abused muscles. He couldn't decipher her expression in the semidarkness, but a connection sparked between them. She was too close.

As if she'd had the same thought, she backed away. He looked down to hide his confusion and immediately noticed his rumpled state. He was a mess. Needed a bath and a shave, and his clothes were covered in dust.

"Coffee." She pressed a tin into his hands and retreated again. "I'm not much of a cook. I think I scorched it."

A sip of the black sludge confirmed her words. He swallowed when what he wanted to do was spit it out. It *did* warm his insides.

"Thank you," he said, voice rusty.

"Thought your pain might be bad after a night out in the cold. You were moaning in your sleep."

His back teeth clenched. He often thrashed around because of the nightmare, but he wasn't about to admit to it—she'd probably ask questions, and he couldn't afford the answers. Not when the answer was that he'd been responsible for the deaths of the two people he'd loved most in the world.

"Thanks," he muttered again, forcing himself out of the bedroll and into the bracing morning air. Taking a moment to stretch the kinks out, Chas absently rubbed a particularly twinge-worthy knot in his lower back while he watched his unusual companion as she used her boot to kick dirt over the graying embers of the campfire.

She looked up at him, this time with her hat pulled low over her brow. He couldn't read her eyes.

"If we find your things quickly, we can make it back to Calvin by breakfast."

His rumbling stomach thought that that was a good idea.

"Your shoulder might act up a bit when we're jostling around on the horse's back, so you'll just have to tell me if you need to stop for a while."

He was ready to have some distance from this confusing woman and the draw he felt toward her.

"I'm sure I'll be fine. Let's go."

Nearly two hours after the tenderfoot's declaration, Danna wasn't so sure his wounded arm was holding up.

She'd kept her mount to a plodding pace—both she and the animal wanted to *move*—but felt Chas O'Grady's body grow progressively stiffer as the morning wore on. She imagined his pain must be getting worse, but he'd yet to say anything.

The morning sun finally peeked over the canyon's rim, but finding anything in the torn-up ground left by the stampeding cattle was proving impossible.

The tenderfoot shifted in the saddle, a soft gasp making her turn her head for a glimpse of his face. A muscle ticked in his jaw. With her late husband, that had been a sure sign he was either mad or hurt.

"You want to stop for a while?" she asked.

"No. I'm sure you need to get home." She did, but she kept quiet. "But my saddlebags had some important documents in them. If they somehow survived, I'll need them."

"Fine."

She knew he was hurting, but if the man wouldn't admit it, what could she do?

Danna kept her eyes on the chewed-up ground. Just looking at how the sandy canyon floor had been marked by the thousands of hooves, she was starting to doubt there would be anything left to find. However, she understood his need to keep looking. She knew what it was like to lose something important and never get it back.

And what were those cattle doing in the canyon anyway? She'd mulled it over all night, awake in the dark, while she'd tried to keep her gaze and her thoughts from straying to the man who'd slept just across the campfire.

She'd spent far too long staring at his broad shoulders—the only thing she could see, as the rest of him had been wrapped in the blanket—trying to pinpoint what it was about him that unsettled her.

For now, she chose to ignore that unruly flash of emotion last night. She simply couldn't be drawn to the near stranger. He made her uncomfortable. That was all.

It wasn't the same feeling she got when in danger. That was a prickling at the back of her neck, beneath her hairline. No, this was more of an intensity. She'd been aware of his every movement, even after his breathing had settled, signifying he'd dozed off.

She almost thought those prickles of sensation were…attraction. But that couldn't be right. She'd never felt anything like this with Fred. Maybe she had been too young when she married Fred, or maybe she had felt something similar at the beginning of their acquaintance and she'd forgotten. She'd been married to Fred for eight years, after all...

The tenderfoot groaned, stifled it and shifted again. "Maybe I should walk for a while. I might have a better chance at spotting my saddlebags that way."

She doubted it, but guessed he must be hurting something fierce by now, so she shrugged and reined in her mount. She'd have a better view from her horse's back, but if he wanted to walk, he could walk. The tenderfoot huffed softly when his shiny boots hit the ground.

"You sure you don't want to stop for a while?"

His only answer was a silent frown. The tenderfoot wore the same closed expression that Fred had worn when she'd asked too many questions. Fine. She wouldn't ask about his arm again, even if it fell off.

She forced her thoughts back to the cattle and what they were doing in this canyon last night. The roundups and cattle drives should have already been completed in this area. The ground above the canyon was dry, not terribly good for grazing. So what were that many animals doing here?

It was a mystery.

"Did you happen to see any brands on those cattle last night?"

"What?" The tenderfoot glanced up at her, focusing those intense blue eyes on her momentarily. "Oh. No, I didn't get a good look at any of their markings. Why? Did you recognize them?"

"No." Danna scanned the landscape, aware that his eyes remained on her, uncomfortable with his scrutiny.

"Why do you want to know?"

"It's a bit unusual for the cattle to be in this area this

late in the year," she said. And she thought she'd heard gunshots immediately before the cattle had stampeded. But in the confusion she couldn't be sure. "Usually, they've been driven to Cheyenne for market. The vegetation starts to get scarce."

"Hmm."

He didn't sound terribly interested, but she supposed he wouldn't be. She guessed he was a professional cardsharp, a gambler. He'd told her last night he was a businessman. Only, who would come to the tiny town of Calvin, Wyoming, to do business? And his fancy city clothes would make him out of place, as well. It was a good thing she wasn't interested in him. A gambler.

Her thoughts distracting her, she almost missed the mangled piece of leather half-buried under the sandy dirt.

"I think this is it," she called out, and he joined her as she dismounted from her horse. He picked up the leather bags, juggling a pouch and canteen when they fell out of the hole torn in one side.

"I can't believe it. The saddlebags are ripped, but everything else appears to be intact." There was wonder in his voice as he riffled through his belongings.

He took an item out—an envelope?—and tucked it into his breast pocket beneath his vest. A second item quickly followed the first. Danna couldn't see what it was, something wrapped in leather and tied with a thong.

Were these two things important? If so, why hadn't he kept them closer in the first place?

"God must be watching out for you, Mr. O'Grady."

The instant Danna spoke the words, his expression closed. "I sincerely doubt God has spared any thoughts for me lately."

* * *

Chas tried to ignore the pain that throbbed up his arm and through his shoulder with each movement the horse made, but it proved impossible, even when he closed his eyes against it. He knew his companion tried to make the ride as smooth as possible—she held her horse to a walk, traversed more ground to go around the gullies—but nothing helped.

He just wanted to get to town and soak his aching joints in a tub of hot water. And find something to stop the growling in his stomach.

They hadn't spoken since he'd gotten back on Danna Carpenter's horse. Her comment about God's favor had thrown up a wall between them, and he found he was glad for the distance. The sense of connection he'd felt with Danna since their chance meeting had him feeling distinctly off-kilter.

After the horror of Julia's death, and his part in it, he'd vowed not to allow another woman close. Not ever. Six years had gone by, and his vow hadn't been difficult to keep. He hadn't met any woman that had compared to Julia.

Until now.

And Danna Carpenter couldn't be more different from his first love. She was tall and slender, where Julia had been of average height and curved in all the pleasant places. Julia had been femininity personified, always dressed immaculately, with lace or jewels accenting her best physical attributes. Danna Carpenter dressed like a man and didn't seem to care about her appearance at all. Not that she had to, with her expressive brown eyes and that crown of long, black hair.

Julia had used her feminine wiles to manipulate him.

And it had cost her life, because he hadn't been able to resist.

Chas shook himself from his thoughts, noticing that the horse seemed to move faster now, although Danna held it in check. Chas locked his eyes on the horizon, hoping they were getting close to Calvin. A small speck appeared, then another and another, and finally they got close enough that he could make out the individual buildings.

His heart sank. The town was even smaller than he had imagined. It might pose a challenge to get the information he needed to make his case and find the rustlers; he wasn't likely to blend in.

Miss Carpenter's horse crossed one dusty street, passed the railroad tracks and turned onto the second. He supposed this must be the main thoroughfare.

Perhaps the town did have some charm, though none of the buildings matched. Half were brick, roughly half were wooden. Most of them were unpainted, as if they'd been constructed hastily and occupied quickly. Likely they had.

He could see several houses on the street behind the buildings, one larger than all the rest. A mansion, in this small town?

Danna reined in her horse in front of the second-to-last building on the street, the most unique one. Its first level was rock, but the second looked as if it had been added on later, and was wood.

A dog bayed from inside, but that couldn't be right, could it? Perhaps it was a child playing.

Danna started speaking. "The livery is at the end of the street. I've got to go in and check—"

"Help! Marshal!" A high-pitched, female voice cried out.

Someone needed help.

Chas jumped from Danna's horse, jarring one ankle and his injured shoulder when he landed. The horse shied at the unexpected movement.

"O'Grady!" Danna exclaimed, but he didn't have time to stand around and help her, and she was a good horsewoman anyway.

Chas darted across the street.

His heart thudding in his ears made it hard to determine which direction the cry had come from, but he thought maybe from the left, so that's the direction he turned. He stalled at the first corner where the boardwalk ended for an alleyway between buildings. Which way?

"Help!" the voice warbled now, sounding a bit muffled.

"O'Grady!" Danna clapped a hand on his forearm, her expression fierce under the brim of her hat. "Don't ever do a fool thing like that again. My horse could've—"

"I have to—" *Help the woman in jeopardy.*

He didn't get a chance to finish his sentence because the voice called out again. "Marshal!"

Danna stuck two fingers in her mouth and issued an ear-splitting whistle. Instantly, the shouting stopped.

While Chas gaped at Danna, a small nut-brown head popped up from behind a pile of crates on the boardwalk in front of the nearest building, a saloon.

"Missy McCabe, come here," Danna ordered.

The head turned into a pair of shoulders, and a little girl emerged from behind the stack of crates. She came to stand in front of Danna with her head down.

Chas calmed the chaos in his head, now that it became apparent that there wasn't a true emergency.

"What is going on?" Danna asked, her voice sharp.

"Sorry, Marshal." The girl responded. Her shoulders slumped even more.

Marshal? A sick feeling began to steal over Chas.

"My brothers *stole* my dolly and I thought—" her lips quivered "—I thought you might put them in jail. Or help me get her back."

Danna knelt to the girl's level, gentling her voice. "Missy, you know I'm busy dealing with important marshal business. I don't have time to chase down your doll."

Chas looked at the woman he'd spent the last twelve or so hours with. Really looked at her.

And was astonished he hadn't seen it before. The gun belt slung low on her shapely hips. The trousers and man's shirt. The flash of sunlight from a *badge* pinned to her shoulder, just visible inside the lapel of her jacket.

She was a marshal?

She glanced at him and he realized he must've spoken out loud.

"Why don't you see if your ma can help you?" Danna advised the girl.

"She won't," the girl mumbled to her bare feet. "They ain't gonna listen to her."

"Perhaps your brothers will tire of playing and bring your doll to you after a while."

The little girl sniffled, eyes pleading with Danna.

Danna sighed. Pulled a penny out of her pocket. "Why don't you buy some candy?"

The girl's eyes lit up.

"And no more screaming around town, all right? Mr. O'Grady thought you were really in trouble."

The girl ran off. Danna watched her, wearing an expression he couldn't decipher. Maybe longing?

He couldn't contain the words inside him any longer. "You're a *marshal?*"

Chapter Three

Danna heard the disapproval in O'Grady's voice. After a night without sleep, plus the other troubles she'd been dealing with, her temper flared.

She hiked up her chin, pinned him with the same stare she'd used on what seemed like every male in town. "I haven't been hiding my badge."

His eyes flicked to the tin star at her collarbone, then away. "You didn't introduce yourself as a lawman."

She hated feeling defensive. Shouldn't have to feel that way. Tried to keep her voice calm. "If you recall the circumstances surrounding our introductions, it didn't come up. Good day, Mr. O'Grady."

Without a look back after her abrupt dismissal, Danna strode to the combined jail and marshal's office and unlatched the door. A large blur of fur and teeth—Fred's dog—nearly knocked her onto her backside and took off down the street, howling at the top of his lungs. She didn't bother to go after the dog, not as exhausted as she currently was. He would come back when he got hungry. Unfortunately.

Dismay filled her as she stared at the chaos inside.

Papers—Wanted posters—were strewn across the floor, some with muddy pawprints obscuring the writing on them. The desk chair had been knocked over. The desk itself appeared not to have suffered, and that was all Danna cared about. She hung her hat on a peg next to the door and slid her arms out of the sleeves of her coat.

The sound of firm bootsteps on the boardwalk just outside her door alerted her that Chas O'Grady had followed her. "Did someone put an animal in here? A prank, perhaps?"

She bristled at his insinuation that someone would play such a prank on her, and that she couldn't handle it if they did. She crossed her arms over her middle. "It's my dog. Was there something I could help you with?" She had to work at keeping her tone businesslike. Fred had always said her temper would get her in trouble. Now, as the marshal, she couldn't afford to let it get the better of her.

O'Grady stared at a point on the floor for a long moment. So long that she wondered if he was going to say anything at all. Finally, he sighed and pulled something out of his shirt pocket. It was an envelope, the one he'd put there earlier when they'd located his saddlebags. He handed it to her, then waited as if he expected her to open it.

So she did, only to find a letter inside. Her mind spun, trying to figure a way out of this situation gracefully. After his earlier disdain at her profession, she had no intention of revealing to him that she couldn't read the letter.

Fortunately, he seemed not to notice her hesitation, but spoke quickly and quietly. "I'm a private detective hired by the Wyoming Stock Growers Association to look out for the interests of cattlemen in this area."

Danna looked over the top of the letter that she couldn't read. O'Grady had half-turned and face the window to the street outside. Not much to see; the jail was one of the last buildings on the street. Most of the interesting happenings in town centered around Hyer's General Store or in the street in front of one of the three bars.

Not a gambler, then? "So you're a Pinkerton? I didn't think they took jobs this far west."

His eyes remained on the window. He didn't crack a smile. "I'm on contract with a different agency, but yes, similar to a Pinkerton. There have been reports of cattle rustling in these parts, and I've been sent to find the criminals behind it."

Now she raised her brows. "I haven't heard any reports of that kind of trouble." She thought back to the spring cattle drives, shaking her head to clear the pain of missing Fred as much as to stir her memories. "A few missing cattle earlier this year, but that could be explained by predators or natural causes. Wandering off. Nothing recent."

His eyes narrowed, but he still looked out the window. "My employers are concerned with more than a few missing cattle, Marshal. If there's something going on here, I'll find it. I'm very good at my job."

She didn't doubt it, but he seemed too citified for this type of work.

He turned, reaching out a palm. She slapped his letter into it, and he stuffed it back into the envelope without care that it was folded correctly.

"I've done my duty and notified the local law." She

easily read the derision when he spoke the word. "And I'll expect you to stay out of my way."

Danna worked at curbing the anger that formed a tight knot in her chest. What would Fred have done when faced with a nuisance like Chas O'Grady? Probably turned the other cheek.

"If there's anything I can do to help—"

Chas gestured to the mess covering the floor. "You appear to be plenty busy. I'm sure I can find my way around town. Good day."

With that, he strode out of the jail.

Danna slumped into the chair behind Fred's old desk. For a moment, when he'd first stated he was a detective, she had hoped that Chas O'Grady might be her ticket to winning the townspeople over. If they saw a man working with her, would they start to trust her to take care of the town? They'd been remarkably cool toward her since she'd been appointed to the position of marshal.

Frustration boiling, she curled her hands into fists on top of the desk. She'd proved herself those first two years Fred had let her be his deputy. They'd accepted her in that position—why was being marshal different?

And why did it hurt so much to find that Chas's reaction was the same as everyone else's? She didn't feel anything for him. Wouldn't.

Weariness swamped her; all she wanted to do was go upstairs to her small room above the jail and sleep. Instead, she rounded the desk and began picking up the loose papers strewn across the floor. What had once been a tall stack of Wanted posters had been spread across the entire floor.

She'd moved the mess to the top of her desk, but had

not started sorting yet, when a commotion outside had her rising from the desk chair.

"Marshal—"

"—that varmint—"

The door burst open and Wrong Tree—Fred's dog—ran in with tail lowered and droopy ears, followed by Will Chittim, the young livery stablehand, and Martha Stoll, one of the crankiest women in town. Wrong Tree scooted behind Danna and underneath Fred's desk, until just his tail was poking out.

"What's the trouble?"

The barber's wife pointed at Danna, face flushed and emotions running high. "Your dog. Your awful, no-good varmint of a dog, that's what the trouble is!" Her voice rose throughout the rant and she ended with a screech.

"Danna—Marshal—" Young Will's voice cracked when he rushed to speak. "I put the dog in your office last night to keep him from runnin' the streets, but someone must have let him out today...."

"I did." Danna didn't mention that he'd almost knocked her over on his way out of the building—she hadn't had a chance to catch him before he'd been gone.

Martha drew in a deep breath. "He was digging up my prize rose bushes. That's the third time this week! One of them was completely ruined. Ruined!"

"Mrs. Stoll—"

"Don't offer me any more of your empty platitudes, young lady."

Danna bristled, both at being spoken to as if she were a child and at the childish title. "Mrs. Stoll, I apologize—"

"I don't accept it!" the other woman said with a

stomp of her foot that would've suited little Missy McCabe more than it did the fortysomething woman. "I want that mongrel eliminated. If you won't do it, I'll make a complaint to the mayor. The dog is a menace to this town."

"I'll take care of it, Mrs. Stoll."

"You'd better." With those parting words, the woman stomped her way out the door, slamming it behind her.

Will ran a shaking hand down his face. "I'm sorry, Marshal. I saw the pup trot by, on up the boardwalk, but I was talkin' with a gent who wanted to rent a horse and I couldn't go fetch him. By the time I got away, he was in Mrs. Stoll's garden. You're not really going to—to hurt him, are you?"

"Of course not."

She didn't like the dog—they'd never gotten along in the eight years Danna and Fred had been married—but she couldn't do a thing like that, out of respect to her husband's memory.

"Not because of you," she told the dog when he stuck his head out from under the desk, looking up at her with false-innocent eyes.

"He hasn't been the same since Marshal Fred's been gone." Will obligingly knelt and scratched under the dog's chin when the mutt approached him.

"Mmm," Danna hummed, watching the two interact. None of them had been the same since Fred's death. The dog was the least of her worries right now. "I suppose I should try and find him a good home out in the country. With lots of space to roam."

"And a nice, big garden to dig up?" Will asked, attention still on the dog.

"We'll see."

* * *

Chas strode down the boardwalk, ignoring the curious glances of passersby. He probably should stop in to some of the stores and start making contact with the owners, but his thoughts were too chaotic and his shoulder ached miserably. Instead, he headed straight for the hotel.

What kind of town made a *woman* its marshal? It was a dangerous job. Dangerous for a man—how could a woman handle the dangers of the job?

All Chas could think about was Julia and how she'd died—his fault. He'd brought her into a location, a situation fit for men only, and she'd been killed. Being a lawman was a man's job. Based on his simple reasoning, Danna could get killed trying to do her job. What was the town thinking to appoint her?

After securing a room—not as grand as what he was used to, but it would do—and a long soak that loosened his shoulder, Chas felt moderately better. Well enough to venture out and find something to eat.

The hotel clerk recommended the café down the street. This time when Chas walked down the boardwalk, he nodded and smiled at the men he passed, as well as tipped his hat to the ladies, soliciting giggles and smiles behind gloved hands from some of the younger women.

In the café, he was seated by a matronly woman and served a cup of coffee by a slender girl who appeared to be related.

It was midafternoon, and the café was mostly empty. Only one other patron was seated across the room, an older gentleman dressed in denims and a light blue shirt. Clean. He had a white hat on the table at his elbow. A wealthy rancher? Chas nodded to the man but chose not to interrupt his meal. Perhaps he would introduce himself when his stomach wasn't so loud.

"Thank you," Chas said when a steaming plate of roast and potatoes was set in front of him.

"Anything else?" the younger woman asked.

"Mmm." Chas hurriedly swallowed the coffee he'd sipped. "I'm new in town and seeking employment. Do you know of anything?"

"Ma might." The girl went into a rear room and the older woman appeared in her stead.

"Ya seekin' work?" She eyed him skeptically. "Not a cowpoke?" He shook his head. Chas's heart sunk as she frowned. "Don't know of anyone in town needin' help."

The door swung open and another man entered, this one in a rumpled, untucked shirt and brown trousers. His fingers were stained with ink. A shopkeeper? The second man joined the first at his table.

"Sorry, sir." The café matron left with a shrug.

Chas went back to his meal, trying to remember his manners. The food was delicious and he wanted to inhale it.

"Marshal's back in town," the new man said to the rancher, the low words piquing Chas's attention, though he kept his face downturned as if he hadn't heard.

The rancher grunted but didn't speak.

"Seems she didn't find no help for hire over in—" He named the nearest town. "Still no deputies to work with her."

Danna Carpenter was marshal *alone?* She didn't have any deputies? Surely that couldn't be right.

"That's a shame. A real shame."

* * *

Two days later, Chas was back at the café, this time during the lunch rush. Frustration over this case had cost him a sleepless night.

No one in town needed help. He'd spoken to every business in town that was a viable option—not the dressmaker's shop or the livery—to no avail. From what he could gather, most businesses in town were family operations or they couldn't afford the help.

However, one suggestion he'd received over and over again was, "The marshal's lookin' for deputies."

It seemed to be a joke around town. He'd learned that what he'd overheard on his first afternoon in town was true. Danna had no deputies.

He'd entertained the thought of working with Danna for scant moments before he'd rejected it. He couldn't work with a woman. Couldn't get close to one, even though she'd saved his life. It was too much of a risk.

His dreams of Julia's death had returned, as if the event had happened only yesterday, another reason he hadn't slept last night.

There was no way he could be a deputy for Marshal Carpenter.

But he didn't know how else to stay in the area, and he needed a reason to stay in town, or folks might start getting suspicious of his purpose for being here.

He needed to gain the trust of at least a few of Calvin's citizens, get the lay of the land and find some clues to the missing cattle.

"—we can't wait any longer—" Low but heated words from the table seated next to him floated to Chas's ears.

"We got our orders. The boss said wait."

Chas threw a casual glance over his shoulder, hand

on his coffee mug as if he was looking for the waitress. Three men at the next table over shoveled their meat loaf into their mouths. The layer of dust covering their denims and chambray shirts, and the shaggy haircuts and scruffy facial hair marked them as cowboys, but these men had a rough look to them, as well.

Chas's senses went on alert. It might be nothing, but usually his instincts were good. He snuck glances out of his peripheral vision, trying to memorize their features without catching their notice.

Two had beards—brown and black—and the third a long, sand-colored mustache that trailed all the way down the sides of his face to his chin. The brown-haired man had a scar running down one side of his face, from temple to jaw. The man with the black beard and hair had dark stains down his trousers that appeared to be spittle from chewing tobacco. The sandy-haired man had unusual pale-blue eyes.

"The other boys'r getting restless. Ready to move on."

The same voice answered, "Boss says wait, we wait."

"But the grass is all dryin' up now." Chas dared a glance at the other table when the door opened and gave him an excuse. The man with brown hair was speaking. "The cattle—"

A sharp grunt from the pale-eyed man silenced whatever the speaker would have said. Chas's ears were attuned to every word now. What cattle were they speaking of?

The blond-mustached man caught Chas's eye. Chas gave him a nod, hoping the other man wouldn't notice that he'd been listening in on their conversation.

"Afternoon." The man said, lifting his coffee cup in salutation. "Ya new in town?"

The other two men looked up. With all three pairs of eyes fixed on Chas, his discomfort grew, especially when he noted the gun belts on each man's waist.

"Yes, I'm new here. My name is Chas O'Grady."

The man with black beard and hair curled his lips in what should've been a smile, but just looked as if he bared his teeth, two of which were missing in front. "Earl."

"I'm Big Tim," drawled the man with brown hair. He was big indeed, looming head and shoulders over Chas. Big Tim did not smile a greeting; he stared at Chas with an unwavering brown gaze.

"What brings you to our fine town? You sound like a city fella. You got fam'ly here?" the blond man asked. Chas couldn't help but notice he hadn't offered a name.

This was where things could get sticky. As a rule, Chas tried to keep to the truth as much as possible—that way, there was less chance of trapping himself in a lie.

"No, no family here," Chas said easily. He used what was left of his roll to sop up the red gravy on his plate. "I'm a businessman of sorts. Got bored in St. Louis and wanted to see some of the West. The horse I bought in Cheyenne expired in the badlands, just the other side of your town. So I'm here now until I find something new. You don't happen to know of any open jobs in town, do you?"

The two dark-haired men went back to their food as if they'd weighed Chas and found he wasn't dangerous. The blond man didn't seem convinced and watched Chas with narrowed eyes as Chas dug a coin out of his pocket to pay for the meal.

"'Fraid not. We're just local cowhands. Trying to make a buck of our own. About the only time we get to town is to find us a little female companionship, if ya know what I mean."

From his correspondence with the WSGA, Chas knew there were two major outfits in the area. Most of the smaller outfits only hired cowboys during the spring and fall, when it was time to drive the cattle to market. "Oh, do you work for Parrott or Brown?"

"Brown."

"Parrott."

Big Tim and Earl spoke over each other, giving conflicting answers. The blond glared at both his companions. "We're between outfits right now," he said. "And dead broke. Sorry we cain't help ya."

Chas nodded at the obvious dismissal and rose to leave. As he walked away, he heard a hiss, "Ya idiots!"

Emerging into the sunshine outside the café, Chas decided to cross to the general store across the street and wait for the three men to exit the eating establishment. If he could see which direction they headed, perhaps he could follow them.

He knew their hard appearances and conflicting answers didn't necessarily mean the men were involved with the cattle rustling, but something didn't ring true about them.

His main concern was that he might not be able to follow them without being noticed. Although the small town of Calvin had a bit of foot traffic on its dusty thoroughfare, it wasn't enough for Chas to disappear, should the need arise. Perhaps he could invent an errand in the same area of town, once he determined the men's intentions.

He didn't have to wait long. The three men stepped

out onto the boardwalk moments later, arguing. He was too far away to hear what about.

Chas pushed off the post under the general store's awning, where he'd been leaning, intending to follow them down the street. A commotion in the other direction arrested his attention.

Two men tumbled out of the nearest saloon, dust flying as they rolled into the street. Shouts and men followed them out—wasn't it a bit early for the saloon to be so full?—and Chas spared a glance back toward Earl, Big Tim and the blond man. They'd ignored the ruckus and continued down the street. He stepped off the boardwalk in that direction.

A new shout, this one in a different octave, met his ears. He stopped, watched in growing horror as a slender figure ran up to the fight. Marshal Danna Carpenter.

From the looks of things, she was going to jump right in.

And then he saw the glint of silver in one of the fighting men's hand.

"Knife!" The word ripped from his lips.

Chapter Four

❧

Danna looked around at the faces lining the street outside the saloon. Most men watched the fight, but some watched her. Waiting to see what she'd do. Like always. Waiting for her to prove herself.

No one joined her just off the edge of the fracas created by the two drunks who'd burst from the saloon. She needed to separate them before they got hurt.

"Stop!" she shouted, but it didn't faze the men. "Ellery! Hamilton! Stop fighting this instant!"

Nothing. She took a breath and waded into the conflict, getting an elbow in her shoulder as she broke the hold the men had on each other. She kept her feet, but barely, getting between the two men.

A flash of metal alerted her to the weapon and she blocked the swipe of Ellery's knife with her forearm against his wrist. The blow hurt, but not as much as a stab wound would have.

"Put the knife down," she ordered. Still no reaction from either tussling man. It was as if she wasn't even here. Hamilton was behind her and got one arm wrapped about her midsection, cutting off her air with a huff.

She had no choice. Danna stomped on his instep. When Hamilton's restraining arm went slack she used all her strength in an uppercut against Ellery, in front of her. Pain radiated through her fist and up her arm. Ellery slumped to the ground in a satisfying heap, though Danna could see he wasn't completely unconscious.

Using a move Fred had taught her, she gripped Hamilton's arm—still around her waist—spun around so she was behind him, and jerked his arm up tight against the center of his back, immobilizing it and hopefully letting him know she meant business. It was helpful she was almost as tall as he was—it gave her more leverage against his arm. Inebriation slowed the man's response, but he finally stiffened against her hold.

"Did you see that?" someone in the crowd asked.

"Not bad for a gal that put curtains up in the jail," a second voice called out.

"Blue, *flowery* curtains," came a hiss, followed by several snickers.

"You finished?" she asked the men in front of her, doing her best to ignore the onlookers. She hoped Hamilton couldn't feel her shaking. That swipe with the knife had been too close for her comfort.

"He shtarted it," Hamilton slurred.

Ellery groaned from the ground, stirring.

"I don't care. You're both coming down to the jail to sleep it off. Then I'll check with Billy Burns about any damages you'll have to pay."

"Whoossh gonna help ya drag both of us down there?" Hamilton's belligerent question resulted in chuckles from those nearby. Ellery pushed to his hands and knees, still gripping the knife. He looked up at Hamilton, malice on his face.

Without warning, Hamilton jerked his arm free, bucking against Danna's hold. His other elbow rammed backward, catching her in the shoulder. Losing her balance, Danna stumbled between the two men once again, determined to end their fight. Meanwhile, Ellery lurched to his feet and lifted his knife.

Danna swung her arm out wildly, praying she wouldn't be cut, when someone close yelled, "Hey!"

The interruption was all she needed. She slammed an elbow into Hamilton's gut behind her, and he folded. From her peripheral vision she could see someone knock down Ellery a second time.

Danna gritted her teeth. She'd had the situation under control and hadn't needed help!

Ellery tried to get up again. A shiny black boot came down on his back, sending him sprawling. A matching one kicked his knife away.

Danna looked straight into the unsmiling face of Chas O'Grady.

Chas was going to be sick right here in the street. He rapidly blinked away his memories of Julia's body, broken and bloodied on the saloon floor, but the sight that greeted him was not much better.

Danna Carpenter had handled the two ruffians, both drunk, with finesse, but he still couldn't erase the memory of that knife slashing toward her. Did she know how close she'd come to dying right here on this dusty street?

He desperately wanted to rebuke her, make her understand exactly how dangerous a position she was in, but he couldn't force the words past the fear lodged firmly under his sternum.

"If you don't mind, I'd appreciate your help getting that man—" she nodded to the drunk underneath his foot "—over to the jail."

Still unable to answer, he pulled the man on the ground to his feet and followed the marshal as she prodded the second man toward the two-story jail building on the edge of town.

Thoughts and memories colliding inside his head, he marched his prisoner along with her. Once both men were locked in adjoining cells, Chas rounded on the marshal.

"What did you think you were doing?" he demanded.

"My job." Her words were said stiffly. Something was wrong. Was she hurt and he hadn't seen it? He looked her up and down but couldn't detect blood on her clothing.

"You all right?" He asked the question without thinking, and stepped closer so he could watch her roll up one shirtsleeve. A large red mark shaped like a hand bloomed on her skin and made him tremble more. He wanted to pull both men out of their cells and give them a thrashing like his older brother had given him once.

"I'm fine. Probably a bruise is all." She lifted her shoulder—trying to keep him from seeing?—and didn't look at him, ran her fingers over the skin on her forearm.

It would turn into a nasty bruise, if the red mark was any indication.

"What did you think you were doing, embarrassing me like that?" she asked, eyes flashing when she finally turned to him.

"What?"

"I had everything under control."

He shook his head in disbelief. In his mind's eye, all he could see was that knife coming toward her.

She slapped her hat down on the desk, stirring a stack of papers sitting on one corner. "I would have been fine." She clapped one hand on her hip. "But you had to step in, and now all those men probably think I can't take care of things myself."

"That's not what it looked like. One of your assailants had a knife." He blinked. Again. Still, the image persisted behind his eyes. She'd almost *died*.

"I know." She knew?

"He almost stabbed you."

"He didn't."

"Because *I* stepped in!" Didn't she understand? She needed him!

She needed him.

The realization sent him reeling. He sat down in the hard-backed chair against the wall next to the door, silent. Danna still spoke, but Chas couldn't hear her words for the rushing in his ears.

How had this happened? He'd been drawn in by another female, when he'd vowed to himself to stay away from all persons of that gender. He couldn't do this.

Was it the connection between them that had sparked to life at their first meeting? Was that connection because she'd saved his life?

He couldn't be her deputy, could he?

A knock sounded and the door opened. The wealthy rancher Chas had seen in the café two days past sauntered in.

"Mr. Parrott," Danna greeted him with a deferential nod of her head. Her shoulders were suddenly straighter.

So Chas's guess in the café had been correct. This man was a wealthy rancher, one of the two who owned the largest spreads around. Was that why Danna had assumed such a reverential manner? Or was there something else about him?

Chas scrutinized the other man as he took off his white hat and tucked one hand in the top of his vest. He was tanned, lines on his face indicating his age was probably midforties.

"Marshal, I heard you took care of a little dustup down by the saloon." Parrott spared a quick glance for Chas. "Everyone all right?"

"Yes, fine," Danna responded quickly. "How's the missus? Anything I can do for you today?"

"Oh, no, dear. The wife's doing well. She asked me to make sure you're planning on attending the dance we're hosting at our place this Friday."

Danna glanced at Chas, but as far as he was concerned, they still had talking to do; he crossed his arms over his chest and stretched his legs out in front of him to show her he wasn't leaving.

Her smile, when she turned it on Parrott, was forced. "I've been thinking on it. I'm not sure I'll be able to get away."

"You work too hard, Marshal. A night of relaxation will be good for you."

The marshal's frown showed she didn't agree with the man, but her voice remained level and calm. "I don't know that I should leave the town unattended."

Her statement almost sounded like a question. Why was she showing Mr. Parrott such deference, when Chas had seen her talk down to other men? Chas had learned there were four men on the town council for Calvin; they appointed the marshal and had the power to remove that person from their position, as well. Mr. Parrott must be one of them, for Danna to speak so respectfully to him.

"Ah. Still no luck with the deputies? I'm sorry to hear it. Well, be that as it may, you can't work every hour of every day. Besides, the wife has a few eligible men she wants to make sure you meet. You *are* considering remarrying, aren't you?"

Chas's breath stuck in his chest. The marshal was a widow, too? What else didn't he know about her?

She cleared her throat, her feet shifting and downturned face indicating her discomfort with the discussion. She gestured toward Chas, who hadn't joined the conversation. "Mr. O'Grady and I were in the middle of something, Mr. Parrott. I'll try to come to the party if I'm able. If there isn't anything else, I'm afraid we'll have to speak later...."

She hadn't given the older man a straight answer about remarrying, but the rancher accepted it with grace as Danna ushered him out the door.

After he left, she leaned against the portal, her head clunking against the wood.

"Your boss?" Chas asked.

"One of them." She huffed and blew a strand of dark, curly hair off her face, then turned her head to look at Chas. "What are you still doing here?"

"Marshal, you can consider us even," Chas said.

"What do you mean?"

"You saved my life. I saved yours."

Her lips twisted. Not a smile. They pinched together. If she didn't like that, she probably wouldn't like Chas's next statement either.

"I think you should hire me on as one of your deputies." Had those words really come out of his mouth?

She first appeared stunned, then skeptical. She pushed off the door. "You want me to deputize you? Why?"

He glanced at the two men in adjacent cells. They continued arguing through the bars, not paying any attention to Chas and Danna. "I need a job, a reason to stay in town. Plus, it will give me some leeway to investigate without any potential cattle thieves being the wiser. You need some help."

She looked as if she would protest, so he quickly went on.

"I've been talking to people around town and found out a couple of families are missing cattle. Problem is, I don't know the lay of the land."

She half-smiled at that, probably remembering his unfortunate tumble down the ravine.

"You can relax a little, go to that party—"

Chas hadn't finished his sentence when she burst out, "I don't need a deputy so that I can attend social functions. If you want to pin a tin star on your chest, you'll have to realize that *I'm the marshal*."

"I do realize that." His temper started to get the best of him and Chas rose out of his seat, moving to stand face-to-face with the marshal.

"That means *I'm the boss*. I make the schedule. I'm in charge. If you can't handle that—"

"I can." He hoped. "I have to put my investigation first, but as long as you stay out of my way—"

Danna shook her head, stepping back and putting space between them. "This isn't going to work."

He blinked and again saw that knife coming straight for Danna's heart. "We'll have to make it work. I'll be in town until I find my rustlers. You'll be my boss—" he almost choked on the word "—until then."

She started to say something else, but the door opened again and a very pregnant woman bustled in, followed by a toddler, a blond-haired girl in a stained dress.

"Fine," Danna's tone emerged, resigned. "Be here first thing tomorrow."

Chapter Five

Danna tucked her chin into the upturned collar of her coat, the chill in the early morning wind stealing her breath. She made this journey almost every morning. It never got easier, standing in front of Fred's grave in the small cemetery just outside of town.

This morning she was especially discomfited. Thanks to her new deputy, Chas O'Grady, private detective.

Intriguing.

She shook off her distracting thoughts. She shouldn't be thinking about another man, even one she planned to work with, while visiting her husband's grave.

"I'm sorry I haven't found your killer yet," she whispered, the wind snatching her words away. Three months, and she hadn't turned over one clue that would lead her in any helpful direction. As his deputy, Fred had believed she could solve any crime. So why couldn't she solve his murder?

She could still see his body lying prone in the field of dry summer grass. Shot in the back. And no one in town or out of town was talking.

Her only hope was to find the horse that matched the funny-shaped hoofprints she'd found near the scene of Fred's murder. The horse was shod, but not well. Something was wrong with one of its shoes. Its tracks made a crescent shape instead of the traditional horseshoe. She'd made a sketch in the leather book Fred had insisted all his deputies carry to take notes on pertinent information.

Since she'd never learned to read or write, Fred had taught her to sketch the important things about crimes she investigated.

But she hadn't been able to track down that horse anywhere.

With a sigh, Danna turned to town. She had one more stop to make before she faced O'Grady this morning.

With the sun barely up, the streets were still quiet. Not many folks stirred this early. Danna wouldn't usually, but she hadn't been able to rest this morning. Too many thoughts crowding in her head, keeping her awake.

She banged on the wind-faded door of a shanty on the edge of town. When her friend Corrine opened the door, Danna lifted the dead rabbit she'd snared with her slingshot. Why waste a bullet if you didn't have to? "Brought you a present."

"You've been out to the cemetery again." Corrine didn't sound surprised. She didn't sound much of anything, her voice emerging a monotone. She edged inside, motioning for Danna to follow.

"Lots of game out there, with the tall grasses" was Danna's reply. She didn't have to make an excuse to her best—and only—friend in town. Corrine knew about loss, too.

Inside the shack, the smell of fresh bread wafted through the small space. Three places were set at the table against one wall, under the only window in the house. Two of the plates were untouched with what appeared to be last night's supper still on them.

Corrine faced Danna, unshed tears reddening her eyes. She twisted a towel between her hands, then one hand moved to cover her large-with-child belly.

"What's this? Did you eat last night?" Danna asked, concern for her friend overriding her lingering thoughts about Fred's murder.

Corrine shook her head, visibly upset. "I—I made a plate for Brent, just in case he came home. But—but then I got so upset thinking about him that I couldn't eat."

Danna nudged her friend into a chair. Another failure on her part. Corrine's husband had been missing since the same night Fred hadn't come home. Unlike Fred's body, Brent had never been found. Danna—and most of the town—couldn't help thinking the two events were connected.

Patting her friend's hand, Danna did her best to comfort the distraught woman. "You need to eat. You've got to think about the baby."

Corrine nodded, but put her face in her hands and began to snuffle. "I don't know how much longer I can keep going. Wh-why doesn't he come home?"

Danna hugged her friend's shoulders, a little afraid to touch the swell of the other woman's stomach. "Shh. Shh. I don't know. Shh." She knew better than to offer promises she couldn't keep, so she kept silent while she rocked the slight woman.

Movement from the bed in the corner caught Danna's eye. Ellie, Corrine's daughter, was asleep but maybe not for much longer. She had to get Corrine calmed down or risk upsetting the three-year-old.

"I don't know what happened to Brent," Danna said softly, still rubbing Corrine's back. "But I promise I'll find out. I'll do everything I can to find him." Dead or alive. She didn't say the words, but Corrine shuddered against her shoulder.

"Do you…" Corrine had to sniffle and swallow before she could continue. She spoke in a voice so low it wasn't even a whisper. "Do you think he killed Marshal Fred and that's why he left?"

Most of the town did. But not Danna. "No. Brent might be a laggard and a bum—" and he was, frequently out of work so that his wife had to take jobs in order to feed the family "—but he's always returned when he's left before."

And Corrine always took him back. Even after weeks apart. Danna couldn't believe her friend would stay in a marriage like that, but what could Danna do, other than help her friend out occasionally? Corrine wouldn't accept what she termed "charity" from anyone else.

"You're right. I know you're right." Corrine pushed away and went to the washbasin. "Not the part about Brent being a bum—" her voice came muffled from the scrap of towel she scrubbed her face dry with "—but that he's always come back before."

Danna hated it for her friend that her lousy husband had done this enough times that she could say that. "Is there anything you need?"

Corrine busied herself wrapping one of the two loaves of bread warming on the stovetop. She shook her head quickly. "No. No, we're fine. Thank you for the rabbit, though. I'll make a nice stew with it."

"Auntie, auntie!" A joyful shout erupted from the bed.

Danna barely had time to scoot her chair away from the table and catch her nightshirt-clad "niece," Ellie, as the girl vaulted from the bed in the far corner of the room and launched herself at Danna. Holding the three-year-old's small, sleep-warm body in her arms fueled a rush of emotion that brought tears to her eyes.

She wanted—*needed*—a family of her own. It was her biggest dream and her deepest regret from before Fred had passed. She'd always wanted to give him a son.

Danna shoved away the familiar longing, stowed it in a deep corner of her heart and made a funny face. "Good morning, Elf. You're late for breakfast."

Ellie giggled, as she did every time Danna used her pet name. She hefted herself up into her own chair at the table and settled her worn rag doll in her lap. "Ma, can I have jam?"

Corrine smiled at her daughter, but when she turned away to slice a piece of fresh bread, Danna could see fresh tears in her eyes. The bulge of her stomach became more defined when she reached with one hand to rub the small of her back. She didn't have long before the baby came. Would Brent return before that time?

A sense of urgency sent Danna to her feet. She reached for the cloth-wrapped loaf of bread Corrine had placed on the table before her. She froze at Corrine's next words.

"I heard about your new deputy. You rushing off to him?"

"Ya got a new dep'ty, Auntie?" Ellie's question echoed her mother's, but her blue eyes held an innocence that Corrine's did not.

Danna sagged against the table. "Don't tease, Corrine. I can't imagine this working out." Not with Chas O'Grady only concerned about one thing: his case. Maybe his presence would allow her to make inroads with the other men. She hoped.

"You'll be fine," Corrine said, reversing roles and patting Danna's shoulder comfortingly. "It can't be different than working with the other deputies back when Fred...was still here."

"Yes, but when Fred was marshal, I wasn't in charge. And this isn't the same situation at all."

More of a trial period. Chas O'Grady would leave once he'd found his outlaws. Danna only hoped she would get the respect she deserved from the people of Calvin, and maybe the help of a couple more deputies.

Corrine narrowed her eyes. "Why? Because he's a handsome fellow?"

"What? No!" A hot flush stole its way up Danna's neck and into her face, mocking her denial. "Even if he is handsome, I have no intention of noticing. He's a city dude. Likely, he won't make it long in our small town." Or for other reasons.

Corrine shrugged. "I don't know why you're getting all bothered. It almost sounds as if you *want* him to leave."

Danna waved her hat in front of her still-warm face. "I don't know what I want. Just to find Fred's killer and find some peace."

She was tired. Tired of working alone. Of facing the censure that nearly all the town showed for her. The town council had thought she could do the job of marshal. Why didn't anyone else? Carrying a gun, enforcing the laws, those were the things she was *good at*. The only things.

"Maybe that's not all that God wants for you," Corrine said softly.

Danna couldn't help it. Her eyes dropped to her friend's pregnant belly. She'd always wanted a family... until she'd made herself stop wanting that impossible dream.

"I have to go," Danna said finally, when she could find words again. She reached down to hug Ellie, who'd watched the exchange with huge blue eyes.

"Bye, Auntie!"

Corrine pushed the forgotten loaf of bread into Danna's hands. "You're plenty smart. You'll figure out what to do."

Danna strode out of the saloon, disgusted. She'd stopped in to find out what the owner would charge Ellery and Hamilton for damages to his properties from their fight yesterday. She'd thought a morning visit would be a mite more respectable. And she'd been the epitome of professionalism, but the proprietor had insisted on leering at her the entire time, and offered her a job as one of his "girls" on her way out.

She was steaming mad, fighting to hold on to her temper.

And that's when she saw Chas O'Grady leaning casually against the outside corner of the jail, in what looked to be a cheerful conversation with two of Calvin's eligible young ladies, Penny Castlerock and Merritt Harding.

Still fired up, Danna stomped right toward the little group.

Penny Castlerock, the wealthy banker's daughter, in her frilly gown, with her hair cascading in copper ringlets from her bonnet, and with a parasol bobbing over her shoulder, was the picture of femininity.

Even Merritt, the schoolmarm who was a little too old to be on the marriage market, was pretty in a slightly faded gingham dress, with her blond tresses bound up in a bun like Danna could never achieve.

She would never be like those women. She didn't want to be like those women. Did she?

The question stopped her in place. She turned toward the general store, pretending to admire the two gowns in its front window.

When she'd become Fred's wife at age sixteen, she hadn't known how to do any feminine things. Keep house, sew a quilt, cook...all those things had been beyond her capabilities.

And Fred had never made her learn. He'd seen her skill with a rifle, and how she could track a coon in a snowstorm, and made her his deputy instead. She'd never fit in with the other women in town, and he hadn't asked her to.

She didn't really want to be like all the others, did she?

In the reflection of the glass she could see Penny leaning flirtatiously close to O'Grady. She couldn't help straining her ears to overhear their discussion.

"Perhaps we need a man's opinion. Mr. O'Grady?" Penny's query was accompanied by a flutter of her eyelashes so big Danna could see it from this distance.

"Yes?"

"I'm trying to decide between these two hats." Now Penny pointed to the window of the milliner's shop, right next to the jail. "Pink or yellow?"

O'Grady considered the store window for a few moments, then said, "I'm afraid I don't know much about ladies' fashion. They both look fine to me."

Danna felt a little gratified he didn't seem to be falling for the girl's overeager manner.

Penny giggled, a shrill sound to Danna's ears, and she had to clench her teeth.

The young woman leaned toward Chas to murmur, "You must not know much about ladies either. You never tell a woman she looks 'fine.' She may look 'lovely,' or 'pleasing,' or even 'handsome,' but never simply 'fine.'" Then she oh-so-casually placed her gloved hand on O'Grady's forearm.

The flirt! Danna thought she stifled the snort that wanted to emerge, but she must've made some noise, for Penny and Merritt turned toward her, and Chas's head came up.

"Well, hello, Marshal," Penny greeted. "Are you shopping for a new gown?"

Danna narrowed her eyes. The girl's question seemed innocent, but everyone in town knew Danna never wore dresses. "No, miss, I'm not. Hello." Danna nodded to the group and considered whether she should walk past them to the jail. Since they'd engaged her in conversation, it seemed rude to go on. She stepped forward, but not close enough to be considered part of their group.

"Do you know Mr. O'Grady?" Penny asked. "You do? Hmm. Merritt and I were just commenting how terribly *brave* he was yesterday to stop that horrid fight in front of the saloon."

The fight Danna had stopped? Merritt shook her head and Danna wondered if she was embarrassed for her friend's overly flirtatious behavior.

Color crept into Chas O'Grady's cheeks. "Marshal Carpenter—"

"You're coming to the dance next week, aren't you, Marshal? Papa said I could have a new bonnet and dress. Which do *you* like better, the pink or the yellow?"

Danna took a cursory glance into the shop window. Honestly, they both looked the same to her. Fussy frills and ribbons. "The yellow is nice."

"Hmm." Penny appeared to be lost in thought for a moment, leaning her head on one gloved hand while she gazed into the window. "Perhaps I'll wait to buy the bonnet." Penny said, giving her parasol a twirl.

Merritt, who hadn't said a word to Danna yet, grasped her friend's elbow and leaned close to murmur something in Penny's ear.

"Miss Harding reminds me that we're committed to tea with my mother this morning. Mr. O'Grady, it was a pleasure to meet you. I hope we'll meet again. Marshal."

The two women walked off arm in arm, Penny shooting a final saucy wink over her shoulder toward O'Grady.

Danna shook her head as she moved past her new deputy and opened the jail door.

"I knocked earlier but there was no answer. I wasn't sure if I should go in and wait for you... I wasn't trying to engage those young ladies in conversation."

"You don't have to make excuses to me." She moved behind her desk, noting the floor was particularly dusty this morning and could use a good sweeping.

"I wasn't. I don't— I'm not interested in female companionship."

Danna shot a look at him and noted his face had

flushed so darkly that his freckles were entirely obscured. "What you do when you're off-duty is none of my concern."

"I'm not interested," his words emerged stiffly now. "I have a job to do, and that's all I care about."

"Fine." She shrugged and pulled open the top desk drawer. The items inside it clinked together and she drew out one of the tin stars. She flipped it onto the desk. "Yours."

He picked it up, looking down at the silvery badge for a long moment. "Why did you become marshal, anyway?"

"Because I was asked." She didn't mean to be short with him, but the events of the morning had worn her nerves thin.

O'Grady exhaled loudly. "I think we've gotten off on the wrong foot this morning. Shall we start over? Morning, Miss Marshal."

She glanced up at him quickly, at his teasing reference to her title, but he didn't seem disrespectful. He extended one hand for her to shake.

She took it, and warmth ran all the way up her arm. She couldn't keep her gaze from meeting Chas's, and his blue eyes reflected the same awareness that was in hers.

There was something between them.

She dropped his hand and hurried to fill the coffeepot Fred had always kept going on the stove. The familiar motions soothed her, and when she finally sat down behind the desk, she was able to appear composed. She hoped. Chas took the chair near the door, clearing his throat.

She shuffled the stack of Wanted posters on the corner of the desk. The silence now stretching between them was awkward, but she didn't know how to bridge it.

"Where'd the two yahoos from yesterday go?" Chas asked, jerking his thumb toward the two empty cells.

"I had to let them go once they sobered up."

He nodded, drummed his fingers on his knee. "It seems like a hard job for a woman."

She answered him in a softer tone than she'd used earlier. "My husband...used to be the marshal. I was one of his deputies."

"How did he die?"

"He was murdered."

He didn't ask if she'd caught Fred's killer yet, for which she was thankful. She didn't want to talk about Fred.

"And you were asked to be marshal? What about the other deputies?"

He didn't have to speak the words for her to hear *What about the male deputies.* She frowned. "I'm sure the town council considered all options, but when they came to me and offered me the job, I couldn't refuse."

"Did none of the other men want to work with you?"

She gave him a speaking look. If they had, she wouldn't have needed him, would she?

"Did you...do something to them? Alienate them somehow?"

She threw her hands up, tone turning exasperated. "Other than being born a woman? I worked mostly with my husband, but I have worked with the other men on occasion. Either they think I'm not competent to be marshal without Fred's support, or they've been paid off." She said the last part in jest. No one in Calvin would do that. Why would they?

She turned the tables on him. "Tell me about

yourself, Chas O'Grady. I should know something about my new employee, shouldn't I?"

He shrugged, but his gaze dropped to the leg he crossed over his knee. "I'm from Boston. Have been a detective the past five and a half years. My mother and father still live in the East."

"No siblings?"

"One living. A younger sister. May we get down to business now? What would you have me do today?"

His choice of words was telling—he had another sibling who had died. As was the fact that he wanted to change the subject, but she allowed it.

"I thought we could ride out to some of the smaller homesteads today and ask about missing cattle. If there really is rustling going on, I have a responsibility to find out."

And it still irked her that the ranchers hadn't reported any missing cattle to her. She was the marshal. She was supposed to take care of those kinds of things.

Plus, by making the rounds of the ranches in the area, she would have a chance to watch for those funny-shaped tracks she'd seen at the site of Fred's murder.

"Fine." He stood and pinned the tin star to his chest. "I'll need a horse."

She'd already thought of that. "My husband's horse is stabled at the livery. You can borrow her until you leave town."

It was best to remind herself that he'd be leaving soon. That way maybe she could keep her heart from getting too attached to her attractive new deputy.

Chapter Six

"Perhaps this time we should try something different. That last man, Gill, knew something. I'm almost sure of it." Chas tried to affect a tentative tone as he offered the suggestion, but he was afraid his irritation leaked out.

At the last two small farms they'd visited, Danna had insisted on accompanying him out to the barn to talk with the men—who hadn't wanted to give any information in her presence. They'd been polite, but hadn't offered one piece of information helpful to Chas or his case.

"What do you mean?" Danna's terse question echoed his own frustration.

"Keep in mind this is just a suggestion…but what if you remained inside and visited with the woman of the house?"

Danna's looked at him askance. "You want me to pay a social call?"

He lifted his shoulders. "Not exactly. Just talk for a bit. She might even offer some news that we could use."

"But you've never even met Mr. Early."

"That's all right. It might be easier to talk him round to the information we need without a woman present."

"But I've never gone visiting in my life!" she burst out.

"Never?" How could that be? She was a woman, wasn't she? Wasn't that what women *did?* His sister loved to gossip with her friends and never missed a chance to pay social calls.

Watching Danna's trim figure out of the side of his vision, he still couldn't believe he'd first mistaken her for a man. Even in the men's trousers and shirt, there was no disguising her womanly form. She was just too shapely. She moved with the horse, her natural grace evident.

She flushed under his scrutiny. "I'm not like other women."

"There is no doubt in my mind that that is true."

She sucked in a breath, face creasing, and he realized how she might have taken his statement the wrong way.

"Wait— I didn't mean—" Chas stifled the urge to curse. "Let's not have another misunderstanding like the first night we met."

She glared at him.

"Let me explain."

Finally, she nodded.

He went on quickly, before she could change her mind. "Obviously, I've never met a woman who dressed…" he waved a hand to encompass her from head to toe "…like that. Or can break up a fight between two drunken men. And I'd be willing to wager you can outshoot me, as well."

She gazed at him questioningly, as if she was half-afraid to see what he would say next.

"You *are* an original, Miss Marshal. I like that."

He liked her, even though he didn't want to. He couldn't allow himself to get close to her.

"Have you ever…" He hesitated to ask, but he found he had to know. "Have you ever wanted to dress like the other women?"

She stared ahead for a long time. When she did say something, it wasn't to answer his question. She nodded ahead, and Chas saw a couple of buildings grow larger as they approached.

"Here's the Early place."

Had he touched a sore spot? He hadn't meant to. It seemed he couldn't keep from saying the wrong thing around Danna Carpenter.

Danna stood behind one of the four kitchen chairs surrounding the small table in the Early kitchen, gripping its back with white-knuckled fingers.

"Thank you…um, for inviting us in. It was very kind."

Mrs. Anna Early glanced at her with creased brows as she bustled to brew a fresh pot of coffee. "Is there sumpin' wrong?"

"No, no." Danna placed one hand flat against her stomach. "I'm just nervous. I'm not— I don't make very many social calls."

The woman turned and smacked one hand onto her ample waist. "I meant is there sumpin' wrong that you want to talk to my husband about. He ain't a thief or nuthin'."

"Oh. Oh, of course not, Mrs. Early."

"Anna. We don't stand too much on formality round here."

"All right, Anna. No, I don't think your husband has

done anything wrong. Mr. O'Grady and I are investigating a possible case of cattle rustling in the area." Danna released her death grip on the chair back. "Is there— Can I help with anything?"

"Don't know nuthin' about any missing cattle. Here." Anna plopped a loaf of bread and a knife on the table.

Grateful for something to do with her hands, Danna did her best to carve slices of the bread without smashing it too badly. Judging from the slightly pinched look on Anna's face, she didn't succeed.

The other woman offered Danna a cup of coffee and sat down at the table. With a soft sigh, Danna sat, as well. "Neighbors have been in a ruckus lately, but I don't know no details. Mrs. Bailey and me don't get along so well."

"Mam! Mam!" A small girl raced into the kitchen through the back door, followed closely by a boy only a little bigger. "There's a dep'ty talking to da!"

Anna turned in her chair and shushed the children. "Shh, you two. Cain't you see we've got comp'ny?"

The two children faced Danna with wide eyes and dirt-smudged faces.

"Hello," Danna greeted them, holding out her hand to them.

Faces solemn, they slowly rounded the table and, one by one, shook her hand with their grubby ones.

"Are you goin' to arrest my da?" asked the little boy, who seemed unable to look away from the badge pinned to Danna's vest. His voice lowered even more. "He didn't shoot that no-account, thievin' Timmy Bailey, ya know. Even though he tried t'other night."

"Joey!" Anna stood up from the table and clamped a hand on her son's shoulder. "He didn't mean—"

"It's okay." Danna did her best to hide her smile.

"I'm not here to arrest anyone," she reassured the boy. "Just to visit. Do you want to eat with us?"

For once, she'd said the right thing. Anna's shoulders released their tension and she allowed the children to sit at the table and have a slice of bread and glass of milk.

"Mmm," Danna hummed as she bit into her slice of bread. "This is delicious. I wish I could bake bread like this."

"Thank you." Anna accepted the compliment with a flush. "My own mam taught me." She sipped her coffee.

"I'm learning, too!" chimed in the little daughter.

"That's wonderful."

"Did your ma teach you?" the girl asked.

"No," Danna said slowly. "My ma died when I was littler than you. I never learned how to cook or sew or anything."

Anna looked a little more sympathetic after hearing that. It gave Danna the courage to turn to her and ask, "So you're having problems with your neighbors?"

Frustrated that Mr. Early had been as silent as a church mouse, Chas waited near the horses for Danna to end her visit.

When she finally stepped out of the Early's small farmhouse, she squinted in the bright afternoon sunlight. Chas was graced with a view of her glorious dark head before she smashed her worn brown hat on.

He offered her a leg up to her horse. She accepted the boost into her saddle with a twinge of her fine black brows and a flash of curiosity in her coffee-colored eyes. She wore a small smile as they guided their horses down the rutted lane toward the edge of the Early property.

"Did it go better than you thought?" he asked.

"You were right." Her body fairly vibrated with energy. Her smile grew until he saw a flash of white teeth—the first real smile he'd earned during their brief acquaintance. He liked it more than he should.

"The neighbors?"

She tugged on her hat brim and the smile faded. "The husband told you?"

"Not in so many words. He was remarkably close-lipped. What did you find out?"

"It seems the Baileys have been riding across the Early property, which wouldn't normally be a problem…"

"Do go on."

"Apparently, they've been driving some cattle in the middle of the night. Some got loose and knocked down a lean-to. The Earlys lost some chickens."

"Seems a little suspicious. Why would they do it at night?"

Her eyes shone at him. "That's what I thought, too. The husband didn't say anything at all?"

Chas drew in his horse to stop next to hers, where the next lane started. "Said he'd heard some rumors of missing cattle, but nothing important enough to re-member. Said he wasn't missing any himself. But said he thought someone in the area had been moving animals."

"The Baileys."

Chas knew his admiration showed in his eyes. The marshal was perceptive and intelligent, two things he could appreciate. He nodded to the dilapidated house not far up the lane. "Let's go."

A half hour later, they met up outside the empty corral.

"Barn's empty."

"House, too. They must've left in a hurry, because the furniture and some of the clothes are still in there."

Disappointment sliced through Chas. He'd been convinced they were on the right path to finding the missing cattle and rustlers, but there wasn't a man or beast on this place.

Danna's frustration knew no bounds as she and Chas mounted up again, halfway between the vacant house and barn. "We should ride down their back pasture toward the Early property and see what we can see," she said quietly, trying to rein in the anger that wouldn't help her solve this mystery any faster.

The afternoon sunlight would last another couple of hours. The breeze tickling the curls that escaped her braid was chilly, but not unpleasant. Sky was clear. They should have plenty of time to scout the Bailey property and get back to town before sundown.

As they neared the creek that the Earlys claimed as their property line, the grass changed from dry and brown to just tufts and then dirt, pockmarked by many hooves.

"This looks familiar," Chas commented, riding up beside her.

"Umm-hmm. Like in the canyon? Not quite so bad. I think this was fewer animals. See how the tracks don't spread very wide?"

"I see it."

"In the canyon, the hoofmarks were spread across the whole canyon floor."

"Is it possible it was the same number of animals, just driven in a narrow bunch?"

She considered it for a few seconds. "Doesn't seem likely. You'd need more cowboys than a small outfit like the Baileys could afford."

But what were they doing moving cattle this time of year? And where had the family gone?

Chas followed Danna across the creek, but she reined in her mount before she reached the bank.

"Look," she cried, pointing to the impression visible in the mud. "It's a crescent." She hopped down from her horse, boots splashing in the shallow water, and squatted next to the single track, peering closely to be sure. She started to shake.

It was the same. She knew it was.

"What is it?" Chas rode past her, up the bank, before he stopped his horse and dismounted. Probably didn't want to get his boots wet.

Danna waded through the creek to her horse and dug in one of the saddlebags, finally locating the small leather-bound book. She flipped pages to the middle, to the sketch she'd made. She turned the book so Chas could see the drawing. "This was found near—" She choked on the words, had to swallow hard before she could say it. "Near my husband's body."

His gaze went from the book to her face and she drew a deep breath, struggling to maintain control of her emotions. She wanted him to know she could do her job, didn't get distracted by feminine emotions.

When she thought she could speak again, Danna worked to make her voice even. "I'm going to track them. You can go back to town if you like."

"I won't let you go alone."

No, she hadn't really thought he would.

* * *

It was after nightfall when Chas and Danna rode up to the livery and dismounted. Chas watched Danna's slow movements, her disappointment evident in the droop of her shoulders.

The tracks she'd wanted to follow had vanished not long after they'd picked up the trail. She had not been happy.

They'd ridden home in silence, Chas allowing her the time to get her emotions under control. He was impressed that she had held back her tears earlier. And he knew what it was to be disappointed a lead hadn't panned out.

Now she reached out a hand for his reins. "The stableboy will have gone home for his dinner. I'll rub these two down and make a patrol of the saloons. Come by the jail in the morning."

Chas flipped the reins into her hand, but didn't let go. He tugged against her hold until she looked up at him, her eyes dark and unreadable. "You take care of the horses, and *I'll* make a round of the saloons."

"I'm the boss," she argued.

"Yes, I haven't forgotten." There was something in the air between them, though the only physical connection was the reins they both held between them. "Let me help you."

"Why?" she whispered.

To keep her out of danger. It was one reason, but another he couldn't voice was that he liked the look she was giving him—a look that said he was offering her a kindness no one else ever had.

She nodded gravely and he made a quick escape before she could ensnare him even more.

* * *

The town was quiet, except for the piano music and raucous laughter coming from the four saloons. Chas stuck his head into each of the first three to make sure things were relatively calm.

It was at the fourth saloon that things changed. Chas stepped inside and stood with his back to the wall next to the door, perusing the main room to make sure things were calm. He was about to turn and leave when he caught sight of the man with long hair and a blond mustache sitting at the bar.

The suspicious man from the café.

Chas glanced around, but didn't see Big Tim or Earl. Pale Eyes seemed to be talking to a man with a scruffy goatee and dark hair. Chas waited to get a good look at the man's face, and when he did, everything seemed to stop around him.

A long, jagged scar down the right side of the man's face left no doubt in Chas's mind that this was the same person he'd come to hate in Tucson.

The man who had killed Joseph and Julia.

Hank Lewis.

Rage roared through Chas, filling his head, pounding in his ears. His hand went to the gun at his belt—then he realized two of the men at the table closest to him had turned to stare at him. What was he doing?

Even though he'd been made deputy, he couldn't shoot a man in cold blood, out in public—he'd hang for murder, even if the scoundrel did deserve to die. He would wait until Hank Lewis went outside and then do it.

But how to stay unnoticed while he waited? Finally, he settled in one corner, waving away the bartender when the pot-bellied man approached.

Nearly an hour later, both Hank Lewis and the blond man from the café stood. Chas waited until they'd left the establishment before he got up from the small table he'd been occupying. When he pushed through the swinging doors, neither man was in sight. Rushing around the side of the building, Chas scoured the shadows, pistol in hand. Nothing.

Back into the street. Empty.

Hank Lewis was gone.

Chapter Seven

"A man in her rooms—"

Danna craned her neck, trying to get a look at the speaker over the heads of the partygoers at the Parrott's dance.

This was the third comment she'd overheard about a person of the male persuasion being seen in her rooms. *Her. Rooms.*

Which was ludicrous, because she wasn't aware any man in Calvin—or Converse County for that matter—thought of her as anything other than *The Marshal.* Certainly not as a woman, not with her job and the way she dressed.

Who had started these horrible rumors swirling around the room?

"Ah, just the woman I wanted to see."

Danna turned at the booming voice of Joe Parrott, to find him approaching her through the crush of people with two of the other three town council members in tow.

"Mr. Parrott, lovely party. Mr. Hyer. Mr. Castlerock." She nodded to the owners of local general store and the Calvin Bank and Trust, respectively, both of them on the town council with Parrott. Neither man smiled at her.

"It's, ah…" Hyer started, "come to our attention there are some rumors going around about you." He looked uncomfortable at having to speak about this.

She stifled the groan that wanted to escape, the anger that made her want to lash out at them. It wasn't *their* fault someone had started malicious gossip about her.

"I haven't had anyone up to my rooms, male or female," she said, working hard to keep her voice level. But she must've spoken louder than she intended, because a woman nearby turned to look. Danna glared at her until she turned around.

"We mustn't have even a hint of scandal amongst the leaders of our town." Castlerock managed to look condescending, though he didn't meet Danna's eyes. She knew he had been the only one of the four council members to vote against her appointment.

Parrott patted her shoulder, giving her a smile. "My dear, we know you are trying your best."

Castlerock snorted softly. Danna eyed him but kept her mouth closed while she tried to think. What would Fred have done in this situation?

"If she can't maintain a good reputation, perhaps she shouldn't be marshal," said Hyer, and Castlerock nodded agreement.

This was getting out of hand. Danna kept her voice even when she spoke, but it was not without effort. "Gentlemen, I haven't done anything inappropriate. As I'm sure this will not be the last time malicious gossip is spread about a woman in a position of authority, I would advise you to ignore it."

Then, shaking from speaking in such an outright manner to the men holding the power to remove her from her position, she turned on her heel and escaped into the crowd.

Chas reined in his borrowed horse, slowing to move through the wagons and horses gathered outside the impressive ranch house. He hadn't known where the dance was to be held, but he'd managed to find a few stragglers leaving town late and follow them.

He wasn't supposed to be here. Danna had tasked him with watching over the town while she attended the dance, but he'd had a little situation and needed her.

Plus, he wanted to mingle in the crowd and see if he could spot Hank Lewis again. He'd patrolled the entire town of Calvin in the last week, become overly familiar with its three main "roads" and couple of smaller, grassy lanes. He'd memorized most of the nooks and crannies behind each store. He'd found no sign of Hank Lewis.

Each day, Chas's rage and desire for revenge had grown. He'd barely had patience to deal with the marshal, and could sense she'd been getting frustrated with him, as well. There had been no further leads about the cattle rustlers. He could no longer bring himself to care about his case. Only getting revenge on the man who had murdered Julia.

Chas took a moment to adjust his horse's saddle, eyes taking in the yard filled with buggies and horses. The dance appeared to be in full swing, with the sweet sounds of a fiddle and banjo floating over the din of many voices.

The six-shooter at Chas's waist seemed heavier than

usual. He kept touching it, reassuring himself he was ready to do this.

Even as his urge for revenge built, he'd been struggling with his conscience. He wanted to do *right,* but he also couldn't forget the promise he'd made to himself when he'd awoken on the doctor's table after Julia's death. He'd promised himself if he ever came upon the man who killed her, he'd return the favor.

Chas was out for revenge, plain and simple. Lewis deserved to die. Eye for an eye. That was biblical, wasn't it?

Chas shrugged off the distracting thoughts and approached the house.

The porch spanned the width of the house, and Chas was halfway up the steps when a shadow moved near the corner of the house. Suspicion had Chas jumping into one of the dark patches in between the rectangles of light shining from the windows. Could it be Lewis? No one with good intentions would be hiding out in the shadows instead of being inside.

Crouching close to the outside wall of the house, Chas crept toward where he'd seen the movement. Subdued voices reached his ear, but he couldn't make out what they were saying. He moved closer, being careful not to make noise and get himself noticed.

"...boys are getting ready to move the cattle after they take care of this other matter. They'll have to take 'em to Rock Springs, instead of Cheyenne, or someone might notice the brands, but it shouldn't be a problem."

Now that sounded promising for his rustling investigation. Chas settled one knee on the wood planks of the porch, giving his other leg a reprieve from the uncomfortable crouch.

"And what about the marshal?" This was a different voice, another male.

"She don't have any idea what's goin' on," the first man replied.

Chas didn't think either of the voices was Lewis, but he couldn't ignore what he was hearing.

"Besides, the marshal's got other things to worry about. She's goin' to be tied up with the robbery. This gossip about her is an extra bonus."

What robbery? Were these men involved in the cattle rustling?

He had no idea if they were armed, but they could be dangerous. Chas leaned his head against the wall behind him, unsure what to do. Two against one wasn't the best odds, and what if Lewis was here and he missed his chance to kill him?

Maybe if he could get a look at one of the men...

He shifted closer until he could see a boot and a dark pair of trousers. The man seemed to be leaning on the adjoining wall, around the corner, so Chas couldn't see his face, but he held an expensive-looking black bowler hat against his leg. In the dim light, Chas thought he could make out a mark of some kind—a tattoo?—on the man's wrist, but he couldn't be sure. The second man wasn't in sight at all.

Just then, two horses rode up into the yard, hooves thundering. If they approached the house, they would see Chas in his vulnerable position. He had no choice but to scramble across the wooden planks and go inside.

Once in the front door, he slipped into the crowd. There were plenty of people around. No one seemed to notice him. He skirted the room, torn between returning outside to try to find out the identities of the two men who knew something about a robbery and cattle moving, and staying inside to find the marshal and look for Lewis.

He was concentrating so hard on his dilemma, he nearly missed the familiar dark braid on the woman with a badge on her chest.

Danna had sensed O'Grady the moment he walked into Parrott's front parlor, even though the room was filled with people. So many people, she was having trouble making her way toward the door.

What was the man doing here? Couldn't he follow instructions? She wanted him available for any emergencies back in town.

He'd been moody and distracted since they'd ridden out to visit the Earlys and Baileys last week, but coming to the dance tonight was outright defiance.

She wasn't sure if she was more irritated by that, or by the distance he'd been building between them. If only her awareness of him would fade, but it had only grown stronger in the past few days.

She'd spent much too long finding her hostess to thank the woman for inviting her, and now all she wanted to do was return to her rooms. She had no desire to confront her deputy right now; she could talk to him in the morning.

Other than the three town council members, hardly anyone had spoken to her all evening. She'd thought she had learned to be tough while being Fred's deputy, but she found herself close to tears at the rejection of the people who had been, if not friends, then acquaintances for the last seven years.

And now O'Grady had shown up and was blocking her exit. She didn't want to see his admiration for

Penny Castlerock or the other ladies in lovely gowns who would undoubtedly flock to him.

Unfortunately, he saw her heading toward the door.

"What are you doing here?" she asked by way of greeting.

Light from the gas lamps highlighted the red in his auburn hair. Sandy stubble covered his chin, making him look disreputable and a bit dangerous. Because of the press of bodies in the crowd, she stood close enough to smell him—leather and soap and man. She didn't want to feel the tingle of awareness that trembled deep in her belly. She focused on glaring at him for not following her instructions.

"We've got a situation in town." His gaze slid right over the top of her head, as if he was looking for someone else in the crowd. Her insides pinched to think it was the banker's daughter or someone else who he searched for. His indifference shouldn't matter to Danna, but it did.

"You couldn't handle it on your own?" If her words were on the caustic side, she hoped it couldn't be heard above the voices surrounding them.

Chas looked down at her, his eyes glinting in the lamplight. "Not this one. What say we switch places? I'll stay here and you head back to town?"

She'd been prepared to leave the party, but his request ignited her ire and made her question him. "What kind of situation are we talking about?"

"I've detained someone." Again, his blue eyes swept the room above her head. Was the person he looked for so important he couldn't have a conversation with her?

Irritation surged and she tried to push past him. "Fine. I'm sure Miss Castlerock is around somewhere so you can admire her new gown."

Before she could get around him, he grasped her elbow. "That's not why I came—"

"I shouldn't have said that." She tried to shake his hand away, but he held fast to her arm.

"Dance with me, Miss Marshal."

His demanding tone sparked something inside her like iron on a tinderbox, and she opened her mouth, but her refusal was muted when she noted the set of his jaw.

"Please," he murmured.

Without waiting for an answer, he swept her into the crowd of dancers. Reacting quickly, in order not to be stepped on by the swirling couples, she clutched his shoulders to keep her balance. The fiddle seemed muted now, or was that the blood rushing in her ears?

Though he was only a couple inches taller than she, his very presence seemed larger. Almost protective. Like she could lean on his broad shoulders and be kept safe.

Belatedly, his hand met her waist and she jumped. No one had touched her since Fred. And how did this touch, in the middle of a crowded room, feel so intimate?

"What's the matter?" she asked, struggling to focus on her words, instead of the unsteady feeling he evoked in her.

"Do you know that man? There, in the corner—with the long blond hair?" He twirled her and she caught a glimpse of a man with stringy blond hair and a long mustache standing near the food tables in the second parlor. Her quick glance revealed he was dressed as many of the cowboys were, in their nicest denims and starched white shirts.

She shook her head in the negative. "I don't know him. Who is he?"

"I've seen him in town a couple of times. Last time with…a suspicious character."

Danna could feel the tension in his grip; she suspected there was something he wasn't telling her. But what?

Chas knew he'd made a mistake the moment he took Danna in his arms. Holding her felt natural, right, the same way it had on horseback when she'd rescued him. And it scared him.

But when he'd seen Hank Lewis's crony across the room, he'd faced an irrational urge to keep her near. If Hank Lewis *was* here, anyone in the room could be in danger. Including the marshal.

If he blinked, he could imagine Danna sprawled across the floor in a pool of blood—just like Julia had been at the hand of Hank Lewis. He couldn't let that happen.

He hadn't counted on what the feel of her in his arms would do to him. The simple smell of soap and woman rose above the other smells of food and other bodies.

For a brief moment, he forgot about Hank Lewis. He couldn't stop himself from gazing upon Danna; he let his eyes roam her face from forehead to chin. She was flushed with the exertion of swinging and stomping around the dance floor. Wisps of her dark hair had come loose from her braid and curled at her temples and over her forehead. At the moment, she wasn't looking at his face, more like his shoulders, and her dark lashes contrasted with the golden skin of her cheeks. She hadn't dressed up like the other ladies here tonight, still wore her trousers.

She was vibrant.

And he wanted her as far away from Henry Lewis as he could get her.

The music ended and they stepped away from each other.

"We probably should head back to town," she murmured, not looking at him now. "And see about this situation of yours."

He cleared his throat. "Yes."

When he regained his senses, looked up again, the blond man was gone.

The situation was…a girl locked in one of the cells.

Danna stopped in the middle of the floor, shock holding her immobile. Dark hair, stringy from being unwashed, obscured her view of the girl's face, but the slight person huddling on the cot behind bars was certainly female, even disguised by the tattered man's shirt and trousers.

Was this what Danna looked like in her marshal's clothes?

"Let me out of here!" the girl shouted when she caught sight of Danna and Chas. She stood up from the cot, and Danna got a good look at her dirt-smudged face. She didn't know the girl.

The girl shook the cell door, rattling the metal. "You can't keep me here!"

"You were caught stealing earlier, so yes, we can keep you here." Chas spoke calmly, ignoring the girl's ire. Again, almost distracted.

Danna turned to him with raised brows. "Which store?"

"Hereford's Grocery. I was walking down the street and caught her myself when she ran out front with a half a ham in her hands."

Danna walked up to the bars, and the girl backed away. As if she was afraid. "I don't know you," Danna said quietly, hoping to calm the girl. "Do your parents live in town? What's your name?"

The girl didn't answer, only crossed her arms over her middle.

"If you don't talk to me, I can't get you back home."

"Store owner didn't recognize her either. She can't be more than fifteen. I would've turned her over to her parents, but there was no one else around, and I couldn't get anything out of her." Chas sat down in his now customary chair and propped his feet on the desk. Danna frowned at him—she'd told him twice not to put his boots there—but he ignored her glare and went on. "I wasn't sure you'd want to leave her locked up all night."

The girl's face blanched at his casually spoken words.

Danna considered it for a moment. "I don't know that we've got a choice. She's a minor. I can't just turn her out on her own. Maybe a night in that cell will make her want to tell us who she belongs to."

Now the girl's shoulders slumped; she seemed to sink into herself.

Danna felt sorry for her. She approached the cell and touched the bars. "If you're afraid your parents are going to be angry, I could talk to them. They're probably worried about you right now."

The girl curled up on the cot, giving Danna her profile. She swiped at her face with one hand, and Danna thought she saw a bit of moisture before it was whisked away. But what choice did she have if the girl refused to cooperate?

Moving to the pot-bellied stove in the corner,

Danna stirred the coals and fed in two sturdy logs. The autumn nights were getting cooler and the girl didn't have a coat; Danna didn't want her to get chilled overnight.

Chas's booted feet hit the floor with a thump.

"You heading out?" Danna asked, intent on her task. His attention had been diverted all evening. She didn't want him to know it mattered.

"Mmm-hmm. See you in the morning." And he was gone.

Danna turned to give the girl one more chance. "I want to help you. Won't you tell me who you are?"

Still no answer. The girl only sunk her chin into her folded arms, a ball of misery.

Climbing the stairs to her room, Danna considered what she could do. The mystery girl couldn't stay in the jail indefinitely, especially if any men were arrested. But who was she? Why weren't her parents looking for her? Was she an orphan?

The questions had no answers, at least not tonight.

Danna toed off her boots and changed into her nightshirt, but her thoughts stayed with the girl below. If she was an orphan, was she lonely?

Like Danna was?

Maybe that was the key to getting the girl to open up. Just spending time with her. Showing her that Danna could be trusted.

Danna pulled on a pair of pants, tucked her nightgown into them. Threw her coat on over that, then pulled the extra quilt off the end of the bed, added Fred's pillow on top.

She ducked back outside and made her way down the steps without really looking, even though the moon was mostly hidden by clouds. She was pushing open the door to the jail when a hulking figure loomed over her.

Resisting the urge to shriek, she reached for her pistol and realized she'd left it upstairs when she'd started getting ready for bed. Could she—

The moon came out from behind a cloud and threw the face of Chas O'Grady into relief. Danna's shoulders dropped and she let out a silent breath. It was just her deputy. But...

"What are you doing here?"

Chas grinned at the marshal's discomfited expression. "Scare ya?"

She shook her head but he didn't believe her. Seeing her vulnerable put a hitch in his stomach, just like he'd felt when he'd seen the mercantile owner grab the teen girl Chas'd taken into custody.

Women. They brought out the best in him—his desire to protect, take care of them. And also the worst—he seemed unable to stay away, even when he knew he should.

He spotted the bundle in Danna's arms and couldn't help his smile. Something warm unfurled in his chest at the realization that Danna had the same thoughts he had about making friends with the mystery girl.

"You felt for her, too," he whispered. "I thought— the girl was stealing food. Figured you'd have to be pretty desperate—hungry—to do that. So I brought some things from the hotel." He held up the burlap sack he carried.

She nodded. "Perhaps, if we show her that we care, she will open up?"

Those had been his thoughts exactly. He could put

aside his quest for vengeance for a few hours. On his walk down from the hotel, the town had seemed almost deserted—probably most folks were still at the party outside of town. Finding Hank Lewis could wait until morning.

Chas pushed the door open and allowed Danna to brush past him. In the warmth and light inside, he held up the burlap sack he'd filled with the goods begged from the hotel manager.

"So you brought some leftovers from the hotel?" Danna asked, probably for the girl's benefit, since they'd just discussed this in whispers outside.

"Unfortunately, the hotel's kitchen was closed—I had to bribe the manager for some eggs and bacon from tomorrow morning's breakfast."

He waved the cast-iron frying pan in the air, moved across the room to the pot-bellied stove. "I borrowed this, as well."

The girl did her best to appear disinterested, but Chas saw the way her eyes tracked both his and Danna's movements across the room. Danna moved to the desk, putting the bundle of cloth and pillow she carried on its top.

The girl's head came up off her folded arms, but she remained motionless on the cot.

Danna moved closer to him, reached for the coffee-pot on the shelf near the stove. "You want me to make some?"

How could he cushion his answer? He didn't have to. Danna's eyes narrowed. "You don't like my coffee."

It wasn't a question. "Your coffee is a little…ah…" He started to say *strong*.

She shook her head, cutting him off. "Don't say it. I'll fetch some water. *You* can make the coffee."

When she brought the pot back in, he had to push back the skillet to make room—the stove was made for heat, not cooking, but it would still work for their purposes. The food should be edible, at least.

"Are you sure you know what you're doing?" Danna asked as Chas cracked several eggs into the skillet, where they sizzled.

"I've been a bachelor long enough to know how to fry a couple of eggs." He added some bacon to the far side of the pan and the scent of cooking meat wafted through the air. When he looked up at her, Danna's mouth was pinched and white.

"My husband used to say that."

"He cooked?"

"One of us had to," she said, and this time there was fond remembrance and a bit of humor in her soft smile.

Chas jerked his focus back to the frying pan and away from her mouth.

A glance from the side of his eyes revealed the girl sat forward on her cot, watching them. If they kept the conversation going, would she eventually say something?

"I thought most mamas taught their daughters how to cook."

"My ma died when I was little."

She said the words so matter-of-factly that he glanced up quickly and the fork scraped across the bottom of the frying pan with a screech. "Sorry." Was he apologizing for the noise or for her mother's death? She always tangled his emotions until he didn't know which way was up.

"Who raised you?" He hadn't meant for the words to come out of his mouth, hadn't meant for the conversation to turn serious, but he couldn't take them back now.

"My brother. Until I was sixteen and he sent me away."

"Let me guess. He sent you to a finishing school, but it didn't take?"

She shook her head stiffly and gave Chas her profile, sitting on the edge of the desk. "No, he sent me away to get married."

The sound of bacon grease popping was the only noise in the room for a moment that stretched long.

Finally, not knowing what to say, Chas scraped the bacon and turned it over. "Almost done."

Danna popped up from the desk and scurried to the door. "I'm going to run upstairs and get a plate for our...guest." She nodded toward the girl now sitting on the edge of the cot.

"Bring a couple," he said, not looking away from what he was doing.

"Hmm?"

"I got a glimpse of that fancy spread at the party, but I didn't get to partake." He pointed the fork he was using to turn the bacon at the girl in the cell. "I can hear her stomach growling from here. I think you're the only one who ate supper tonight."

"I didn't eat either."

"Why not?"

When she didn't answer, he looked up from the popping grease in the pan to see her turn for the door with a faint trace of a flush on her face. "I'll get the plates."

She closed the door behind her with a snap. A few moments went by and Chas heard movement above his head.

Chas took a moment to try and make sense out of

Danna's comment. From the way she'd said it, it seemed as if her brother had pushed her into marriage. But why? And was it inappropriate for Chas to ask more questions of his boss?

The door banged open again and Danna reappeared, holding tin plates and cutlery in her hands. "Are you burning that bacon?"

She was going to ignore his question if he let her. So he didn't. "No, I'm not. Why didn't you eat supper at the dance?"

She shrugged, but she wouldn't meet his eye either, as he waved her over. He waited her out, scooping eggs and bacon onto the plates she held.

"Goodness, there is a lot of food here. I was too busy avoiding rumors to stop and eat," Danna said, all in a rush. "Someone believes they saw a man in my rooms, and it has scandalized everyone from town. Even the council members cautioned me about my behavior."

The thought of someone calling on Danna put a hot rock in the center of his chest, but he instantly knew she wouldn't allow any inappropriate behavior around her. She was too straight-laced for that.

He tried to make a joke out of it. "I'm sure once the idea of you accepting callers gets around, things will settle down."

If he'd hoped to calm her ire, his statement hadn't worked. She sputtered. "I haven't had any callers—or any men in my rooms—and I don't *want* another husband."

The pressure on his chest eased a bit. Chas took the girl's plate before Danna could dump it on him in her annoyance, and brought it to the cell. The teen still sat on the cot, her eyes fastened on the food in his hands, hope shining from their depths.

"For you."

She was slow to get up, hesitated before she accepted the plate from his hands, but then began shoveling the eggs into her mouth with her fingers, not even using the fork.

Chas turned away to give her privacy. Danna sat behind the desk, eating slowly, staring off at a point across the room. Had he offended her by his teasing comment? He could easily see her getting remarried— she was uncommonly beautiful, with her dark hair and eyes. The way she dressed couldn't disguise it, men's clothes couldn't hide it. And her sense of duty was strong. Her dedication to the people of this town proved it; as a wife, she would never betray her husband.

Scooping the last of his eggs—he hadn't done too bad of a job—into his mouth, Chas let his gaze linger on Danna where she sat behind her desk. As he watched, she slid open the top drawer and fingered something just inside.

He'd snooped one afternoon when she'd been out visiting a sick friend and knew that the only thing in that drawer was a worn leather journal. Her husband's journal. He'd glanced through the first few pages then decided it was too personal to keep reading.

This wasn't the first time Chas had seen Danna touch the object. Did she miss her husband? Did she keep the journal near as a reminder of him?

It was another reminder of how deep her loyalty ran. Even after the man's death, she sought to uphold his honor by defending this town.

"I suppose your sister is a good cook? Pays lots of social calls?"

Danna's quiet question surprised him. He didn't want to talk about his family, about home, but he could feel the teen's eyes on him, though he didn't turn and look at her.

"Erin? Yes, I suppose my mother has been instructing her on how to best run a household." Although his wealthy Boston parents would have a very different opinion on what that entailed from anyone in this small town. "She was only fourteen when I left home. Still having lessons with her tutors."

And it made him ache to think about home. He couldn't speak of it any more. "It's late," he said, pushing off the wall where he'd been leaning. "Wouldn't want any more rumors to get started about you, Marshal." He winked at Danna.

Chas collected the frying pan and fork he'd borrowed from the hotel kitchen and moved toward the door.

Danna had gathered the plates and utensils on the desk and took the bundle she'd carried into the jail over to the cell.

"I brought you a blanket," Danna said, offering the girl a folded quilt. "I know the cots in those cells aren't the most comfortable, but this will have to do if you won't tell us your name or where you come from."

The girl slid her hands through the cell bars and accepted the quilt and pillow.

"My name's Katy." With those softly spoken words, she went to the cot and began spreading out the quilt.

That was it. Just Katy.

The next morning, Danna finished a quick sketch of the man Chas had pointed out to her at the dance. She wanted to put his likeness on paper while it was still clear in her mind. If Chas thought the man was a suspicious character, perhaps she had a Wanted poster on him.

Her next task was to flip through the stack of hand-drawn faces and see if she could match her sketch to any of them.

However, it was a little hard to concentrate, with Katy humming a bawdy tune that she might've learned in a saloon.

Danna didn't move from where she sat with elbows propped on her desk, but flicked her eyes up to watch the teen.

Katy seemed much more relaxed today than she had last night. The shadows behind her eyes had lifted somewhat, and her humming—a scandalous tune—showed her mood had lightened. Now all Danna needed to do was find out where she belonged and get the girl out of her jail.

"I brought breakfast." The cheerful, masculine voice preceded Chas into the jail as he backed through the door, two piping plates in his hands.

She looked down at the Wanted poster, but she couldn't make her eyes focus on the face it depicted. Chas's casual statements last night about his sister's tutor and running a household had thrown another obstacle in the way of her silly emotions. He obviously came from money. Somehow he'd ended up here in the West, but his roots mattered, even if he didn't talk about home much.

If she was right, and his family was well-off, she would never fit in. She was no lady. That was if her silly, female emotions ever came to anything.

Not that her silly emotions *would* ever come to anything.

A gilt-edged china plate—much nicer than the tin

ones she owned—plonked onto the table and her head came up.

Chas quirked a half smile, just a corner of his lips turned upward. "I grabbed breakfast at the hotel. Didn't figure you had."

His kindness flustered her; she could feel a flush creeping into her cheeks. He didn't seem to notice as he crossed to glance out the window.

Chas kept one eye on Katy again shoveling the food into her mouth, ignoring the fork he'd put on her plate. Was she still *that* hungry?

In the reflection of the window's glass, he caught a glimpse of Danna with her head bent over the papers on her desk. Before he'd turned away, he'd seen her blush.

She was sweet on him.

The thought was terrifying. Surely he was mistaken. She couldn't be.

"I think I've found your man with the blond mustache."

He turned to find Danna waving a piece of paper in his direction. "You're kidding."

Surprised she didn't want to read the poster's information first, he took it from her outstretched hand. He did indeed look down into the face of the blond man he'd seen in the café and then in the saloon with Hank Lewis.

"Well, what does it say?" Danna demanded.

"Jed Hester," Chas read aloud. "Wanted in Kansas, the Indian Territory and Colorado. For robbery. There's a reward."

"Robbery? Not rustling? Are you certain it is the same man you've seen around town?"

"I'm sure," he replied grimly. "But what is he doing

around this area?" And what was his involvement with Hank Lewis? Hank had been a cardsharp in Arizona. At least, that's what he'd been doing just before he'd killed Julia and Joseph.

"How many times have you seen this man?"

"Three."

"Then he isn't just passing through."

"It would appear not."

What did it all mean?

"Do you mind if I borrow this?" Chas indicated the Wanted poster with Hester's likeness on it. "I might check around and see if he is staying at the hotel or boardinghouse."

"Do you think that's likely?" From her skeptical frown, it was obvious Danna didn't think so.

"No, but it wouldn't hurt to ask."

"Marshal?"

The quiet voice from the girl huddled in a blanket next to Danna's bed brought Danna from the brink of sleep instantly. It was the first time Katy had spoken since telling Danna and Chas her name the night before.

"Hmm?" Danna levered herself up on the bed with an elbow, in order to see the girl, though she could only make out an outline—Katy appeared to be curled in on herself, though the room was warm.

A barroom brawl earlier in the evening had filled the two cells, and Danna's conscience wouldn't let her leave the girl in the jail. Danna'd brought Katy into her room above the jail, telling the girl sternly that she was still under Danna's custody.

"Did your brother love you?"

It wasn't remotely the question Danna had been

expecting. Stunned, half-asleep, she spoke before thinking about her words. "I suppose he must've."

"Then why did he send you away?"

Danna had asked herself the same question for years after she married Fred. She'd never come up with a satisfactory answer. She hadn't spoken to her brother much since she married Fred—hadn't seen him in years now—so the subject was never brought up.

"My brother had lived on the ranch his whole life. Didn't even go to school. I don't think he knew what to do with a sister—a girl."

Katy was quiet for so long that Danna almost drifted off to sleep again. When she finally spoke, her voice was almost a whisper, tentative.

"What would have happened to you if…if there wasn't a husband to take you in? If you had nowhere to go?"

Aha. Now they were getting to the crux of the matter. Danna suspected Katy was speaking of her own situation. Finally.

"Well, Katy… I guess if I hadn't married Fred I probably would've found a family that I liked and that liked me and I would've stayed with them and helped work their farm. I was used to outdoor work from being on my brother's ranch."

"What if you didn't know how to work?"

Danna followed her instinct and reached down to rest her hand on the girl's shoulder. At first Katy flinched but then seemed to calm.

"Honey, if you're worried about what's going to happen to you, you don't need to."

Danna felt more than heard the girl take a shuddering breath.

"Do you have any family?"

"N-no," came the whisper. "My p-pa died."

"What about schooling?"

"I can't read, but I can cipher some."

"Well, come tomorrow we'll see if we can find you a place to stay and some work to do. You promise not to steal anymore?"

The girl grunted and Danna decided to take it for a yes. She should probably feel good that she finally had a plan on what to do with Katy, but something about it sat like a stone in her stomach.

Was it because the girl reminded her so vividly of herself at that age? Alone, uncertain, unloved?

It was a long time before Danna drifted off to sleep.

Chapter Eight

Danna moved wearily up the stairs to her room above the jail, looking forward to her bed and some rest after breaking up a barroom fight after one gambler had declared the man playing against him was cheating.

She'd nearly taken a broken bottle to the ribs. Chas would've been upset if he'd been there, but this was his evening off. Finally, in the wee hours, the saloons had closed, and she was free to get some sleep.

She pushed open the door, being careful to stay quiet so she wouldn't wake Katy, whom she'd settled earlier in the evening. A sliver of moonlight from the open door fell on the blanket Katy had used the past two nights.

The girl was gone.

A horrible feeling clenched Danna's insides in a fist. She struck a match and lit the oil lamp she kept on the small round table in one corner of the room, only to find the entire room was empty.

The blanket was folded neatly, extra pillow in the middle of Danna's bed. No signs that the girl had ever inhabited the room with Danna. She'd left?

It had been dark when Danna had brought her up here for the night. If she'd left, she probably wouldn't have gotten far. But why would she go?

Questions swirled in Danna's mind as she raced back outside and clomped down the steps, her boots echoing loudly in the quiet darkness.

She slipped in between the small space between the stairway that led up to her rooms and the outside wall of the milliner's building, pausing before she reached the boardwalk.

Something felt wrong. Call it instinct, call it something else, but her skin crawled and she felt in her bones that something was going on tonight. Something that she hadn't felt two minutes ago when she'd gone upstairs.

Taking her time, just like Fred had taught her, Danna peeked around the corner of the building, but the street was empty, the buildings dark. Yet something still wasn't right.

Danna crept down the street, taking care to stay in the shadows under the building awnings, keeping her bootsteps muted against the boardwalk.

As she crossed Third Street, she thought she glimpsed a flash of light from inside the Calvin Bank and Trust. She froze, eyes glued to the front window. Was someone inside? Straining her ears, Danna heard a soft whicker. A horse?

Everything was still. Then—*there*. The flash of light came again.

From this distance, she couldn't make out any details through the bank windows. She needed to get closer.

A prickle of unease skittered up the back of her neck, a sure sign that something was wrong.

She needed to be sure, needed to see into the bank.

She crouched down and crept along the boardwalk, keeping close to the front of the grocery. She jumped when something warm bumped into her leg, but was able to stifle a scream.

"Wrong Tree!" She hissed the dog's name, and he sat in front of her. He was supposed to be at the livery with Will. "Go home." He looked up with his tongue lolling and tail sweeping the dirt-packed lane. "Go. Home."

He whined, and turned his head away from the jailhouse, toward the saloon across Third Street from the grocery.

"I don't have time to deal with you right now," she hissed, and tried grasping the piece of rope around his neck to usher him a few steps toward the jail, but he immediately turned back toward the saloon, and this time he barked.

"Hush!"

Danna released him, ignored him when he galloped away. She had work to do.

The bank had two entry points that she knew of. The main customer entrance at the front, as well as the employee entrance at the rear. Both of those doors were on the east side of the building, so it was possible someone could be watching both exits at once from the alley between the bank and the doctor's office next door. It would make it harder for her to get near the building.

And the bank's entire front wall was composed of large windows. If they had a sentry inside, there would be no sneaking up on the building from Main Street.

The closest she could hope to get without being seen was the doctor's office. And it had no windows that looked toward the bank.

But it was only one story tall. If she could get to

the roof, she could use her field glasses to see into the bank. And she'd have her rifle in case she needed it.

It wasn't much of a plan, but she had to try. She didn't have time to track down Chas at the hotel if the bank was being robbed.

Chas had had a bad feeling all evening that Hank Lewis was in town. This was his third patrol through Calvin's streets tonight, and he was exhausted, his eyes tired from scouring the shadows and darkness for trouble that might or might not be there. He'd never told Danna about the conversation he overheard at the party, so he'd been taking extra patrols on his own.

Everything was quiet, the streets deserted, the saloons finally having closed down for the night.

Then he saw movement on top of one of the buildings a few blocks down.

Heart pounding, Chas pulled his pistol from his gun belt and ran across Main Street, then jumped up onto the boardwalk. He chose the building on his left simply for its nearness—the other building had an empty lot next to it, and he wasn't keen to walk across the open land.

At the corner of the bank building, he paused with his back against the bricks, beside the bank of windows that stretched all the way across the front of the building to its front door.

Noise from inside the building surprised him into stillness. Scuffling...and voices.

From this position, Chas couldn't get a look at the roof of the building next door. It would require him to cross in front of the five large windows overlooking the boardwalk. Was there a lookout up there? Was this a bank robbery?

Chas peeked around the corner and through the window closest to him. He thought he could make out some movement, but the inside of the building was too dark for him to be sure.

The soft neigh of a horse brought his head up. Were the robbers ready to move out if they robbed the bank? If this was Hank Lewis and his gang, Chas needed to stop them.

But he didn't have time to rouse the marshal from her sleep.

Ducking low, he half-crawled, half-shuffled across the boardwalk toward the front door of the bank, pistol in hand. If he could just get a glimpse inside...see the layout of the bank, or if there was a sentry standing just inside the windows...

From this angle down low, and farther along the bank building, he could now see the roof of the building next door. He caught a flash of movement. Was that a hat? A glint of moonlight on metal told him there was a weapon up there. Then the figure shifted and he caught a glimpse of a dark braid under the hat.

Danna? No—it couldn't be!

He blinked, straining his eyes for another look, but he couldn't see anything. Had it really been her, or just an illusion prompted by his imagination?

Before he could raise his head above the windowsill to try and see inside, a shot rang out, followed by the sound of breaking glass.

He froze, his mind going back to the day Julia had died.

Julia fell to the ground at his feet, blood seeping from underneath her crumpled body. He followed her to the ground, moaning her name.

But she didn't hear him. She was already gone.

* * *

Danna took her carefully aimed shot and watched the person-size shadow disappear from the bank's side window at the same time it shattered. Had she hit him?

She left her rifle on the doc's rooftop—out of the way of any would-be robbers—and dangled her feet off the edge, then dropped. Landing in a crouch, she spun to face the man on horseback who'd been watching three other horses, in time to see a blur of snarling dark fur launch across the alleyway.

Wrong Tree!

Horses whinnied and then thundered off, hoof-beats fading into the night. She hoped the lookout that had been posted with them was gone, too. *Thank you, Wrong Tree!*

She fumbled for her pistol, moving toward the broken window. With a little hop, she vaulted the lip and slammed right into a moving body.

A dog barked. Horses whinnied. Then came the sound of hooves pounding against the dirt-packed streets.

Chas fought the paralysis—mental and physical—that held him pinned in a ball on the boardwalk. All he could see was Julia's form crumpled before him; his bloodstained hands...

"We got comp'ny!"

The muffled shout shook Chas from the dark place he'd sunk into, his memories of the day Julia died.

A woman's shriek brought him to his feet, though it almost cost him his last meal. He shook with the adrenaline and revulsion coursing through him.

He clutched his pistol against his shoulder, knowing he had to go in there. He couldn't save Julia, but he could rescue Danna.

He used his elbow to break the glass in the window, and then rolled over the sill.

It was even darker inside the building than out. He could make out sounds of scrabbling to his right and started to step in that direction when he was tackled from behind.

Danna grappled with the man trying to take her arm off, using both her shoulder and elbow to try to find a bit of leverage. The man grunted, but instead of releasing her shoved her into the wall, and she cried out.

Her gun had been knocked from her hand when she'd barreled into this human ox, and she could really use it right about now.

Over the sounds of their struggle, she heard glass breaking and a muffled shout. "Danna!"

Chas O'Grady? What was he doing here? He was liable to get himself killed!

The large man's rancid breath hit her full in the face and she reacted, knocking her head into his. He let go of her arm, cursing.

She dropped to the floor, scrambling for her weapon. The ox man walked into her, knocking her flat. Where was her gun? It couldn't have gotten far.

"Let's go!" A third voice rang out from behind the wall separating the bank's teller area from the vault room.

The man Danna had been struggling with turned, but she swept her leg out and caught his ankles. He stumbled, but didn't go down. She tackled his knees and he fell.

* * *

Chas and his assailant were evenly matched. He couldn't get the kid—the man *felt* young, as if he hadn't had time to grow to his full size yet—to go down and stay there.

"Shoot her!" someone shouted.

"No!" The cry ripped from his throat. The exchange was enough of a distraction for him to lose track of the fight. He registered a sharp pain in his temple and knew no more.

Danna heard the sound of a body hitting the floor, but she was too busy struggling with the human ox to do more than hope someone on the street would hear the ruckus and come in to help her.

Something metal clanged against wood. Oh, no! Had the big man somehow gotten hold of her gun?

He shoved her away and she slid, rolling to one side. Light from a torch glinted off the barrel of a pistol, held in the man's beefy hand. Pointed right at her.

She saw the slight movement of his hand as she leapt to her left. The crack of the bullet whizzed close by, but didn't hit her. She ducked behind the teller counter.

A deep thud and soft moan turned her head. The light illuminated two bodies lying on the floor. Was one of them her deputy?

"Get out, get out!" shouted the voice from the back.

From her vulnerable position crouched on the floor, Danna saw the huge shadow of the man she'd been grappling with move away—the robbers were leaving?

Two pair of boots thumped against the wooden floors, one with a noticeable drag to one of his footsteps.

Silence fell.

Danna knelt behind the desk, trembling. She'd nearly been shot. In all the years she'd worked at Fred's side, she'd never been so close to dying before—except two weeks ago, when she'd nearly been run over by a stampede.

She was aware of her heart drumming in her ears, pounding about as loud as the gunshot had been. She couldn't believe she was alive.

Another moan from nearby drew her gaze up from her shaking hands. The body closest to her was moving, his head rolling from side to side.

"Mama," he whispered.

She crawled toward him, frowning when her palms met with something warm and sticky on the floor. Blood? She hadn't been shot, but apparently this man had.

The body she reached wasn't her deputy's, but she saw his tousled head a few feet away and sucked in a quick breath. What had happened? How had he known something was wrong and come in here? Had he been shot?

A shaft of moonlight filtered through the shattered window and illuminated her deputy's face, slack and unconscious. No blood marked his body, thankfully.

The unknown man groaned again and she crouched next to him, kicking away the weapon lying nearby. Even a wounded man could shoot.

A quick examination told her he was in serious danger. Blood seeped from a wound in his abdomen.

Danna bit back a cry and reached into her pocket for her bandanna. She pressed it against the man's stomach, trying to stanch the flow of blood. Wounds in the torso were hard to treat. If she didn't get help, he might not make it.

"Marshal?" came a wavering voice from the vault room. Danna wished she'd have found her pistol, but there wasn't time to locate it now. She kept holding pressure on the man's wound.

A light appeared somewhere behind her and bounced and shook on the walls until she could see the face of Zachariah Silverton, the bank manager. Danna swallowed a groan. Zachariah was not known for his calm during an emergency.

"Silverton, I need you to bring the light closer, then run for the doc. This man's in a bad way." She used her marshal's voice, the one Fred had taught her to cultivate on a laughter-filled afternoon so many years ago.

"Th-th-they made me open the vault. They held a g-g-gun on me. Said they'd sh-shoot me."

Splendid. He was so shaken up he didn't seem to have heard her.

"Zachariah. Zachariah!"

He started and finally looked up at her. The lantern he held wobbled so much she was afraid he might drop it.

"Bring the light here. Put it on the desk."

He did, his eyes growing large in his face when the light showed the bloody body under Danna's hands. The lantern banged against the corner of the desk and he nearly dropped it before he settled it on the edge of the nearest desk. He backed away, overturning a wooden chair and almost falling.

"Zachariah." She waited until he focused on her face before she went on. "I need you to go find Doc."

He nodded, his head bobbing awkwardly as he didn't look away from her.

He edged toward the vault room and the door there.

"Hurry! This man needs help."

He turned and bolted, shoulder banging into the door frame as he passed out of sight. The sound of his boot-steps faded, and Danna could hear Chas's deep breathing from feet away, and the wavering breaths of the man underneath her hands.

Her handkerchief soaked through, she looked around for something else to help stop the flowing blood.

She needed the doc now. This man was dying.

Chas heard noises as if from far away. Shouts, voices, then moaning. A ringing filled his ears, his head ached.

He remembered. Following Danna into the bank, right into the middle of a scuffle—a robbery. Was she alive?

It took some effort, but he cracked one eye open. Light sent shafts of pain pulsing through his head, but he refused to close his eye, now that he had it open. He rolled his head to one side and saw the broken window he'd busted through before he'd been attacked.

Where was the kid now?

He turned his head in the other direction and forced both eyes open. There was a body, lying on the floor. And…Danna leaning over him.

He closed his eyes against the intensity of his relief. She was all right.

But the kid didn't appear to be. What had happened? Had Danna shot him?

Confusion and pain beat at the inside of his head, muddling everything.

He tried to lever himself up with one hand, but throbbing pain made it impossible and he slumped to the floor.

"Stay still for now." Her voice sounded curt, angry. "Are you hurt?"

Was he? All he could feel was the pounding in his brain. "Took a wallop on the head."

"You must've got knocked out just before the man I was fighting with let loose with his gun. It's a good thing, too, or you might've ended up shot like this poor soul."

"He got shot?"

Her lips flattened. "Yes. Not by me."

Chas's throat closed. More bloodshed. He hadn't been able to prevent it. Gingerly, he sat up, head spinning.

"O'Grady, stay where you are."

Hurried steps pounded on the boardwalk and Chas turned in time to see two tall forms pass the broken window. They clattered inside.

"M-marshal, I got the doc."

A nervous-sounding man hung back, while an older man with a bushy white mustache and full head of silver hair came to Danna's side.

"Can't get a good look. Need more light," mumbled the man that must be the doc.

"Silverton," Danna barked. "Bring the light down here."

Silverton didn't move. His face was a pasty white, and Chas wondered if he was about to faint. Chas stood, fighting his equilibrium as it tried to keep him on the ground.

"O'Grady!" Danna barked his name, but the rushing in his ears made it hard to tell if she said anything else.

He used one hand to hold on to the desk, to make

sure he didn't embarrass himself and fall. With the other, he picked up the lamp and handed it to the doc.

"You don't look real good either, son."

And Chas blacked out for the second time.

"—robbed—"

"Four or five men…"

"—headed out of town—"

An irate voice yelled over all the other chatter. "Where's the marshal?"

The other voices receded into more of a whispered murmur. Chas forced his eyes open, noting the pain in his head wasn't as bad as it had been before.

The bank was lit up now, several more lamps joining the first. A short, balding man stormed through the now open front door, past Chas where he lay half-behind one of the desks, to where Danna stood conversing with a man Chas didn't recognize and the man named Silverton near the rear of the building.

"Marshal—"

She ignored him, continued her conversation with the two other men in low tones.

Chas pushed himself up to a sitting position.

The man Danna had ignored obviously wasn't used to being treated that way, because his face turned a deep shade of purple and he began to splutter.

Danna nodded at something the doc said and turned. "Yes, Mr. Castlerock?"

Ah. The owner.

"Marshal, why aren't you out catching the men who did this to my bank?"

"Mr. Castlerock, I've been tending to a man with a bullet wound in his gut. My deputy is injured. I'm doing the best I can." She walked past him, toward

Chas. "I'll let you know when I have something to report."

The man sputtered, but Danna's gaze was fastened on Chas as she crouched next to him.

He couldn't look away from her face. Unscathed. She was perfectly unharmed.

He had to swallow back the emotions that wanted to burst from him.

She wasn't touching him—he suddenly realized it was because her hands were covered in blood—but apparently the connection between them didn't require a physical bond. *He* could feel it, anyway.

It unnerved him. Look at what had almost happened to her earlier—he'd frozen up, couldn't come in to the bank and protect her. She hadn't been killed, but she *could've been.*

He needed distance.

Forcing himself to stand, he closed his eyes to counteract his roiling stomach.

"All right?" Danna's soft-spoken question came from too close.

"I will be. You?" He opened his eyes, but didn't look at her. The dizziness began to fade.

She shrugged; he saw the movement out of the corner of his eye. "Maybe a little bruised. No worse than breaking up a saloon fight."

It made him itch that she spoke of throwing herself into danger so casually. What could he say? She was the marshal.

He followed her out the front door, boots crunching on glass from the window he'd broken.

Danna knelt in front of one of the watering troughs usually reserved for horses to drink from. She spoke as she scrubbed her hands. "I'm going to take a swing

around town, make sure they haven't holed up anywhere. I doubt they would, but best to make sure. I'll
gather a posse and ride out at first light."

She hadn't looked at him the whole time she'd been
speaking, but now she glanced up. He could see weariness etched in the lines bracketing her mouth. "You
should have Doc check out that bump on your head.
Maybe rest awhile. I want you to sit in the doc's office
until the man who got shot comes around. If he does."

Chapter Nine

The door to the jail half-open, Chas picked his aching head up off his arms when he heard a distinct set of bootsteps approaching. Danna was back.

And then a second set of footsteps—this one much heavier than Danna's steps—thudded on the boardwalk, coming from another direction.

"Marshal, did you catch the men who robbed my bank yet?"

The bank owner. Castlerock.

"Not yet, sir." Weariness was evident in Danna's voice.

"I want my money recovered and the men apprehended."

"They will be, sir."

"Soon, or I'm going to call for your job."

Now her voice lost what was left of its politeness. "I'll be in touch when I have more information to share."

Through the open doorway, Chas saw her push past the larger man, and then she stepped through the door, her huff of annoyance audible as she closed the door with a snap.

"Problem, Miss Marshal?"

She was apparently so tired she didn't even react to his teasing use of her title, as she always had before. She moved to her desk quickly and started opening drawers, making a pile of items on top of the desk. He recognized the leather journal from the top drawer, a pair of field glasses, a length of rope.

Chas glanced out the window. The sky was lightening. Dawn would be here soon.

"When's the posse get here?"

"There won't be one." Her actions contradicted her flatly spoken statement; she seemed to be preparing to leave for a length of time.

"You found them, then?"

She laid her hands flat on the table, closed her eyes, head tucked so her chin rested on her vest. "No one will ride with me. But I'm going anyway."

"What, alone?"

She must have heard the sharpness in his tone—the same sharpness that speared his insides at the thought of her chasing down Hank Lewis with no one at her side—because she looked up with a glare.

"Is it such a surprise? You didn't—don't want to work with me either. You're only here because you need my help getting around the countryside."

She went back to her packing as if he hadn't lodged a protest. "The tracks close to town were obscured, but I picked up four sets of hooves—four horses—outside of town, heading toward the mountains."

"You can't go after them alone. You'll be outnumbered."

She didn't seem to hear him, was muttering under

her breath as she loaded her chosen items into a pair of saddlebags.

Something whined outside the door and Danna whirled to open it. The ugly mutt he'd met on his first day as deputy sauntered in.

"Wrong Tree! I'd forgotten about you, boy. Where've you been since last night?"

She awkwardly patted the top of the dog's head, ruffled his ears. "You helped me last night, didn't you? Chased off that lookout. But how did you get loose from Will Chittim?"

The dog only lay down at her feet and offered his belly to be scratched.

"He likes you," Chas commented, the only words he could force past the lump of fear lodged in his throat.

"He never has before," came her response, as she stood and went back to the desk. "He was Fred's dog before we married. He's been staying at the livery."

The dog lolled its head toward Chas, as if inviting him to take Danna's place and scratch him. Chas knelt to oblige, and the dog grunted its appreciation.

Chas stood when Danna finished packing her saddlebags and turned for the door. "I'm going with you."

"Your head still hurt?"

Her eyes were too perceptive not to catch him if he lied. She could probably see the pulse pounding in the left side of his temple. "Yes, but I can ride."

She shook her head. "You're not riding along. There's a storm threatening and I've got to move fast. If you get dizzy and fall off your horse…" She shuddered as she considered the possibility. "You're too much of a liability."

"I won't fall off. I'm not letting you go alone. We should really have more men, as well."

"You're welcome to try—go and talk to the same men I've just been to see. Maybe they'll listen to an *outsider* instead of a *woman* when you ask for their help."

The bitterness in her voice scared him; she was normally even-tempered, even in the face of the others in town doubting her. If she was giving chase to Hank Lewis and a gang of violent men with her emotions leading her, she was liable to get killed.

The chill that thought sent through his blood shook Chas to the core. He grasped the marshal's arm just above her elbow.

"Would your husband have gone off to face multiple armed men alone?"

It was the wrong thing to say. He knew it as he watched her fist clench against the wood of the door. She looked over her shoulder, her face set and fierce.

"Fred would've done whatever he needed to do to apprehend these men."

"And you need my help," he said it softly, as close to pleading as he'd ever come. "I'll ride with you. I won't take no for an answer."

Danna rode a few paces in front of her deputy, eyes on the terrain in front of her horse. She might be watching for tracks, but she was extremely aware of the man behind her.

He'd been vehement about not letting her do this alone, but she was concerned about that bump on his head.

So far, he'd been true to his word and not fallen, but his face was gray with the strain. Of course, that could be from the cold that had fallen as the temperature continued to drop.

They needed to round up the bank robbers and fast, or risk getting caught in the snowstorm banked in gray clouds getting closer as time went on. A stinging cold wind, strong enough to cut through her leather slicker, had descended about the time they'd ridden out of town.

Plus, she disliked riding into the mountains, ever since she'd been injured and lost, riding after a lost cow and calf, just before her brother had sent her away to marry Fred. After riding all day and into the early afternoon, they were already well into the foothills and she was starting to get jumpy.

And even though it irked her to admit it, her deputy had been right when he'd said Fred would never have walked into a situation like this alone.

It still hurt that the men from town—men her husband had counted on, had worked with—denied her request for help. Hadn't she proved herself enough yet?

Chas made a low sound and Danna looked back to find he was hunched in the saddle with the collar of his jacket turned up.

She drew up on the reins, halting her mount. Chas followed suit.

"You okay?" she asked.

He nodded, but it didn't reassure her, not with the strain on his face. She knew he most likely couldn't find his way back to town on his own, and she didn't want to leave him when he had a head injury—if he became unconscious and fell without anyone to assist him, he could die out in the elements.

But if they stopped now, they'd lose the trail.

There were no good options.

He rested the reins against his thigh and raised his hands to his mouth, blowing on them. "I'm fine, just cold," he said, voice muffled by his hands. "Do you really know where we're going? I still don't understand how you can know which way they've gone."

She dismounted, her joints protesting the movement after being in one position for too long, and motioned Chas to do the same. "It won't hurt to get down and get some blood flowing, warm up a bit."

When her deputy hit the ground, she motioned him to her side, a few feet in front of the horses. She squatted and pointed to the leaf knocked from its branch about a foot off the ground.

"See how it's broken off—this jagged edge here? Something stronger than the wind had to do that." She walked forward a few paces before bending over a patch of soft dirt that showed a partial print from a horse's hoof. "This track didn't come from a wolf or a bear."

Chas knelt beside her and traced the imprint with his forefinger. She tried not to be aware of his close proximity. She failed.

"How did you even see it?" He looked up at her, his hat shading his eyes so she couldn't read them.

"It's a learned skill. The more time I spend in the woods, the more I can tell what is the natural way things look, and then it's easy to spot things like broken leaves or footprints."

"Where did you learn all this? Following your husband around?"

She shook her head. "My granddad taught me and my brother a lot before he died. The rest is a matter of staying in practice."

She pointed to another pair of hoofprints a few feet further along. "These are shaped a little differently.

See here? It's a different horse, but the tracks are just as fresh. I've seen four different prints, best I can tell."

"Amazing," O'Grady muttered.

His tone reminded Danna of his voice when he'd called her a doll on the first night they'd met. But surely his sentiments weren't tender toward her, not after seeing her do a man's job?

Her emotions certainly didn't need to get any more tangled regarding her deputy. She knew he was leaving when he completed his assignment. He was a city boy; she was happiest on the trail, like they were right now.

They would never suit.

But her heart didn't seem to want to listen.

"We need to keep going if we've got any hope of catching up with the robbers." Danna swung her foot into the stirrup and boosted herself into the saddle, not looking back.

The sky kept getting darker and darker, and Chas watched Danna get jumpier and jumpier the farther they rode into the foothills.

She hadn't spoken to him again since they'd taken off for the second time. He couldn't get a good look at her face, couldn't tell if she was getting antsy because of what she was "reading" on the trail or for some other reason.

Her constant reactions to little things, like the snap of a branch in the wind, put him on edge. Plus, he was bone-aching cold, and the wind seemed to keep getting worse the longer they were in the saddle.

"Can we stop for a rest?" he called out when he couldn't take her silence or the cold any longer.

She wheeled her mount around but showed no signs

of getting off. Great. Her jaw was set tight, almost like she was holding back a scream. "I hate to stop now. Once it starts snowing, we'll start losing the trail."

"Do you think we're close?" he asked.

"I don't know." Her fatigue and frustration were evident as she shifted in the saddle, wiped her face with a gloved hand. "I've lost two of the sets of hoofprints. I don't know if they've split up or if I'm so tired I'm not seeing straight anymore."

Part of him wanted to comfort her, to make everything all right again. Another part wanted to find Hank Lewis at all costs, and enact his revenge.

"Danna," he said quietly, and she raised her eyes to meet his. "Why don't we rest for a few minutes and you can catch your breath?"

She tapped her thigh with a fist. "I'd rather keep moving."

Something cold stung his cheek and he raised his face to the sky. Snowflakes whipped downward in a crazy dance toward the ground. He looked to Danna to see her face fall. "I think we're out of time."

"Not if we hurry!" She jerked on her mount's reins and kicked him hard, spurring him into a gallop.

Chas followed, but his heart wasn't in the chase any longer. He still felt an urgency to find Lewis, and he *would* find him, but his concern for Danna was more pressing at this moment.

He concentrated on keeping pace with her, not an easy feat, since her horse's legs were so much longer. Her braid flew out behind her, the tails of her long coat flapped in the wind. Snow and sleet stung his face as they raced through the trees and hills.

He was forced to fall back, his mare lathered and

getting winded. He managed to keep Danna in sight, but fell farther behind.

He'd topped a ridge when he saw her lying on the ground, a dark shape against the gathering snowdrifts.

Chapter Ten

In a blind panic, reckless, Chas kicked his horse, riding past where Danna's horse limped on three feet, several yards away from where her body lay. He threw himself to the ground before he could stop the beast; it slowed to a stop near Danna's horse.

"Danna," he cried, dropping to his knees and not even noticing the wet from the ground.

He took her shoulders and turned her over, being as gentle as possible. Other than a scrape on one cheek, her face was unmarred. Her dark eyes blinked open, focusing on his face.

Her hat had fallen off and her hair fell loose in the wind, dark strands tickling his fingers as he clutched her shoulders. She gasped for breath.

"Danna!"

She struggled against him, and for once he was thankful for her stubborn independence. "I'm all right. Just winded."

She pushed his arms away, tried to sit up, finally catching her breath.

The sense of relief he felt nearly crippled him. She

was all right. Again. Did the woman have to *constantly* put herself in danger?

"Let me—" His throat threatened to close, so he cut off his sentence as he ran his hands through her hair that had come loose, checking for bumps on her head. Large, fluffy snowflakes continued landing in her hair, stark white against the dark locks.

"I'm all right, Chas."

Her quiet words stopped his erratic movements but not the frantic beat of his heart. Before he could think, he leaned in and took her mouth in a kiss.

He felt her surprise in her utter stillness, was conscious of her hands trembling against his chest. When he pulled back, hands on her shoulders, she stared at him with large, dark eyes.

"What…was that?"

"Relief," he said quickly. "Probably shouldn't have done that—we work together—"

She stood up, cutting off the rest of his words—not that he knew what he was saying—and moved toward her horse.

Danna couldn't stop shaking. Not from adrenaline or fear from when her horse had thrown her.

From Chas's kiss.

The kiss that he thought was a mistake.

She went to her horse, immediately noting that something was wrong. A quick examination revealed it had thrown its shoe. She patted its neck, intensely relieved that nothing worse had happened, like a broken leg.

"He won't be able to carry a rider, not with a thrown shoe."

Chas had moved to his horse, too. He wouldn't look at her. She closed her eyes, realizing he must regret kissing her.

"So what do we do?"

"We can both ride out on your mount, but the snow's getting worse."

It was—coming down now in clumps, the cold wind buffeting it in all directions.

"I think we're better off buckling down here for a while. We wait until the worst of the storm is past."

She wouldn't be able to track the bank robbers farther in this weather either. It galled her to have lost them, but the circumstances seemed to go against her mission to capture them.

Shelter was scarce this high in the mountains, but Danna scouted their best option. She showed Chas the best places to find dry kindling in this kind of wet weather, then picketed the horses in a spot where the ground dipped away, providing a wall to shelter them from the worst of the wind.

Nearby, she found a hollow between a hill and a large fallen tree. It would give her and Chas the most protection possible. Hopefully, they wouldn't be stuck for long. Especially with the awkward tension now between them because of that kiss.

He'd pulled away so quickly…had he been able to tell how it had affected her? Her heart had beaten like a big bass drum she'd heard once at a parade in Cheyenne; she hadn't been able to breathe correctly.

It was nothing she'd ever felt before. Not even with Fred.

She couldn't be falling for her deputy. She just couldn't.

Quickly getting a fire going, Danna secured the wood Chas brought to her and motioned him to sit close to the flames. She spent a few more moments carrying their gear over, including the saddle blankets that they would use to keep warm.

Chas watched the marshal move around the improvised campsite as if nothing was out of the ordinary. The kiss they'd shared didn't seem to affect her at all.

He wished he could forget it as easily. How she'd felt in his arms, her scent... His head pounded, but not with pain.

He shook those traitorous thoughts away as she sat down, near enough to touch.

She tipped her head back and glanced at the sky. He watched, entranced, as snowflakes fell on her face and into her dark hair that she seemed to have forgotten hung loose past her shoulders.

"Snow's coming down faster." Her voice was hushed, awed. "It's a good thing we didn't try to go back. If we couldn't find our way, we might freeze to death. Your head all right?"

"Fine." He didn't know what to say to her. He was completely off-balance from that kiss.

She tucked her knees up toward her chest, wrapping her arms around them and loosely clasping her hands toward the fire. "It's my fault." This was said so softly that Chas barely heard the words over the popping of the fire. "We should've turned back earlier. But I wanted to race the snowstorm."

"Do you think the bank robbers holed up somewhere? Why would they come up into the mountains like this?"

"I don't know. There are lots of caves in these mountains, even some old trappers' shacks where they could've taken shelter."

She was silent for a long time. Chas watched the fire until he finally felt compelled to say, "It's not your fault we got stuck here. The weather…"

She shook her head. "Fred would never have gotten in a pickle like this."

"You compare yourself to him too much."

Her eyes flashed up to his and he saw the surprise in their depths. "I do?"

"Mmm. All the time. You make coffee like Fred used to make it. Patrol the town at the hours he used to patrol. What's wrong with making the job your own?"

A flush ran up her jaw and into her cheeks. He hoped he hadn't offended her with his words.

"I don't know," she said, unclasping her hands to hold them toward the fire. It made him realize the air was biting cold on his exposed skin, mostly his face, and he shifted closer to the fire's warmth.

"Fred was a good marshal. He'd been doing it for years. A good teacher."

The affection in her tone when she spoke of her husband wasn't surprising, but his reaction was. He felt *jealous*. He tried to ignore it. "You're not the same person he was. No reason you have to be marshal the exact same way he did. The town council appointed you for a reason."

"Why did they?"

Her abrupt question seemed to surprise her as much as it did him. She went on a rush. "You asked me about my appointment before, and once I started thinking, it really didn't make sense. Why me, instead of any of the

other men Fred used as deputies? Why not hire someone from another town?"

"Maybe they asked those others and none of them
wanted to be marshal."

Her brows wrinkled in skepticism. "That doesn't
seem likely."

"Perhaps…perhaps they simply considered all the
candidates and decided you were the best."

Something changed in her eyes, some softer emotion
that he didn't recognize. Didn't want to recognize. "I'm
still sorry you're caught in this snowstorm with me."

He shrugged. "I guess there could be worse things
than being stuck in the wilderness with a beautiful
woman."

She turned her face away, but not before he saw the
flare of hurt in her expression. "I'll thank you not to
mock me, even though we shared—even though you
stole that kiss earlier."

What? She thought he was jesting?

The cold, and his still-roiling emotions from earlier,
made him scoot across the damp ground, reach out for
her, pull her flush against his chest. All the while bracing for an elbow or a fist he was sure would be coming
his way. "I wasn't mocking you," he said quietly.

"What are you—"

"It'll be warmer this way," he interrupted her before
she could finish her protest. He settled his arms loosely
around her and rested his cheek against her brow. The
softness of the hair at her temple made him close his
eyes. He forced them open, forced away thoughts better
left alone. "Who'd have thought this city boy would be
camping with a pretty marshal in a snowstorm?"

She was silent for so long he thought she wasn't going to respond.

"I'm not...pretty." Her whisper was nearly inaudible.

He looked down at her. Was she blushing? Yes. Warm color lit the side of her cheek. How could she doubt herself?

"Yes, you are. Why, at least half the men wanted to dance with you the other night at that rancher's shin-dig."

She didn't speak, but somehow he knew she didn't believe him.

"Didn't your husband ever tell you how pretty you are?"

He nearly bit his tongue as the words escaped him. He didn't want to talk about her dead husband.

"Fred told me that I was a good shot. That I could outride him most days, and that I had a good memory for details. He told me the truth."

"Well, he didn't tell you everything. Your eyes and your smile are...incredibly lovely." His voice stuck on the word, so caught up was he in making her believe him. He went on, voice lower. "And your hair...like silk..."

He didn't dare touch her hair, not the way he wanted to, although a few strands tickled his chin and neck.

One of the horses blew and Danna turned her head, her temple grazing Chas's jaw. They both remained quiet for a long while, Chas simply enjoying the opportunity to be close to her and the marvel of the falling snow. He *was* warmer now, with the small fire blazing and Danna near.

The woods were silent until she burst out, "If they wanted to dance with me, why didn't they *ask?*"

* * *

For a moment, Danna felt Chas's breath catch in his chest and she thought he was going to laugh at her.

"Maybe they're a little afraid of you," he suggested. "Or it could have something to do with that weapon you carry and the badge you wear."

"Or because I don't dress like the other women?" she asked, knowing her curiosity betrayed that she wasn't entirely indifferent to how the people in town treated her.

Most days she ached to belong. To walk into one of the stores and be welcomed like the other wives and daughters, not with the grim, condescending smiles she always received.

"Maybe," he responded. "Although I can't really picture you jumping into a brawl at the saloon in a skirt."

She leaned her head against his shoulder to gauge if he was mocking her *now,* but he wasn't smiling, he was staring out into the night. Why was it that being close to her deputy like this made her want to open up to him? He wasn't even holding her tightly; his arms loosely covered hers. His head rested against hers in an almost brotherly way.

But the thrills coursing through her veins didn't feel sisterly at all.

He blew out a breath. "If you want to blame anyone, it's really *my* fault we're stuck out here."

Her brows scrunched as she followed his change of topic. "What do you mean?"

"Outside the bank. I was there sooner, but…I froze."

"I wondered how you came to be there."

"I was patrolling. I've been…anxious since that blond man has been around town."

Something about the way he finished his sentence was off. She sensed that he'd started to say something else.

"I saw a light in the window. And I thought I saw you…on the roof?"

She nodded. "I was there. I was out looking for Katy—Katy!" How could she have forgotten the girl? Yes, Danna had been extremely busy with the robbery and its aftermath, but—

"What about her?" Chas asked.

"She'd disappeared. That's how I stumbled on the bank robbery. I was out looking for her. I'd tucked her in and left, and when I came back she was gone. I haven't even thought about her…." Guilt pressed heavy. Danna should have remembered the girl, should have told *someone* before she left town.

"She'll be all right. She'd survived until we found her."

"I hope so," Danna said. It was true, but it didn't make her feel any better. "I'm sorry. I interrupted you earlier. You were telling me why you thought the robbery was your fault?"

He shrugged, eyes on the fire. "I heard your shot, heard scuffling, but before I could make myself go inside, I just…couldn't move."

Again, she sensed he hadn't said what he wanted to say. She waited for a moment to see if he would.

"Even if you'd come into the building right away, we were outnumbered," she said finally. "And since I didn't know you were there, I might've shot you." She was just glad she hadn't known about the hostage— Silverton—that the robbers had left behind.

"How do you do it? Walk into dangerous situations like that alone? You could've been killed."

"I wasn't alone. God was with me."

He snorted his disbelief and she drew away from him; he let her go easily.

"It's true. He is with me every day, every moment. You don't have to believe for it to be true. It just is."

He didn't reply.

"When He calls me home, I'll go. But I'm not going to stop living life—that includes doing my job—until then."

He flipped a twig into the fire; the moisture in the twig sizzled for a moment before it was engulfed in flames. "I used to...be religious."

She stifled the urge to tell him that her relationship with God was more than "religion," but something held her silent.

"Then someone I loved—someone I was close to—died."

A wife? She couldn't bear the thought. "God didn't make her die."

He was silent for a long time. "No. No, he didn't."

He didn't say more, and with the closeness between them broken, she shifted over to reach the saddle and opened one of the saddlebags. There was hardtack and jerky inside a wrapped pouch. Fred had always insisted on traveling with a little food in case of emergency. It wouldn't be much to eat, but if she needed to hunt up a rabbit for supper, she could. At least it gave her a distraction right now. She handed a portion of the dried meat to Chas, who took it and ate silently.

Where was the canteen? She reached back into the saddlebag, but this time her fingers brushed against soft leather and she pulled out Fred's journal. She'd forgotten sliding it into her bag this morning.

She flipped open the journal and ran her fingers over the writing. How many nights had Fred sat at his small desk in their room above the jail, writing in this book?

She blinked away her memories and returned the journal to her saddlebag, where it would be safe from the snow still falling.

"You ever read that, or just like touching it?"

Danna looked up with surprise to find Chas's eyes on her.

"I've seen you handle that book several times, but never read it."

It was already a night for sharing confidences. What would it hurt to reveal this, too? "I can't read," she answered quietly, a little ashamed by the admission. "It's one of the many things I don't know how to do. Cooking, sewing, keeping house. It was good my husband was a bachelor for years before we married, or we'd likely have starved."

Chas felt the tension crackling in the air between them. It mattered to Danna how he reacted to her revelation that she couldn't read.

He noted the distance she'd put between them when he'd rebuffed her mention of God, saw how she stared into the fire with her arms crossed protectively over her middle, a shiver coursing through her.

She thought he would think less of her because she couldn't read? Or cook?

"Not knowing those things hasn't stopped you

being marshal, hasn't stopped you doing a good job of it either."

"You really think so?"

"Yes." He was surprised to find out it was true. He *did* think she did a good job. Her loyalty to the people of Calvin couldn't be questioned—she'd ridden out into a blizzard trying to chase down those thieves!

Now that he took the time to think about it, he should have recognized the clues right in front of him. The way she'd squinted at his letter of introduction from the detective agency, that she'd pushed the Wanted poster for Jed Hester to him to read.

"Come back over here. It's cold," he said when a second shiver shook her shoulders. She shifted into place at his side and he couldn't ignore the brush of their shoulders. She spread one of the horse blankets over both their legs. Chas knew it was just to keep them warm, but the intimacy of the action had him scrambling for a distraction.

He choked out the words, "Now that I know you a little, I can't imagine you doing anything else."

Sitting so close, he had only a profile view of her face, but still he saw the wry smile. "Can't picture me as a seamstress or cook?"

"Perhaps a ranch foreman…or running your own spread."

Her lips quirked, but didn't quite form a smile this time. When she spoke, her words held a wistful quality. "When I was a child, I often dreamed of having my own homestead. Raising cattle."

"What changed?"

She was quiet for a long time. "I got married."

He remembered her previous statement that her

brother had sent her away, not to finishing school but to get married, and desperately wanted to ask what had caused the rift between them. She seemed to know.

"When I was fifteen," she started, "I took a horse from my brother's barn to chase down a heifer that was due to calf any day. I ended up in the mountains alone and my horse threw me. I was…injured."

"Is that why the mountains bother you?"

She looked him full in the face, her eyes asking him how he knew that.

"You've been jumpy all afternoon. Reacting to little noises, shadows."

A flush crept up her cheeks and she rested her head lightly on his shoulder. So he couldn't read her expression?

"Maybe I *am* a bit anxious. Anyway, because of my injuries I couldn't get home. It took my brother nearly a day and a half to find me." She inhaled deeply, her shoulder moving against his chest. "I'd never seen him so angry before."

"And that's why he sent you away? Because he was angry?" The question was out before he considered that she might not answer.

She hummed. "I think…I think also he didn't know what to do with a sister. If I'd been born a boy—or maybe if he'd had more time with my parents—he might have known how to handle me."

She yawned, and for the first time Chas realized how tired she was, how tired they both were. After being up all night dealing with the robbery and its aftermath, neither one of them had had any sleep, then they'd ridden all day. No wonder she was exhausted.

"Should we rest awhile?" he asked. "The blizzard doesn't seem to have slowed any."

Her head came off his shoulder. "One of us should probably keep watch. We don't know if the bank robbers are near or made it farther away—once night falls, which won't be much longer, our fire will be a beacon in the darkness."

She sounded bone-tired.

"I can stay awake for a bit," Chas said, shifting his arm around to support her shoulders a bit more.

"You're sure?"

"Yes."

She didn't speak again; her head lolled against his shoulder and her breathing evened out. That quickly, she'd fallen asleep. It told him just how much she trusted him. It was a sobering thought.

Mind whirling, he watched the flames flicker, shadows dance against the trees.

He was getting too entangled with the marshal. Everything she'd shared tonight had served to open his heart toward her. Before, he'd thought her crude, out of place as she fought to be marshal, but that impression had been completely wrong.

He couldn't imagine her brother sending Danna away. She was so strong, unbelievably beautiful, independent. She'd taken the circumstances life had given her, like the loss of her parents, and gone on. Not just existing, but *living*. She'd made a place for herself, provided for herself…

She was amazing.

How could someone who claimed to love her abandon her?

His thoughts went to his sister in Boston. Hadn't he

done the same thing and left her to the devices of their overbearing father and matchmaking mother? What if she needed him?

Not for the first time, he thought of sending for her. He could make a home for his sister in St. Louis or another western town, if need be. The question was, did she hate him the way his parents surely did?

The chance that she hated him was too great. There was no resolution for the situation between himself and his family.

He thrust thoughts of Boston, of *home,* away, focusing instead on the problem of his growing feelings for the marshal.

But there was no resolution to be found for that either.

Chapter Eleven

Dawn arrived with a lightening of the steel-gray sky and the absence of snow falling.

Chas woke to a hand on his shoulder—much pleasanter than a kick to his boot—to find himself wrapped in one of the horse blankets and the fire already extinguished.

"You all right?" Danna asked, crouching near. "Is your head paining you? You were mumbling in your sleep."

The nightmare. Just before Danna'd woken him, he'd watched Julia fall away from him, lifeless....

Chas scrubbed a hand over his face. "I'll be all right in a minute." It was a lie. He'd never be all right again, not without Julia.

He squinted up at the sky, then back at Danna who had moved back to the horses, one of which was already saddled up. She must be ready to leave.

He remembered waking her several hours into the night, when he could no longer keep his eyes open. She'd gone after more firewood, and he'd wrapped himself in the blanket to lie down and wait for her—and that's the last thing he remembered. Had he slept the rest of the night through? And only had the nightmare there at the very end?

It seemed impossible. The dream usually recurred multiple times, making his sleep broken each night.

With the return of his nightmare came the return of his hatred for Hank Lewis.

"Any chance of finding fresh tracks in this snow?" Chas gestured to the several inches of powder accumulated on the ground. A smaller layer dusted his blanket.

She considered him. "Depends. If they were nearby, it's possible we could pick up their tracks. We should get back to town soon…but we could spare a little time scouting, I guess."

Too soon—although the sky had lightened considerably—Danna declared they had to return to Calvin.

The disappointment was sharp in his chest, but he had no choice but to follow orders. Plus, they only had the one uninjured horse between them. Danna's original horse followed behind, its reins held loosely in her gloved hand.

By midday, they had descended out of the mountains and were only a few miles out from Calvin.

Riding double in the silent, snowy landscape was much different than when they'd ridden into town coming out of the canyon.

He was different.

The dynamics of their relationship had changed last night, as well. They were no longer simply marshal and deputy. Two people couldn't share the things they had and remain in a cordial working relationship.

But he was unsure about defining their relationship as "friends." He cared about what happened to

Danna—wanted her to be safe in her job—to be sure, but it couldn't be more than that.

He wouldn't let it.

Couldn't.

Because the only other woman he'd cared about—loved—had died, and it was his fault.

Safely back in town, Chas and Danna parted ways at the livery. He desperately wanted his bed, but a grumble of his stomach had him stopping in at the café first.

He still didn't know what to do.

He needed to find and kill Hank Lewis.

He needed to protect himself, protect his heart. And that meant distancing himself from Danna Carpenter. Because he could see himself falling for her if he stuck around. And he couldn't afford to lose another person he loved, not after what happened to Julia.

Inside the café, he was greeted by the smell of frying meat and the familiar waitress.

"Afternoon, hon." She set a mug of coffee down and motioned him to sit at one of the few empty tables. "Meat loaf or stew?"

He grunted what must've been a satisfactory answer, because she smiled at him and left.

How could he find Lewis? At this point, he didn't even care about the job he'd been assigned. James could send someone else to find the rustlers.

"Marshal come and claim that boy yet?" a male voice asked from a table nearby.

"No, he's still in the doc's office. Heard he's in bad shape," another voice answered.

A plate of steaming biscuits covered in thick gravy, eggs and fried ham appeared in front of him and Chas tucked in to the fare, trying not to listen to the talk swirling around him.

Someone slurped their coffee.

"…said she gut-shot him. Poor soul didn't have a chance."

Chas choked back words in Danna's defense. She'd been *alone* for most of that robbery. It was a miracle she hadn't been killed.

"I've seen her shoot. Wouldn't want to be on the other end of her gun, that's for sure."

"Nor her temper. I heard she let it fly at Harold's wife once for no reason a'tall."

A young woman breezed through the door and joined the waitress a few tables over. "Mama! You'll never guess who I saw riding into town this morning, proud as could be. The marshal!"

Chas's head came up; he fixed his gaze on the pair. The mother appeared harried, carrying two plates to a table at the far side of the room, while her daughter followed at her elbow.

"Put your apron on. We've got a full crowd," the waitress said, not appearing to pay attention to her daughter's words. She stopped for a moment at Chas's table to refill his coffee.

"But, Ma! She was out all night—with *her deputy*. Everyone saw her leave town."

The men sitting nearby who'd been talking about the marshal now sat silent, staring at Chas.

Danna wasn't going to like this one bit.

Danna darted toward the jail and the safety of her rooms. How could those hurtful rumors have spread through town so fast?

Her visit to the doctor hadn't provided any good

news. The outlaw was still in serious condition and hadn't roused except for a few lucid moments. And on her way to her rooms, she'd heard two different people speaking about her reputation being compromised after being out all night with her deputy.

She couldn't help the anger that clenched her fists. She neared the jail and quickened her steps, wanting nothing more than to escape to the privacy of her rooms.

She hadn't paid any attention to who might have seen her yesterday when she'd left town. No one else would help her. What was she supposed to do?

She'd been so relieved to have his help, she probably wouldn't have cared if the town had staged a parade to see them out of town. And she'd never expected to be caught in the snowstorm. Hadn't even considered she had a reputation to be damaged.

Nothing inappropriate had happened. And yet, rumors were swirling through town. She'd never had to worry about rumors or inappropriate behavior when she'd worked with Fred. No one would have dared start a rumor about her; Fred wouldn't have stood for it.

But how did she stop something like this?

Chapter Twelve

Up early after a restless night, Danna came down the stairs from her room, intending to run a quick patrol. She'd let the gossip scare her into hiding last night, afraid of coming face-to-face with her deputy. She couldn't bear it if he realized her feelings for him and pitied her.

But she needed to find Katy and make sure the girl was okay.

Boots hitting the boardwalk, she drew up short at the sight of two men obviously waiting for her outside the jail.

One of them cleared his throat. "Mrs. Carpenter." Mr. Castlerock.

"Marshal." Mr. Parrott.

Her heart sank as she realized both men were members of the town council.

"We need to speak to you for a few moments, on official business."

She motioned them toward the door, quickly unlocking it. They both filed inside behind her.

Still dark inside due to the early hour, Danna lit the

lamp on her desk by touch and then the two that hung on each side of the room.

The men stood inside the door, Parrott looking decidedly uncomfortable, while Castlerock wore the familiar scowl.

She didn't know whether to sit or stand, so she did what Fred would've done and perched against the side of the desk with her hands clasped in front of her. "What can I do for you gentlemen?"

Surprisingly, it was Parrott who spoke, not Castlerock. "We're, er...that is, the town council is..." He took a deep breath, as if preparing to deliver bad news.

Danna braced for the worst. They were going to demand her resignation. They'd warned her not to be a subject of the gossip, but this hadn't been her fault.

"Well, let's just say there is a bit of concern that you haven't made much progress on the bank robbery." He glanced at Castlerock and left Danna no doubt as to who was really worried. "The people of Calvin need to feel they're safe in this town."

"Have there been any complaints about the job I'm doing?" Danna asked, not sure she wanted to know the answer.

Parrott's eyes shifted to Castlerock again, and away. "Not *officially,* but—"

"Perhaps the town council could show its support by recommending that able-bodied men volunteer to be deputies," Danna interrupted, her temper rising, because Castlerock was now using the council to further his own agenda. She forced her voice to stay even, not betray her emotions. "More manpower would certainly help."

"Yes, well—"

"Have you contacted the sheriff?" Castlerock put in.

Even in the dim light from the lamps, she could see his face had begun to flush. He shifted on his feet, agitation visible from his actions.

"Of course," she replied, though it was getting harder to keep her tone calm. "I wired over to Glenrock yesterday afternoon when I got back in town. I haven't received a reply, but I would assume he'll get here when he can."

She hadn't wanted to ask the sheriff for help. He had a whole county to watch over. And Fred had never relied on the sheriff for help. But she'd wired him anyway, knowing she didn't have much choice without finding the robbers.

"You lost their tracks? What are you going to do next?" Castlerock continued questioning her, his eyes and face hard.

Danna stood, propelled by her anger. "I don't recall the town council ever questioning Fred about how he did his job."

He took a step closer. "Answer the questions, Mrs. Carpenter. I want my money back."

Danna registered that this was the second time he'd called her by name instead of *Marshal.* Had a decision already been made about her career? Or was Castlerock simply trying to intimidate?

Parrott was no help to her now, as he stood stoic behind Castlerock, though his expression seemed a little apologetic.

Danna expelled a rough breath. "My deputy and I tracked the robbers as long as we could, but we lost the tracks when the snowstorm hit—"

Castlerock exploded. He turned to Parrott, nearly yelling in the other man's face. "Do you see? She shouldn't even *be* marshal. *My money* is no closer to being found."

"Hold on—" Danna tried to speak but Castlerock ignored her.

"I want her resignation."

Silence descended in the wake of Castlerock's demand. Danna stood frozen, unable to believe he'd said the words aloud. Until now, she'd thought she still had time. That she would be able to find the robbers and that she'd...*what?* Be a town hero, like Fred had been?

What would she do now?

Parrott finally moved. He stepped between Danna and Castlerock and held out a hand toward each of them. "Now, George, we'll proceed as the council already decided."

Danna wanted badly to sit down on the desk behind her. In her exhaustion, and with emotions stampeding over her, her legs threatened to fold. But she refused to give either man the satisfaction of seeing her weak. She would hear the remainder of what they had to say standing. She locked her knees.

"Marshal," Parrott said, "The town council is concerned. We'll give you a few days—"

"Three," Castlerock interjected.

Parrott went on, shooting a quelling look at the other man. "A few days to find the bank robbers. If you can't...I'm afraid we'll have to start looking for a replacement."

Surprise surged through her, along with a renewed sense of hope. There was still time for her to solve this.

Parrott cleared his throat. Apparently, he wasn't done. "There is another matter we need to discuss."

Castlerock's eyes gleamed. "I can't wait to hear her excuse for this."

"Hang on." Parrott tried to calm the other man. "I'm sure there's an explanation. Marshal? Did you spend the night alone with a man?"

Danna couldn't believe it was coming down to this. "We had no choice," she said, and lifted her chin. "We were caught in the snowstorm. But nothing inappropriate happened."

The two men shared a speaking glance. "I'm afraid it doesn't matter if anything happened, Marshal," Parrott said. "We can't have even the appearance of impropriety. Where is this man now? Because I'm afraid he's going to have to marry you."

Chas rapped on the door and pushed it open. "Mornin', Miss Marshal. I know it's early—"

He let the surprise he felt show on his face, as Danna's head came up from her conversation with two older men, one he recognized as the owner of the bank that had been robbed. The other looked vaguely familiar, probably from the dance several nights ago.

"O'Grady." That growl from Danna didn't sound too pleased to see him.

"Hello, hello." The taller of the two men moved toward him and extended his hand for Chas to shake. "I assume you're the groom. Joe Parrott. Nice to meet you." Although the man's words were delivered with a smile, something about him seemed off.

"Hmm?"

Face pale, Danna ran a hand over her face. She appeared exhausted, with deep lines etched around her eyes. Had something else happened last night?

The banker moved forward, appraising Chas with a

flickering glance. "I'm afraid the marshal's reputation is tarnished beyond repair, thanks to your little jaunt out into the woods that lasted all night. I'm afraid she either has to get married—to you—or be removed from her position."

The man's supercilious manner irritated Chas even more than Joe Parrott's false cheerfulness. Then he registered what the other man had said.

"What?"

"Chas—" Danna started.

The rancher interrupted whatever she planned to say. "Perhaps we should leave the two of you to discuss what arrangements should be made. Mr. Castlerock and I will notify the preacher. Shall we meet at the parsonage at, say…two o'clock?"

With that, the two men excused themselves, Parrott sending a shrewd glance over his shoulder.

Once they had gone, Danna slumped in the chair behind her desk and rested her head on folded arms. "What are we going to do?"

Numb, Chas dropped into his usual straight-backed chair near the door. "We can't get married."

"Thank you very much for that!" she sniped, but her words were muffled by her arms, and was she… It almost sounded like she was…

"You're not crying, are you?"

She raised her head far enough to glare at him and he was enormously grateful to see that she wasn't crying, but the terrible emotion revealed on her expressive face didn't do much to relieve the ache in his stomach. She laid her head back down on her arms.

A terrible racket came from outside and then someone pounded on the door. Danna called a somewhat muffled "Come in!" without raising her head again.

A man—the bank manager from the robbery—pushed the door open and shoved Danna's ugly dog inside the room. The mutt stopped his baying and howling when he entered the room and moved to Chas's side, sitting on his boot.

"Um, Marshal, I'm real sorry to bother you, but your dog was, um, serenading me from my front porch this morning. I thought you might be looking for him."

Chas idly scratched the top of the dog's head. His brain was still spinning, not entirely on what was happening before him. Marry the marshal?

"I'm really sorry about the trouble," Danna said, still not raising her head.

Silverton shared a glance with Chas, brows furled. "Marshal…um…are you…I hope you don't mind me asking, but…are you all right?"

She didn't respond. Chas started to get really worried. He'd never seen her this hopeless before. Even when she'd planned to ride out after the bank robbers alone, she'd been more determined than anything else.

It was as if she was giving up.

But he couldn't marry her.

He liked her, admired her even. But he couldn't *marry* her.

Could he?

"Married?" Silverton echoed as Chas finished an abbreviated retelling of what had just happened.

Danna couldn't look at either of them. Did Silverton have to sound so appalled? Was she so undesirable as a wife that the man had to use such a shocked tone just talking about marrying her?

"Yes," she said, hiccupping a little as she finally sat up. "Hitched. Wed. United. Till death do us part."

She stood up, shaky, and started pacing across the open floor in front of her desk. Silverton wisely moved out of the way.

"They said I am no longer above reproach." She laughed bitterly. "Other towns have made marshals out of criminals, killers even, but Calvin's town council is going to remove my badge because of a bit of scandal."

She really couldn't believe it. Hadn't she given her all to this town, to her job?

"But they can't do that. They can't force you to get married."

"They want to."

"I could leave," Chas said, the words halting Danna. She faced the wall, thankfully, so neither man could see the hurt she knew etched her face at his statement.

"That would solve *your* problem, but what about the marshal? If she doesn't marry you, they'd probably still call for her job."

Why did Silverton have to sound so reasonable about it? She wanted to rage at the unfairness of this happening. She'd just been doing her job. She and Chas hadn't done anything immoral. And to bow to the council's wishes...it made it seem as if the gossip was true.

Oh, God. The cry came straight from her heart. Her breaking heart.

"Danna." A touch on her shoulder. She turned to face Chas, doing her best to keep her emotions from showing in her expression.

He looked more serious than she'd ever seen him before. "I can't leave—I have to see this case through," Chas said, voice low. "I have to find...the rustlers."

His hesitation over those words meant something, but her mind was too muddled to sort it out right now.

She rubbed a hand over her suddenly aching eyes. "But you don't want to marry me."

His silence was answer enough.

He didn't get a chance to answer because Silverton spoke. "You could possibly have the marriage annulled later. Coercion is a valid reason for annulment in this state. I'm not a lawyer, but…"

Danna turned in a slow circle, perusing the room that had belonged to her and Fred, and after tonight would belong to her and Chas.

They were going to go through with the wedding. And hope that the marriage could be annulled later, after the bank robbery and rustlers and everything else had been sorted out.

Problem was, she didn't know how to keep her heart from being involved. She was already half in love with Chas O'Grady.

She closed her eyes, forcing the troublesome thoughts to the back of her mind. Concentrating on her surroundings.

The room wasn't very homey. In fact, it was almost bare. She'd never had the inclination to weave rugs or hang curtains—the ones she'd hung in the jail downstairs had been out of necessity. The quilt on the bed had been a gift at her wedding to Fred.

Plain writing desk, table and two chairs, stove, small cupboard. Nothing frilly or womanly here at all.

The one decorative item was the wooden chest sitting at the end of the bed. It had been her mother's, and was the only thing she'd taken from Rob when she'd left home at sixteen.

Sitting on the end of the bed, she ran her hand over

the smooth wood. She flipped the lid open and clutched the side of the box as memories rushed over her.

She couldn't remember her mother, except for a sense of warmth and a vague, feminine smell. But she remembered being young—five, maybe?—and going through this very chest. She knew that under the wedding dress were a few letters tied with a ribbon, a family Bible, a portrait of her mother and father, a partial piece of lace. Pieces of her mother.

Rob had come in as she was going through the contents of the chest, and when he'd seen what she was doing, had erupted in a fit of anger. She hadn't realized at the time that he'd been hurting, too, missing her parents. She'd only known she'd done something wrong.

She hadn't touched the chest again, not until Fred had moved it into the tiny cabin they'd lived in at the time. A wedding present from Rob, after he'd shipped her off to Fred, made her Fred's problem.

Now she touched the pale-blue fabric lightly, then picked up the dress. Her mother's wedding dress. She hadn't worn it when she married Fred. It had been too long, and at the time she couldn't bear to have it hemmed.

But she'd grown two inches in her seventeenth year, and filled out some, too. It might fit now. And a woman shouldn't be married in pants, should she?

Danna considered it for a long moment, before sliding out of her shirt and trousers and slipping the dress over her head. Her hands trembled as she buttoned it up, smoothed out the lines from where the dress had been folded.

She turned to the small looking glass Fred had used for shaving, almost afraid of what she would see.

A woman—with large, dark eyes. Glossy hair,

almost black in color, pulled back from her face. Skin tanned by hours outside. But in the dress, she looked like a woman. Not like the marshal.

Danna slowly unbraided her hair, ran her hairbrush through the thick, long locks. She watched the mirror, the play of light on her hair as it shifted over her shoulder.

Chas seemed to like her hair down. When they'd been trapped in the snowstorm, with her hat gone and braid unraveled, he'd touched her hair more than once.

She tried to imagine walking through town with her hair down past her shoulders, like this, and couldn't do it. It would have to be enough that she wore the dress.

She searched in the trunk until she found a piece of ribbon. Pulling her hair into a bundle, she tied it off at the nape of her neck. When she looked at the mirror, a few tendrils had come loose, but most were held by the tie.

She smoothed a hand over her brow, noticed she was shaking.

Was this really the right thing to do?

Danna delayed long enough past the appointed hour that Chas questioned whether she would come at all. He halted mid-pace in the center of the room when a soft knock sounded.

The preacher ushered her inside, talking quietly with her. Chas was peripherally aware of a soft gasp from behind him from either Parrott or Castlerock, but his senses were filled with Danna. He couldn't take his eyes off her.

She wore a delicate blue dress.

He'd been attracted to her when she wore trousers, but with a long skirt swirling around her legs and the bodice of her gown clinging in all the right ways, she took his breath away.

Chas took advantage of her attention being still focused on the preacher, and used the time to examine the two curls trailing down her cheek, following the line of her jaw and down her neck.

He swallowed hard.

"Thank you," she said, and turned to the room.

Grateful she hadn't caught him with his mouth hanging open, Chas cleared his throat and prayed his voice wouldn't crack when he spoke.

When she looked up and met his gaze, he knew she wasn't as calm as she seemed. Her eyes shone with panic, then flickered to the two council members standing behind Chas, before she blanked her expression.

"You look lovely," he said, and his voice emerged steady. Nothing like the raging turmoil he felt inside. How had it come to this?

Her hands shook when the preacher directed Chas to take them. His might be shaking, too. It was hard to tell.

They faced the preacher, who held the Good Book in his hands. The vows they spoke only took a few minutes, and it was done.

"You may kiss the bride," the preacher said.

Danna's eyes met his—the first time she'd looked up during the whole ceremony—and he could easily read the trepidation in their depths. She started to shake her head. "We don't—"

He stopped her protest with a gentle touch of his mouth. It was nothing like the way he'd kissed her on the mountain. That had been a kiss of relief, a way of expressing the emotions that had pounded through him.

And yet...when he brushed his lips against the velvet

softness of hers, raised his hand and cupped her jaw…
it was the same.

The emotions bursting in his chest were enough to
make him feel like he was in front of that stampede
again, with his heart drumming in his ears. Sweat
popped out on his brow. He stepped away, unable to
take his eyes from her face, the contrast between her
lashes and her cheeks.

Beautiful.

His wife.

For now.

"I'll need you two to sign the marriage license and
we'll be done."

The preacher had a document in front of him on the
table. Chas took up the pen the other man had produced
and scribbled his name on the line the man indicated.
He passed the pen off to Danna and she squinted down
at the paper, hesitating.

Something inside him opened, wanting to protect
her from the men who stood close and who probably
didn't know she couldn't read.

Chas touched a finger to the line where she needed
to sign. It was a simple gesture, but she looked up at
him with something other than the panic or anger that
he'd seen in her eyes since the men had left her office
this morning. Appreciation.

Chapter Thirteen

❧

Fingering the simple silver band she'd put back on—
she'd removed it a few weeks after Fred's death—to
signify she was remarried, Danna approached the jail,
slowing her steps. She supposed Chas would be back
from gathering his things at the hotel soon.

She'd needed some space after the wedding—and
the kiss—so she'd gone on a patrol, keeping her eyes
peeled for any signs of Katy. She hadn't found the girl
or any sign of her.

And now she had to face her new husband. Who
hadn't wanted to marry her.

She didn't really want to be married again either,
she reminded herself.

Except she loved him.

A boy she recognized as belonging to one of Corrine's neighbors came running down the street as she
neared the jail.

"M-miss Marshal," the lad stuttered, "Missus Jackson needs you. Her baby's comin'."

Corrine was indeed in labor, crying out in pain, even
as Danna let herself into the shanty. A neighbor stood

over the kitchen table, but the instant she saw Danna, she turned for the door.

"Glad you're here. I've got my own young'uns at home, cain't stay. I'll take that'un for the night."

With that, the other woman swept out of the shack with three-year-old Ellie in tow, leaving Danna with the wailing Corrine.

"What—"

"Danna!"

"I'm here!" Rushing to her friend's side, Danna saw the face creased in pain, the sweat on Corrine's brow, the marks where she'd obviously clutched the sheets in her fists. "What can I do?"

Corrine let out a long breath, muscles easing. "Nothing yet. I think we have a bit to go, even though the pains have been coming all day."

"Should I get the doctor?"

"He's tied up at his office. The young man from the robbery took a turn for the worse. He's in surgery."

That wasn't good. The "young man" was quite possibly the only lead Danna had to find out where the outlaws were going with the bank's money.

"What about your neighbor…" And why had she rushed out like that?

Corrine clasped Danna's hand as another pain came. Her lips pinched white. "She doesn't… She thinks… Brent killed…your husband." The words came out in spurts and gasps as Corrine panted through the contraction.

Danna found a clean cloth on the end of the bed— someone had prepared things at least—and dabbed at her friend's forehead. "Shh. Shh. It's okay."

The contraction eased and Corrine relaxed again. "I don't suppose there's any news…?"

Danna wished she had something positive to tell her friend, but there was nothing. "I'm sorry."

"And Mrs. Burnett—" the preacher's wife "—is visiting her sister out of town," Corrine spoke as if the question about her husband hadn't been asked. "So I sent the neighbor boy to fetch you. Will you stay with me? Help me labor this baby?"

Tears sparkled in Corrine's eyes.

A lump of responding tears formed in Danna's throat. "You don't even have to ask," she told her dearest friend.

It was dark outside again.

Hours later, Danna trudged toward her room above the jail.

She hadn't wanted to leave her friend, but Corrine insisted she and her new baby boy would be all right for a few hours—long enough for Danna to get some rest.

The labor had been long. Danna had done her best to distract her friend from the pain, telling her about the recent events as marshal, even about the wedding. But Danna had seen it in Corrine's eyes that her friend just wanted her missing husband.

And it hurt that Danna hadn't been able to produce him for her. The guilt ate away at her.

In those last few moments, the baby had come quickly. He'd been a squalling, wriggling mass of flesh and goo. He'd been the most handsome thing Danna had ever seen.

Even now, the memory had her clutching her empty hands together.

For so long, Danna had wanted a family of her own. More than just a husband. Fred had wanted a family, too—a son—and she had wanted to give him one. She'd wanted to be more than just the marshal's wife.

And, yes, a part of her thought that if she had a child she would be able to relate to the other women. Not be so much of an outsider.

But she'd never so much as missed her monthly time, never suspected she was pregnant. Fred had never spoken his disappointment aloud, but she knew he must've been. Oh, he'd never come outright and say he regretted marrying her, but sometimes she wondered…

And then he died. And she had no one.

But this business with Chas O'Grady and a temporary marriage was stirring everything up in her heart again.

She wanted children of her own.

Why wouldn't God give her even one dream of her heart?

She rounded the corner past Hereford's Grocery and looked up. A light shone out the window to her rooms. So her new husband had made himself at home already? Then it hit her.

Chas had left a light on. For her.

Chapter Fourteen

Danna couldn't believe Chas had come to help her with Corrine this morning.

Watching him charm Ellie over a bowl of porridge, all her buried longings to be part of a real family, to have a family of her own, surfaced painfully.

Danna tried not to imagine what it would be like to hold a son of her own, the way she cuddled Corrine's son next to her sternum. But the image wouldn't be shaken.

The little one stirred and began to fuss, which seemed to wake Corrine, so Danna left the boy to be fed and joined Chas and Ellie at the table.

"There's some more porridge left," Chas said, glancing at her, then pushing a bowl in front of her. "You look exhausted."

Danna flushed.

"Did you not sleep well last night?"

It had been particularly hard to quiet her thoughts, even after Chas had settled on the floor and left her the bed. He'd been apologetic when she'd entered her room above the jail. Apparently the hotel manager had

taken it upon himself to have Chas's belongings delivered, and he hadn't wanted to embarrass Danna by
refusing.

His concern, then and now, was disconcerting. She
wasn't prepared for it.

She shifted her shoulders, trying to remove some of
the knots from them. "I'm all right."

He rose and stepped behind her, his large hands closing over her shoulders, making her jump. Their warmth
burned through her shirt. His thumbs made comforting
circles, fingers relaxed her aching muscles.

His touch made her feel as if he cared. And that was
dangerous to her emotions. When was the last time
she'd been touched like this? Tears burned her eyes
when she couldn't remember.

"All right?" Chas asked.

She couldn't answer. The intimacy of the moment
was suddenly too much for her. She wanted it to be real.

And knew that it couldn't.

She pulled away, returning to Corrine in the corner.
Her friend watched with weary, wide eyes, but thankfully remained silent.

Chas watched Danna retreat across the room. Even
with the physical distance between them, he still felt
as if they were connected by an invisible cord, one
stretched thin with emotion and expectations.

His chest felt tight. Breathing was hard.

It got worse when Danna turned, holding the little
one in the crook of her elbow.

Danna watched the doctor rouse the outlaw who'd
been shot, Chas at her side. The doctor thought the

young man had made it through the worst of his injury, but Danna knew that type of wound could be tricky. She couldn't wait any longer to question him.

"He's conscious," the doctor said over his shoulder, and she and Chas both stepped closer.

"Where were they going to take the money? From the bank?" Chas asked quietly.

The other man spoke, his voice so soft and raspy that Danna could barely make out his words. "Cabin... mountains."

"Where?"

"A little stream," he paused, his head rolling to the side, and he groaned. "Big, gnarled oak tree."

The description was too vague. Danna knew the mountains, the terrain, but she needed more landmarks than that if she was to track them down.

"Who was leading the gang?" she asked, leaning down a bit so the boy didn't have to strain so much to talk.

"H-hank. Lewis."

Chas inhaled loudly.

The kid closed his eyes. Moaned.

"Anything else?"

"Supposed to...meet with..."

That was it. He'd fallen unconscious again.

"Sorry, Marshal," the doc said, and sounded it, too. "If he comes awake again later, I'll send someone for you."

Chas turned away, his blue eyes dark like a coming storm.

Danna was disappointed, too. The kid was their only lead, and she felt she was running out of time before the town council might demand her badge.

* * *

Danna allowed Chas to steer her into the café for a midday meal before they returned to the jail.

Instantly, all eyes were on her. Eugene Hamilton, who ran the freight office and was one of the drunks she'd arrested last week, raised his brows. The milliner's spoon clanked against her bowl. The nearest conversations stopped.

She wanted to turn around and walk out the door. But Chas had crowded in behind her and she had no choice but to move toward an empty table in the corner. She lifted her chin high and walked, reminding herself she'd done nothing to be ashamed of.

Chas's hand branded her lower back and she felt him close behind her. She reached for a chair, only to have her hand swallowed up in his. His shoulder brushed hers.

"I'll get the chair for my wife."

She sank into the chair as he pulled it away from the table. His wife.

The waitress stopped short, close to their table but not quite there. "You got married?" The girl gasped the question, then seemed to realize what she'd done, for she came the rest of the way to the table, stammering. "I—I'm sorry. Didn't mean to be rude. C-congratulations."

Heads at the two nearest tables turned.

Chas smiled widely. "Thank you."

The girl set two menu cards on the table and Danna saw her hands were trembling. "Would you like coffee or water?"

Danna mumbled what she hoped was an appropriate response. She nodded to the pair at the next table over and they had the good grace to look away.

She hated this. Hated all the eyes on her.

Chas reached across the table with his palm turned up. Danna raised her brows at him and he wiggled his fingers at her. "Give me your hand."

"What?"

"Your hand."

She gingerly placed her hand in his and his fingers closed around hers. The strength and firmness of his hold reminded her that she wasn't alone in this. She met his eyes across the table and they held. His blue and her brown.

His talents and hers. They would take on the robbers together. Take on the rumors together. A team, like she and Fred had been. Only, this was temporary.

A shadow fell over her shoulder and Danna looked up to see the one person she least wanted to see right now. Castlerock.

"Marshal." He nodded to her, then Chas, his lips a thin line. "Any news?"

Danna tried to reclaim her hand, but Chas clasped it too tightly, and she didn't want to draw more attention than they already were.

"Not yet."

It was too much to hope the banker would leave them in peace. He tapped on the edge of the table. "While I am *delighted*—" his sarcastic emphasis on the word suggested just the opposite "—that you've resolved your personal issues, there is still the matter of my missing money."

Danna bristled, but it was Chas who answered in a cool voice. "The marshal hasn't forgotten about your money."

"Is that so? And how is her investigation going at the moment? Well enough for her to dine with her new husband, is it?" Castlerock's voice was rising, as was the blood to his face—it began to mottle red and white.

Danna stood, extracting her hand from Chas's. He moved to stand beside her and touched her side lightly, but she moved away from him.

She was the marshal; she would handle this.

"I don't remember my first husband being questioned while in the middle of an investigation, and I'll thank you not to question me, either. I *will* apprehend the men responsible for the theft, or you can fire me."

"You can be assured, I will. You're on borrowed time, Marshal." Castlerock's threatening words weren't spoken very loud, but Danna knew every ear in the room was attuned to their conversation.

She sensed Chas shift next to her. They'd spent enough time talking, so she sat down. Castlerock huffed at the obvious dismissal and stalked off.

Their food arrived, the waitress whisking it on the table and leaving quickly.

Chas stared down at his plate while he ate, a contemplative look on his face. After a while, he commented, "The banker seems awfully interested in muddling with your investigation."

Appetite gone, Danna played with her fork. "He's interested in looking out for himself," she murmured, not wanting others to hear the disparaging comment.

"I didn't see it before…" Chas said softly, as if to himself. He lifted his face and turned his gaze on her, food forgotten.

"Can you remember specifically what all those men who refused to be deputies had to say?"

What did that have to do with Castlerock? "No, not really. Why?"

"In the beginning of my own investigation, I started

asking questions around town. About the rustling problem."

She knew her face showed the puzzlement she felt. He went on.

"And the responses I got were a bit…unusual."

"In what way?"

"Everyone I spoke to seemed loath to share information. I could understand if one or two didn't want to talk to me, but this was every person I talked with."

Danna still didn't see what this had to do with the robbery or Castlerock. That seemed to be the same response she'd gotten whenever she tried to talk to anyone from town, ever since Fred's death. Chas was staring off into space again and she cleared her throat.

"Sorry," he said, shaking his head. "I'm trying to understand how it might be related. Perhaps we should…" He nodded toward the door.

They settled their bill and were soon on the boardwalk heading toward the jailhouse. Chas offered his arm again and she took it. Anyone who looked at them would think they were out for a stroll, but when he spoke his urgent tone belied the casual air he put off.

"At the dance—I overheard two men talking about it."

"About the robbery?"

"Yes. They weren't part of Henry Lewis's gang. I didn't recognize the voices and I couldn't see faces, but they seemed to know an awful lot about what was happening. Unfortunately, I had to go inside or risk being found out.

"And the other day, in your office, something seemed…I don't know, *off* about Joe Parrott. I couldn't place it at the time, and then we got distracted, but does he have a tattoo or a mark on his left wrist?"

She nodded. "There's some sort of mark, yes."

"I think he was one of the men I overheard at the dance. What if the town council has set you up to fail? And they've bribed the former deputies not to help you?"

"Why would they do that?"

"I don't know, but there's something going on in this town that's bigger than some missing cattle and a bank robbery."

Chapter Fifteen

Danna perched on the edge of the bed, flustered and ill at ease. Last night, after helping Corrine birth her baby, she'd fallen into bed exhausted.

Tonight she was alone with Chas.

And it was completely different than when they'd been stuck in the snowstorm. They hadn't had a choice that night, and they didn't have one tonight either, but she still felt...discomfited.

A soft knock on the door announced his presence and then he was there, filling her small upstairs room with his broad shoulders and his very presence.

He took off his hat once he was inside, and ran his hand through the auburn curls plastered to his head. She'd seen him do that before. Did it mean he was as nervous as she was?

Chas looked around the rooms, and Danna refused to be ashamed of the simple furnishings. They might not be as fancy as something he'd find in Penny Castlerock's home, but they were functional.

She'd been thinking on Chas's suggestion that the town council could be dirty all afternoon, and she just couldn't see it. Wouldn't Fred have had some suspicions, if that was the case?

Chas reached into his chest pocket and withdrew a small bundle, distracting her from her thoughts. "I— This is for you."

He stepped forward to hand her the cloth-wrapped item, then stuffed his empty hand in his trouser pocket. "It's not much of a wedding present, but I thought perhaps it was something you'd get some use out of."

A gift? For her?

Heart pounding, Danna unwrapped the small bundle of cloth to find a pair of spectacles with round lenses and thin wire frames. She looked up at Chas, puzzled.

"What—"

"To help you read."

The words stretched in the sudden stillness between them, the last thing she'd expected him to say. He'd been so kind, so considerate all day.

And now he'd touched on the one thing she'd never been able to accomplish, no matter how hard she'd tried. Would he be ashamed of her, like Rob had been?

She averted her face, set the spectacles on the desk before her, her fingers flexing against the wood.

"I've seen you...the way you squint sometimes..." His voice trailed off, and she glanced at him to see his gaze focused on the wall, as if remembering something. "Just like a friend I used to know."

"There was no school here when I was a child." Danna spoke, her eyes trained on his shoulder. "Fred tried to teach me...for months after we were married. I never took to it."

He turned to her, watched her face. And picked up the spectacles from the table to hold them out to her again. "My friend could see fine at far distances—maybe better than I could. But up close—" he held his hand about a foot in front of his face "—everything was a blur."

She didn't take the spectacles from him; neither did he lower his outstretched hand.

"I can't do it," she said.

"Wouldn't you like to read your husband's journal?"

She glared at him. "That book is not your concern."

"Will you just try?" His hand remained extended, his eyes serious.

Exasperated, she took the spectacles from him, expecting him to gloat, but he watched her in silence.

She slipped them over her nose, tucked the curves behind her ears. Reached for the sheaf of papers in one of the desk drawers. When she looked down at the top sheet, she expected to see the same thing she always saw—blurry lines that didn't make any sense. To her surprise, the words came into sharp focus. She could make out each individual letter clearly.

She looked up at Chas in amazement. "I can see!"

Danna slept with her face to the door, one hand tucked under her cheek. With her face flushed from sleep, she looked young. Not old enough to be married, or in charge of keeping in the peace in this town.

Chas watched her for a long time, this woman he... had feelings for. He'd been fighting against himself all evening, against the greed inside that claimed "she's mine."

She was his, but not forever. Just for long enough that she didn't get herself killed. Then they'd get an annulment and he'd leave.

He still felt warm from the giddiness she'd shown when she'd tried on the spectacles. They'd sat together at the small table, heads together, reviewing the alphabet and sounding out some small words. Each inadvertent brush of her hand had sent his senses spiraling.

Now he looked down at the leather-bound book he'd palmed as Danna readied for bed earlier. Part of him felt guilty for what he was about to do, but the other part wanted to know if her first husband had left them any clues.

He flipped the book open, toward the end. The writing was cramped, but readable. It seemed to be the middle of an entry.

…when will she understand that she is loved, both by her Heavenly Father and by me? She is so alone. She needs to be able to rely on someone greater than herself. But she won't open her heart—I still can't find a way inside, not after searching for the key all these years.

Neither can anyone else. I saw Mrs. Poe approach her in the general store today, but Danna ignored the older woman's overtures of kindness.

It is as if she can't see her own worth. I have never been able to get her to open up about her relationship with Rob. The man was my best friend, but didn't know anything about females—not like I knew much either, before I married Danna.

Chas slapped the book closed. It felt *wrong* to read the inner thoughts of the man who'd been Danna's husband. And yet a part of him wanted to know more. More about what this other man knew about Danna. Part of him seethed with jealousy that Fred had known Danna intimately, had known her secrets.

But not all of them. Chas remembered the night—

was it just two nights ago?—he and Danna had spent tucked next to the small campfire she'd built. She'd told him her brother had basically thrown her away. From her first husband's words, it didn't sound like she'd ever told him.

And several things she'd said about herself made him think she *didn't* know her own worth, like the husband said. She saw herself as a deputy, a friend. Not as a woman.

Maybe, after they caught Lewis's gang and he finished his job for the WSGA, he would have time to prove to her that she was a beautiful, capable *woman*. He could show her she deserved love.

And maybe he'd find a lost treasure mine while he was at it.

Chas slapped the lid closed on his wishful thinking just as he'd closed the journal a moment ago. He wasn't here to woo Danna. He was here to help her with her problem. Then he was gone. He had to finish his job, and then he'd likely never return to Wyoming.

That was it.

No happy ending for him.

He didn't deserve one.

Danna woke with a start, instantly alert.

What was that noise?

She rolled her head across the pillow and saw that Chas's head tossed, though he appeared to be asleep. His face creased in a frown.

What did a man like Chas dream about? They still hadn't talked much about *him*.

Had he moaned? Or had she imagined the noise?

The sound came again, and this time she knew it was Chas. She slid off the edge of the bed and quickly

pulled on her overshirt and trousers and tiptoed closer
to where he sprawled across the floor. She didn't want
to wake him if she didn't have to.

His head thrashed on the pillow, his lips moving,
brow wrinkled.

She reached out her hand to touch him, wake him,
but she froze when his moan turned into a word.

"Julia."

Feeling as if she'd been punched in the stomach, she
backed away until her calves hit the bed.

Who was Julia? A sister? Friend? Wife?

She was shaking. She clasped her hands together
in front of her to try and stop them trembling. She'd
known he had a past she knew nothing about, but for
him to call out another woman's name...

A sudden noise from street level made Danna jerk
her head toward the window. That had definitely been
a horse's whicker.

She carefully pulled the edge of the curtain back.
The moon was only half-full, but it was enough to see
the three men on horseback, just below her window.
Wearing bandanas over their faces.

With no time to categorize her emotions, to stifle
the hurt that his dreamed woman had caused, she fell
back on the training learned from years of working
with Fred.

She darted across the floor, slapped her husband's
shoulder and held a finger to her lips when he started
awake.

"There are masked men downstairs. I don't know
what they want, but I don't wish to be trapped up here
with only one way out."

She was gratified when he rose without a word and
reached for the weapon he'd left on the table.

He glanced at her over his shoulder and she prayed he couldn't read the turmoil in her face.

"I'm going out the window. You'd better sneak down the stairs, and quick."

As quick and silent as she could, Danna slid the window all the way open and swung one leg over the sill.

"Wait!" Chas had found his voice. He grasped her arm above the elbow. She flinched but forced herself not to pull away. She couldn't read his face in the darkness, but the rasp of his breath was rapid, almost anguished. "Please—be careful."

She nodded, not sure if he could even see her in the dark, but she couldn't make words emerge from her suddenly parched throat. He sounded as if he cared.

She pulled away from his grasp and slipped out the window.

Chas woke from one nightmare to be thrust right into another.

The stench of blood and death was strong in his mind, and he didn't have time to shake it off before Danna was halfway out the window.

He clung to her for too long, afraid this whole thing was going to end badly. He couldn't watch another woman he...*cared about* die.

When he opened the door with a soft snick, he didn't even have a chance to step outside before he heard the thump of boots on the wooden staircase. He shut the door with another near-silent click, and latched it, for all the good it would do.

Now what?

He made for the window, swung one leg over to try

to find the footholds Danna had used a moment ago. Where was she?

"What are you doing?" A sharp hiss from above his head answered his unasked question. She was on the roof.

"How did you get up there?"

Before she could answer, a loud thump announced someone was attempting to force their way inside the marshal's room. Chas needed to get out of the window, which was in direct sight of the door. He swung his other leg over the windowsill and then was supporting his weight with his posterior and a white-knuckled grip.

"Chas—"

He didn't hear the rest of Danna's words, because the distinct sound of wood splintering—the latch?—obscured her whisper. He slid off the windowsill, now hanging by his fingertips. Dangling like a monkey he'd once seen at a circus.

He didn't think it would hurt too much if he fell to the ground—he couldn't be more than eight or ten feet up. He was more afraid of the noise he'd make if he hit the boardwalk.

Angry voices from inside the room preceded the sound of boots stomping, moving toward the window. Chas knew he'd run out of time to make a choice.

He let go.

This was a disaster.

The two men in her rooms weren't making any effort to be quiet. Their rapid, pounding bootsteps told her their exact locations inside. She even heard them swear when they realized the room was empty.

She could drop off the edge of the roof and have the element of surprise, but she wasn't sure her husband could keep himself from getting killed. Clouds blew in and covered the moon, provided poor visibility, and she couldn't see Chas on the ground.

She waited for the exclamation that would come when they discovered a man hanging in the window, but nothing happened.

And she was afraid to call out again with the two men inside. From the angry buzz of their voices, they'd discovered no one was home. Where were the two other men? And where was Chas?

How she wished Fred was here; she'd even settle for one of his deputies. She could trust Fred to take out the two other outlaws and leave these two for her. But she knew Chas had different instincts, and she couldn't be sure how he would respond. He could get them both killed.

She closed her eyes. No more time to decide.

Careful to stay light on her feet, she darted across the roof and grabbed the rope she'd left earlier, then hopped down to the stair platform. She slammed the door closed. A muffled curse came from inside. She looped the rope around the doorknob and tied off the end to the beam supporting the stair railing.

The door rattled under her hands as someone started pounding from the other side.

Running down the stairs, she paused behind the corner of the building and strained her ears to hear over the drumming from upstairs. She had no desire to run smack into any lookout they'd thought to leave nearby.

She unholstered her pistol and held it at her side. Hearing nothing, she skirted the building, keeping to the shadows close to the wall. Where had her husband gotten to?

The three horses now stood saddled and ready to go in the alleyway between the jail and the saloon behind it. One of the shadows behind the horses moved, and she was able to make out a head and shoulders of someone standing on the other side. She edged closer.

"Hold up a minute." The harsh, deep voice, undeniably male, came from behind the horses.

The pounding from upstairs ceased, and in the silence Danna heard the unmistakable sound of a pistol hammer being cocked. She froze a few paces from the horses, crouching close to the ground.

"Where's the marshal?"

"Don't know." And, lovely. Chas's voice answered the unknown man.

"You was jest in her room. Saw you twist yer ankle comin' out the winder."

Even better. It sounded like her husband was hurt on top of being caught. She should have tried to do this on her own.

"Earl!" A voice drifted down from the open window above Danna's head. "We're trapped in here. Come let us out."

"Cain't. I got a dep'ty down here. I'm trying to find out where the marshal is. Unless you know where she keeps the keys to them jail cells."

"Sorry, no."

Light brightened the night, coming from the window above. Danna tucked even closer to the ground, going to her knees and supporting her upper body with her left hand so she still had her gun available.

"Jest conk him in the head if ya need to."

"So what're we s'posed to do?"

This time two voices came down from the window at the same time.

Exasperation began to leak from the man named Earl's voice. "I dunno. Bang the door down, why don'cha?"

A guttural growl was the response. The thumping started up again, this time louder than before.

Danna began to crawl toward the horses, hoping Earl and Chas were the only men there. Would Chas be able to get himself out of this?

"I'm gonna ask ya one more time. Where's the marshal? I aim to get my colleague outta jail. Tonight."

He'd come for the injured outlaw? He must not know the other man was shot, was located at the doctor's office. Not if they'd come *here* looking for him.

Danna's grip on her pistol wavered and the gun thumped against the boardwalk. She cringed and stopped moving, praying this Earl character hadn't heard.

"What was that?"

Danna rolled, coming close to the hooves of the nearest horse, but she should be out of sight, as long as the outlaw was looking over the backs of the horses.

Through the horses' legs, Danna could make out one pair of feet and shins. She didn't remember O'Grady wearing spurs, so this must be Earl.

The sound of wood splintering followed by a loud *whoop* came, and Danna bit down on her lower lip to hold in the exclamation that wanted to escape. She'd have had those two hog-tied or locked in a jail cell by now, if she hadn't been wasting time trying to rescue her husband.

So what should she do now? She could intercept the two men as they came downstairs and rounded the corner. She knew she could get the jump on them, but where would that leave Chas?

Her thoughts circled frantically, and she knew she needed to take action soon, or risk the two men from upstairs coming upon her from behind.

Earl's patience seemed to be running out. His feet shifted restlessly. She couldn't tell if he had a weapon pointed at Chas, but if he did, the chance he'd miss from this range was slim indeed.

"Where's. The. Marshal?" Earl's voice was clipped and Danna knew Chas's time was running out.

So she made the decision. She couldn't leave him to the outlaw's mercy.

Tucking her gun in its holster, she crept beneath the hooves of the first horse, moving as slowly as possible. She prayed nothing would spook the horses. If they startled, they would crush her.

She groaned when she realized the other two horses weren't lined up; one of them stood slightly behind the other, which would put her more out in the open.

She could also see her husband's booted feet near the corner of the boardwalk by the clothing store. He stood with all his weight on one foot; the other was raised off the ground. Her view was blocked by the horses, so she couldn't determine if he had other injuries.

A shot rang out and she jumped, but somehow managed not to startle the horses. Was Chas hit? When she looked, he was still standing. Relief threatened to send her to her belly, so weak were her limbs.

"Tell me what ya know or the next one won't be a warnin'."

She willed Chas to start talking. The shot would have alerted those in the buildings close by—Henry Shannon at the leather goods store and the Quinns at the dress shop—that something was happening. She could count on them to protect their own property, not necessarily to help her. Maybe these outlaws would turn tail and run if enough people started stirring.

If she and Chas could make it through the next few minutes without getting killed, they had a real shot at capturing these guys.

"Last I knew, she was on the roof."

Yes! Finally, he was using his head.

Knowing the two other outlaws could be coming up behind her anytime, Danna made her move. She sprang up between the horses, vaulted over the nearest one and used her foot on its saddle as a springboard to launch herself across the back of the second one. Her momentum took the outlaw to the ground, and she pinned his gun arm with her weight and both hands.

The horses shied at the unexpected movement and trotted out into the middle of the street.

"Danna!"

Chas's exclamation was immediately followed by his presence behind her. He kicked away the outlaw's gun and knelt next to her, stuffing the other man's hat against the lower part of his face as a gag.

"What were you thinking? You could've been killed!" he railed at her.

At this close proximity, she could see the anger in his drawn brows and clenched jaw.

"So could you!" she returned. She took one of the rawhide strips she'd tucked into her pocket and tied the man's wrists together. "Were you *waiting* for him to shoot you?"

The man continued to struggle and was getting louder, so she conked him in the head with the butt of her gun. He stilled.

"I can't believe you hopped—"

"What's going on?" A voice and flickering light

emanated from the saloon. It illuminated Chas's face, showing an emotion she couldn't identify. It looked a lot like whatever had been on his face while he'd been dreaming, before he'd called out another woman's name.

Ruthlessly, Danna pushed down the emotions rising in her throat.

Shouts from farther down the street alerted Danna that the other two robbers had seen the horses in the open. She ducked behind the corner of the building, yelling "Watch out!" to Mr. McCabe and simultaneously pulling her deputy along with her.

Multiple shots rang out, and fire ripped through the inside of her upper left arm. She was hit!

Stifling a cry, she turned to check on Chas. "You okay?"

"Yes'm. What do we do now?"

"I doubt they've figured out that the kid was at Doc's office, so we're good there. But if they start shooting, innocents are liable to get hurt."

"What should we do?"

"Let's herd them toward the railroad tracks. Hopefully, one of us can cut them off in front. If they manage to escape, I can track them down as long as the weather holds."

Chapter Sixteen

"Can we please stop now?"

Chas pushed his hat off his forehead to get a glimpse of Danna, and the action dumped icy water from the brim down the back of his neck.

He may not know much about tracking, but surely the driving rain had erased any tracks that might have been left from the two men who'd disappeared after making it out of town last night.

Danna wheeled her mount toward town without speaking. She'd been silent since they'd mounted up outside the livery.

At least they had one outlaw in custody. This one uninjured. He was one of the men Chas had spoken to in the café on his first day in town. If they could just get him to talk.

Chas was the first to admit he didn't know much about women, but he gathered her silence meant she was upset. But what was she upset about? Losing track of the two other outlaws? He counted it a blessing that she hadn't been hurt.

Still wrapped in his thoughts, he barely noticed

when they arrived in town and dropped their horses off with the boy in the livery. He did notice when Danna stomped off down the boardwalk without him.

"She's sure got a bee in her bonnet this mornin', huh?" the livery hand asked, as he took the bridles of both horses. "I'm guessin' ya'll didn't catch up to them robbers." He seemed disappointed. Was he one of her admirers?

Chas frowned. Danna hated people in town talking about her. "That's the marshal's business."

"Well, I reckon everyone's going to be in the marshal's business if she came back to town without them."

That's what he was afraid of. He hurried off after Danna.

"Danna. Danna!" He shouted her name the last time, his frustration making his temper spike.

She spat her next words over her shoulder, her eyes inscrutable under the brim of her hat. "Please refrain from spreading my business all over town."

He caught up to her in front of the jail building, and grabbed her arm to force her to face him. Something flared in her eyes and she jerked her arm away. "Don't."

"Are you angry with me? Why?"

"Who is Julia?"

He looked down, unable to contain the surprise and pain he knew would show in his face.

With his face turned down, he noticed the pink stain on her white shirt inside the flap of her jacket. "Are you—hurt?" He could barely force the words out, so sudden was the sensation of the breath being squeezed from his lungs.

She shrugged off his hand, and it was only then he realized he was clutching her shoulder. He forced himself to focus, deny the roaring in his head. Danna was injured and needed his help.

"Let's get you to the doctor." He tried to steer her toward Main Street, where the doctor's office was, but she continued on the way she'd been walking.

"It's just a scratch. I'll take care of it myself."

He didn't believe her, but she left him no choice other than follow her up the stairs to her room. Was she angry enough to deny him entrance? Apparently not, because she left the door ajar.

Danna turned her back and took off her long coat, revealing a bloodstain along her left side. Judging by the location of the crimson mark, the wound seemed to be on the inside of her upper arm.

Chas bit off a curse and strode over to her. He gripped her shoulders and spun her so she faced him. He wanted to see her eyes, needed to gauge how bad it really was.

The sight of her blood did things to his insides that he hadn't felt since Julia. But having tender emotions for Danna was impossible, wasn't it? He'd promised himself he was never going to fall in love again.

Danna half turned away from him, shaking loose of his grasp. "I'll undress and take care of this, if you don't mind." She motioned with her head and hands and he understood he was to turn around, so he did.

Staring at the broken latch on the door made him angry, so Chas began methodically taking off his coat, boots, vest. He left the rest of his clothes on, even though his pants were soaked through and his shirt nearly so.

"How did it happen?" he asked, not sure he wanted the answer. It seemed everything had gone wrong last night. How much of it was his fault?

A drawer opened and closed somewhere behind him, and then something—cloth?—rustled and a soft tinkling noise came. What was she doing?

Her voice sounded muffled. "When that first volley of shots came..." now clearer "...the bullet grazed me. It's not that bad." But her voice was tight, as if she might be fudging the truth a bit. He couldn't read her well enough to tell.

She said something else, but her voice was too low to make out the words. It sounded like "I can't afford it to be bad."

"Not that bad," he repeated. Not that bad. Only shot a little. *A scratch.* He felt as if the top of his head floated away from the rest of him as his temper ignited. "How do I get myself into these situations?"

No answer came, either from above or from Danna.

Perhaps he could ask Danna to give up her quest to apprehend the robbers. Instinctively, it sounded like a bad idea. But what if he put her on a train to Boston? Just because he hadn't talked to his parents in years, they probably wouldn't turn away his wife.

Too bad Danna would never agree to go. He *did* know her well enough to know that.

Another part of him wanted to hunt down Lewis's gang himself, and show them as much pain as they'd caused Danna. His feelings now superseded the desire for revenge he'd felt after Julia's death. Lewis needed to pay.

"I can't quite—" Danna's voice interrupted the roaring tempest of his thoughts.

"Do you need help?" He waited for her answer before he turned around.

Danna sighed, a little huff of air to let him know

she wasn't happy about it. "Yes. It's difficult for me to reach the wound."

He faced her, and had to swallow hard. She wore an undershirt and had the quilt from the bed wrapped around her; only her shoulder and injured arm emerged. It was her hair that unmanned him, the dark locks falling in waves down her back. She must've loosed them from the braid so they would dry.

His knees threatened to knock together as he approached her. She flushed under his gaze and averted her face, pointing to the array of doctoring supplies she'd laid out across the bed.

"You'll need to clean it out first," she said. "The wound isn't bad, but if infection sets in…"

"Yes, I know." And he *did* know how bad infection could get. He'd met plenty of men missing limbs or on the brink of dying because of infection from injuries. "I can't believe you went all morning with a *bullet wound* and didn't tell me."

He located an antiseptic and some clean cloths and moved in front of Danna so her crown was at his chin. He began by wiping the blood off the inside of her arm. He was entirely too conscious of how soft her skin felt against his palm, and how she smelled sweet, even though the rain must've washed away any scent of soap or perfume.

"There wasn't anything you could do, even if I did tell you."

"You would've told your first husband."

"Fred—" She bit out the one word. That was it.

He kept his gaze on what he was doing, but he could see her jaw flex from the corner of his eye, as if she'd chomped down on what she really wanted to say.

He leaned away so he could look her in the face. He didn't release his hold on her upper arm. "Say it."

Her gaze didn't waver from his. "Fred would've known without me telling him."

Well. Chas looked down to apply the antiseptic to a rag, pretending her words didn't sting. He dabbed the rag against the bloody furrow in her skin—she was lucky the bullet hadn't entered her flesh—and heard her soft intake of breath.

He hated that she was injured. Hated that they hadn't been able to capture the outlaws. Hated that he had no control over any of this.

He moved to stand behind Danna, in order to get a better look at the other side of her wound.

"This was my fault," he muttered. Maybe he never should have come to Calvin in the first place.

"No, it's not."

Danna's soft but firm words startled him. He didn't realize he'd spoken aloud. Their eyes met in the small looking glass hanging above her desk.

"What?"

"It's not your fault I got shot," she said, and the look in her dark eyes confirmed her words. "That was my own incompetence."

"You're not incompetent." Now it was his turn to reveal his confidence. And he *was* confident in her ability. He just wasn't sure she could take on Hank Lewis and come out of it alive.

She looked as if she wanted to refute his words, but instead she took a deep breath and said, "What about Julia? Who is she?"

Chas closed his eyes. He should have known Danna wouldn't forget about her earlier question. But what should he tell her?

The truth. The simple words reverberated in his head.

"She was a childhood friend." The words stuck in his throat like molasses, gummy, in a way that meant he had to push each one out. "Our parents traveled in the same social circles. When we got older, we became sweethearts."

Danna had been still before, but now went completely motionless. Chas tried to control the bitterness he knew was seeping into his voice. She'd asked, after all.

"And then...and then our parents arranged a marriage."

She nodded. But he wasn't finished.

"For Julia and my brother."

Now her spine went rigid beneath the hand he'd placed there as he doctored her arm.

"She was my brother's wife."

"But you loved her."

Yes, he had. It had been his downfall. "Yes, and I killed her, too."

Chas's words, so casually spoken, turned Danna's world topsy-turvy.

She spun and pushed away from him, creating distance between them while he watched her with stormy eyes.

Where had she put her gun? There it was, on the other side of the bed, beneath the coat and shirt she'd shed when she'd come inside. Could she reach it without arousing his suspicions?

He set the rag he'd been using to doctor her scratch on the table, turning his shoulders so she couldn't see his face. She edged closer to her weapon.

"Julia and Joseph hadn't been married for six months

before he came up with some hare-brained idea to head west and make his own fortune, even though he was in line to take over our father's empire." He looked up for a moment. "In Boston."

Danna sat down on the bed, stretching one leg out to try and reach the gun.

"Julia received a couple of letters, and then all correspondence stopped. She was sure my brother was caught up in something immoral or illegal, or both."

He paused. Ran a hand through his damp hair.

"She asked me to find him for her."

"And you said yes?" She needed to keep him talking. He wasn't looking at her, not really, and she almost had her gun in hand.

"Of course. At the time, I thought it would be a better choice. It was too hard to be near her in Boston, and know that I couldn't be with her. At least not in the way I'd dreamed about since my eighteenth birthday."

He went silent, now staring at the wall. Lost in the past?

She couldn't imagine him hurting a woman. Not one that he claimed to love.

"So you came west looking for your brother. Did you find him?"

He turned back to her, his expression revealing he'd forgotten she was even in the room. His eyes had gone from stormy turquoise to darkened sapphire.

"I made the mistake of telling Julia what train I was taking out of Boston. She showed up, sat down right next to me a few minutes after the train left the station."

"What? She traveled with you?"

He nodded, a small smile quirking the corners of his lips. "I didn't know she had that much gumption. She'd always done what her parents wanted."

Even marry Chas's brother, came the unspoken emphasis.

"I tried to put her off at the next station, but she would have none of it. She insisted she could handle the travel, the long hours. She said she'd stay in the hotels and let me find Joseph. That she just wanted to be there when we found him."

"And you gave in." Danna forgot all about her pistol and allowed her shoulders to relax beneath the quilt. She had a suspicion about the direction his story was taking. And she began to ache for him.

"I was stupid," Chas spat, his brows slashing downward. "I should've known she was fibbing."

"Most women have certain…wiles they can use to get men to do what they want."

Chas looked up at her, as if surprised she was defending him. She was a little surprised herself. She motioned for him to go on, but he continued to stare at her. She prompted him, "So when you found Joseph…"

He shook his head, eyes again going to the floor, to the past. "I found him in a saloon, in the middle of a poker game, surrounded by—"

He cut himself off and flushed a little. As if she didn't know what sort his brother would have been surrounded by in a saloon. She nodded for him to go on.

"He didn't even look like Joseph. The Joseph I knew was always overly conscious of his clothing, always neat and groomed. This Joseph had a scraggly beard and unkempt clothes—his shirt was torn in two places—and he smelled like he hadn't bathed in weeks. I barely recognized him. It was obvious he'd fallen in with some unsavory characters."

Danna knew that feeling, knew how it burned inside. Like when the person you thought would always take care of you suddenly didn't want you anymore. You couldn't help loving them, but *oh*, it hurt.

"Before I even spoke to him, the man sitting across the table accused Joseph of cheating. He probably was."

Chas went silent again. Danna saw the muscles move as he swallowed hard.

"And Julia came into the saloon behind you." She could guess the rest, but perhaps it would be cathartic for him to tell it.

He nodded, his throat still working. Finally, after a long moment, he continued. "The men had their guns drawn before I even knew she was there. She was shot twice. There was blood everywhere." He rasped the words now, rushing, as if he couldn't stop. "I got hit, too, but I didn't even feel the bullets. I tried to save her, but I couldn't."

Again his throat worked. Danna expected to see tears on his face, but though his eyes were luminous, no moisture fell from them.

What would it feel like if Chas loved *her* the way he'd loved his Julia? Would she feel treasured, the way she never had with Fred?

Finally, she had to ask. "And your brother?"

"Dead before he hit the ground."

Chas rubbed both hands down his face, and Danna worried there was more to the story. He spoke evenly now, the words seeming to come easier to him. "I haven't been home since it happened. I promised myself I'd find the man responsible and kill him. And now I'm so close."

"Hank Lewis?"

He nodded.

No wonder he'd been so fixated on the man, enough that he could draw an accurate portrait.

"You know I can't let you kill him," she murmured, and hoped he wouldn't erupt in a fit of temper.

He shook his head, not quite meeting her eyes. "Then you'd better hope you find him before I do."

The air crackled between them.

Danna stood, breaking the awful tension between them. "Will you wrap my arm? I want to go talk to the man we locked up last night. And maybe see if our boy over at Doc's is awake."

He returned to her side, and the heat of his hand on her bare skin made her wish they didn't have places they had to be.

"Would you really arrest your husband?" He didn't look up, but his words held a tinge of amusement.

She shrugged. "I'd prefer not to have to make the choice."

"I know. I know. Your first husband was perfect." He said the words as if he was joking, but to her trained ear, it sounded as if the words were tinged with a hint of jealousy. Chas was jealous of Fred?

She tried not to examine the warmth spreading through her. It made her want to reassure him.

"I never said that. Fred never would have spoken about what you just shared with me."

"Really?" he asked.

Now it was her turn to share. Seemed like she owed him, after everything he'd told her. "We didn't talk about our feelings, or…things that were hard for us." Like Rob, and how much it hurt when he hadn't wanted his sister anymore.

"I haven't told anyone else."

"Not even your parents?"

"I told you I haven't been home since it happened."

"How long ago?"

"Four years."

"You haven't even sent a letter or a telegraph to let them know you're all right?"

"I can't."

"Why not?"

"I just can't. Leave it be."

It sounded as if Chas needed to find a way to forgive himself for Julia's and Joseph's deaths. That one event was keeping him from his family, and it didn't sound as if he'd found any healing.

"Do you think your husband *wanted* to talk about those other kind of things?"

Chas's words brought her out of her thoughts. What a funny thing to say.

"I doubt it. Fred wasn't the type of man to keep things inside. If he wanted to say something, he usually did."

"Maybe he wanted to, but he wasn't sure how you'd react."

Chas tied off the white cloth he'd used to wrap her arm. His hand remained on her shoulder, thumb brushing the edge of the cloth. His touch sent shivers down her spine.

"Thanks." Was that really her voice, that breathy whisper?

Their eyes met and held, and Danna found herself wishing for a repeat of the kiss they'd shared in the preacher's parlor.

Chas must've seen her wish reflected in her eyes, because he leaned in until his chin brushed hers and his breath warmed her lips.

But at the last second, as her eyes were closing, he jerked away and moved to the opposite side of the room.

"We should—"

"Oh—" Her voice emerged broken, so she cleared her throat before speaking again. "Will you go down and check on the prisoner? I'll finish getting dressed and join you in a minute. We should check on the wounded outlaw, too."

He nodded, again not looking at her, already half-turned toward the door.

She dressed quickly and then stood inside the door with her hands pressed to her stomach, trying to breathe.

She felt as if she would fly apart with one wrong breath, one wrong move. Her husband was in love—with a dead woman. A woman that Danna would never be able to compete with. No, it sounded like this Julia had been cultured, refined...*manipulative*.

Danna shook the jealous thought away. She needed clarity. She knew she had no hold over Chas. They'd agreed to annul their temporary marriage after they found both the robbers and the cattle thieves.

She couldn't go back on their agreement, not now. No matter what she'd started to hope in the last two days...

She needed focus, needed it desperately. What she really needed was to catch the remaining two or three outlaws, keep Chas from killing Lewis, sleep for two days straight, and *then* work through her feelings about Chas.

She needed divine help.

Danna turned and fell to her knees at her bedside. She poured out her heart, begged for God to help her with the tasks she found to be insurmountable. What she couldn't ask for in words—for Him to love her—she secretly hoped He heard anyway.

When she got up to face the town and her job again,

she found her cheeks were wet, but she felt as if a weight had been lifted from her shoulders.

Until she got to the bottom of her staircase and it dropped right back in place. A crowd of people jostled between the jailhouse door and where she stood, murmurs rippling through it. "Gone." "Marshal's done." "…resignation."

The jailhouse door stood open and her heart hit her toes. She found Chas in the center of the crowd, pushing his way toward her. In tow was the man she both did and didn't want to see.

Sheriff O'Rourke.

Chapter Seventeen

The crowd parted for Danna's passage. She met Sheriff O'Rourke in the middle. Over his shoulder, she could see Chas's grim expression.

"I'm afraid we've got a bit of a problem," the sheriff murmured.

The crowd went silent around them, but the last thing Danna wanted to do was discuss any business with the nosy busybodies who resided in Calvin in attendance. She nodded toward the jail. "Let's go inside."

She followed the sheriff back through the group of residents, having to elbow through a couple of times, when their curiosity made them push in to try and get more information. They knew better than to ask her for details, but several men shouted questions at the sheriff. Thankfully, he didn't respond.

Once she stepped up on the boardwalk, she noticed Chas had halted outside the doorway. She motioned him toward the door. "I'd appreciate it if you'd—" *Support me.*

The words stuck in her throat, but Chas must've known what she meant, because he stepped right behind her as she entered the jail and placed a hand at her hip.

The sheriff stood at the cell door where she'd placed the outlaw who'd threatened Chas last night. The *open* cell door.

"Oh, no." The words fell from Danna's lips as a near silent whisper, but Chas was close enough to hear. His hand at her waist squeezed in a comforting way before he let go.

The outlaw she'd captured last night was gone.

O'Rourke appeared to be examining the lock mechanism on the cell door, and Danna stepped up right beside him.

"I rode up about twenty minutes ago and came in here first to find you." The sheriff turned his face up to look at her, but the edge of his hat brim shaded his eyes and she couldn't make out his expression. "I've been on a case and only got your telegraph yesterday."

She nodded, words still failing her as panic gripped her throat. The town would call for her badge now for sure.

The sheriff continued. "Outside of the lock's a little scratched up, like someone tried to pick it. See here..."

O'Rourke pointed to the outside of the locking mechanism, where there were indeed several deep gouges in the metal.

"They're impossible to overcome," she returned, finally finding her voice. "Fred had a friend who could get through any kind of lock or safe, and he couldn't break through these."

She looked over to Chas, who stood behind the desk. While she watched, he bent and reached for something behind the desk. What was he *doing?*

"Was there a spare key, then?" the sheriff asked, diverting her attention from Chas for the moment.

"Yes, it was—"

"In the third desk drawer, in a hidden compartment," Chas finished.

She'd never told Chas that. "How did you—"

Words failed her again as he held up the desk drawer, revealing the broken compartment.

"But who could've come in and done it?" Danna wondered aloud. She stomped over to where Chas stood behind the desk and groaned when she observed the mess of Wanted posters, papers and other paraphernalia strewn across the floor. Apparently, whoever had released the outlaw had felt it necessary to dump the contents of all the desk drawers.

"We accounted for all of the men in Lewis's gang," she continued, looking to Chas for confirmation.

He nodded, face grave. "All the men we knew about."

"...we knew about," she repeated softly. She moved to the center of the floor and gazed between the cell and the desk, contemplating what that meant. There were one or more members of Lewis's gang they didn't know about. And now their best chance of tracking down the bank's money had waltzed right out the door.

"Perhaps you should've left a guard," O'Rourke said, and his tone had Danna looking up to examine his face. Instead of the concern he'd shown up until a few moments ago, his expression and voice were hard as steel.

She knew it was over.

"I didn't have anyone to leave behind."

Two hours later, it was done.

Danna had surrendered her badge and her responsibilities at the request of the town council. The county sheriff was taking over the bank robbery investigation. She and Chas had three days to vacate the rooms above the jail.

Chas stood silent by her side, aching to do something. Knowing that at least part of this mess was his fault. His only consolation was that Danna hadn't gotten herself killed.

They'd returned to her rooms without speaking. Once inside, she'd wilted onto the bed, not looking at him. He stared out the dingy window, trying to figure out a way to comfort her that didn't involve touching her. He'd nearly kissed her earlier, and that would've been a grave mistake, more so because he was leaving soon.

What he needed to do was figure out a way to track down Hank Lewis, take his revenge, and move on to the next job. Alone.

Problem was, he was tired of being alone. Spending time with Danna had shown him how lonely his solitary life had become. He wasn't sure he could return to the way things had been before. Without Danna in it, his life seemed empty. *Was* empty.

But he'd made a deal with himself. Ensure Danna's safety, then leave so he didn't endanger her again. He never reneged on a promise, not even when fulfilling it felt like he'd taken a bullet to the gut.

He just needed to figure out a way to extricate himself from the situation gently.

"—for me?"

He started, realizing he'd missed Danna's words. He had to clear his throat before he could speak. "Sorry. What?" He made his voice as apologetic as possible, and faced her, leaning against the windowsill.

"I said, why didn't you speak up for me?" she asked, her eyes betraying her hurt.

The emotion on her face hammered him. He never saw her so vulnerable, and somehow he knew he was the only person she'd shown it to. It made what he had to say so much harder.

"I thought...I thought their decision was best."

Her lips opened in a silent gasp. She seemed unable to speak for a moment, but then gathered her composure. "What?"

Tears glittered on her eyelashes. It cut him to the bone. She'd stood silent and proud while her job—her entire life—had been stripped away. But now *he* had reduced her to tears.

He was a cad. The worst sort.

Danna had the strangest urge to get up and shake some sense into Chas. But her muscles had atrophied in the short time since she'd slumped onto the bed, and she found she couldn't move.

In light of everything that had happened in her life in the past few days and weeks, she should've been too numb to feel any more hurt.

But it seemed as if every piece of her ached.

She was confused. On the mountain, during the snowstorm, he'd said he thought she made a good marshal.

"If you didn't think I should be marshal, why did you marry me? It was only to save my job?" she asked, the tears in her voice betraying her.

He was silent for a long moment. "I needed you to help me find Hank Lewis. I have to... He killed Julia. I can't forget it." It went unsaid that he couldn't release his need for revenge.

"Julia," she whispered. She should have known.

It had all been for her. He'd loved Julia—still loved her—so much that it colored all of his decisions. Danna would never be able to compete with a memory.

"If you want, I could write a letter to my parents in Boston. I have a little money left, and if I sent you to them, I know they wouldn't turn you away."

She knew it cost him to make his offer, considering he hadn't made contact with his parents since his brother died.

"What would I do in Boston?" she asked with a little teary laugh. She stood up and turned away, wiping at her cheeks. She didn't want him to see how much this was hurting her. Not now.

"You could see the sights," he said, and his voice was low. "Remarry."

She laughed again, and this time it was bitterness coloring her voice instead of tears. "If no one in the Wild West will have me, I doubt I could find a husband in a city like Boston."

"Danna…" He spoke her name like it hurt him to say it, but she couldn't bear to face him.

"Thank you for the offer, but I can't accept." She turned to face him finally, and looking into his craggy face hurt as much as she thought it would. She forced a small smile to her lips. "I think I'll stay with Corrine for the time being, if she'll have me."

He swallowed once, his eyes never leaving her face. "And if her husband returns?"

Finding Brent would give her something to work on.

"Then I'll find something else."

"What about…your brother?"

The thought of going to Rob and admitting her failures tasted a lot like dirt. She shrugged anyway. "It's a possibility."

He looked like he wanted to say something else, but she couldn't handle much more of this.

"You don't have to worry about me," she said, stealing his chance to ask her something else. "O'Grady," she added his surname, needing the distance. But it made her tear up when she said it, so she soldiered on quickly. "I'll be fine."

A sharp twinge in her shoulder and arm had her clutching the offending appendage. Chas's brow wrinkled.

"You should have the doctor look at your wound," he said. She couldn't help but notice he didn't offer to look at it again himself.

Maybe it meant he *had* felt something when he'd doctored her up before.

"What will you do? Hire a tracker to go after your outlaw?" The words were out before she could catch them, and she knew they made her sound like a weak woman, but there was no taking them back.

"Maybe. Goodbye, Danna."

The door closed with a final click, and she knew he'd closed the door on their relationship, such as it was, as well.

Chapter Eighteen

Danna waited in a chair in Doc Critterdon's outer room, ignoring the room's two other occupants. She didn't particularly want to talk to anyone in Calvin right at this moment. Not while the shame still made her cheeks color at each knowing look people gave her.

She'd been too upset earlier to visit Corrine. She didn't want to disturb her friend's fragile happiness with the new baby. So she'd come here to the doctor's office instead.

And waited.

Finally the doctor emerged from one of the two examination rooms and motioned her inside. She didn't waste any time in telling him about the injury, showed it to him and mentioned what Chas had already done for it.

The doctor hummed low under his breath as he recleaned the wound and began to wrap it again.

"Not any worse than you've had before," he said when he was done, moving to the counter to pump fresh water to wash his hands. It was true, this wasn't much worse than what she come to him with before, when Fred hadn't been able to fix her up at home.

"No sign of infection," he continued. "Just keep it clean."

She nodded. "How's the outlaw that got shot up?"

The doctor frowned. "Somewhat better. The sheriff came and got him, even though I recommended keeping him here for observation for a while longer."

"What?" Danna knew her shock was apparent in her voice but couldn't stop it. "O'Rourke took him? When? Where?"

"Hours ago. Said he was taking him to you at the jailhouse."

A niggle of suspicion tickled Danna's overwrought brain. She hadn't heard any movement or voices in the jailhouse when she and Chas had been fighting, or after he'd left. Had she been so wrapped up in her own misery that she'd somehow missed activity beneath their feet?

Surely he hadn't meant to take the outlaw to the county lockup in Glenrock, not in his injured condition.

An awful idea had begun to dawn on her. What if O'Rourke was in on it?

The doctor wrinkled his forehead. "I'm sorry you didn't get to question him again. He did say some things in his delirium that first night...something about a hideout in a big cave. Something about Glenrock."

Her heart started thrumming like the wings of a hummingbird. She knew that cave. It was near where she'd hurt herself—a few miles from her brother's ranch. If what the outlaw had told the doc was true, there was a chance she could still recover the bank's money. She probably wouldn't get her job back, but it galled her to leave the job undone. Especially because of how Castlerock had treated her, and hadn't thought she was capable of doing her job.

The doc must've seen the change of attitude in her expression, because his hand tightened on her arm. "You aren't going to do something foolish, are you?"

She smiled a wan smile. "More foolish than anything I've done in the last few days?" *Like marrying a man I barely knew? Or worse, falling in love with him?* She knew her voice held a tinge of desperation, and she worked to remove it as she reassured the doc. "No, sir."

The thud of her boots sounded heavy and final on the boardwalk as she made her way to the livery. She would find that money or die trying.

Will wasn't in the stable when she arrived. The building was deserted and shadowed, but she found the little paint mare she'd used before, and saddled her.

Riding out of the livery, she glanced up at the sky and found it gray and threatening. Which meant she needed to remember to pick up extra supplies and her rifle before she headed out of town. She turned the mare toward her room. She would do this one last task perfectly, the way Fred would've. And that included ordering her steps from the very beginning.

Chas had gathered up all his belongings—two saddlebags' worth—and now stood in the doorway to Danna's room, looking over the small, bare area.

It didn't even look like a female lived there, without any frilly embellishments or fine china to be seen. Knowing Danna the way he did now, he wasn't surprised at the lack of femininity. She was much too practical to waste time on frippery, and she would see it as showing weakness, which she couldn't afford to do.

But underneath her strong exterior existed a sensitive, beautiful woman.

Why else would she have donned a dress for their wedding day?

Was he making a mistake, going to Cheyenne to hire a tracker?

He didn't know. Every choice felt wrong. Protecting Danna had turned into betraying her. He didn't know anything anymore.

Except that it had scared him—absolutely terrified him—to see the blood on her blouse earlier. She wasn't shy about putting herself in harm's way. As marshal, she would do so every day.

Even in their temporary marriage, his heart couldn't take the strain. Things were better this way. The distance between them would grow when the annulment was filed. Better to cut ties now.

Only it didn't feel better. It felt awful.

The sound of approaching boots on the stairs alerted him to her presence. Perhaps that's what he'd really been waiting for before he left. One more chance to see her again.

She was focused on something, intensity radiating from her drawn brows and pinched frown. She didn't see him until she'd stepped into the room and kicked the door partway closed.

When she did realize he was there, she froze, surprise and something else flashing over her features. Hurt, maybe?

He hated hurting her. But he didn't know what else to do, how to fix this mistake. And marrying her had been a mistake. The only things he would bring to her life would be danger and maybe even death.

"You still here?" she asked, and her voice held no emotion, though he knew it had to be hidden behind her brusque tone.

He swallowed. Raised the saddlebags so she would see them. "My train leaves soon. I'll be back from Cheyenne in a couple days."

She nodded and kept her gaze away from his, striding across the room to the bed. She tossed her hat onto the coverlet. Next, she took off her coat and laid it on top of the quilt before pulling a sweater from one of the drawers in the stand next to the bed. It was hastily pulled over her head, causing several tendrils of her dark hair to escape the braid hanging past her shoulders.

Chas cleared his throat, unable to forget the way her hair looked as it cascaded down her back in those thick, rich curls when undone.

"I guess this is goodbye, then," she said and her tone implied she had nothing more to say.

He watched her yank off first one boot, and then the other, and add a second pair of thick wool socks before jamming the boots on again.

He knew he should turn and walk out the door, but something made him stay. Probably the same thing that stuck in his throat and made it so he couldn't speak. He wanted to show her how much he cared about her, but it would only make things worse.

And she didn't seem to want to talk to him right now, anyway.

Chas turned to go, whispering, "Goodbye, Miss Marshal."

Danna's entire body shook as she scooted down the stairs and untied her mare from the hitching post out front.

She gulped air, working to calm herself—physically at least—because the horse would be able to read her agitation, and she had no desire to fight the mare. Judging by the clouds darkening the sky, she had a few hours to find the outlaws before the storm hit. She'd need the animal's cooperation to make it up into the mountains in time.

Danna didn't speak to anyone she passed on Main Street on her way out of town. Contrary to what she'd told herself all this time, their acceptance *did* matter to her. Once she captured the bank robbers, she would move somewhere else. Maybe try her hand at ranching. Fred had left her a little savings, and she hadn't spent much in her short tenure as marshal. She could buy herself a little homestead and a few cattle…

She didn't know if she could do it. After all, it had been years since she'd worked with Rob on his ranch. But after the way the town had treated her, maybe a solitary life was for her. And there was little chance she'd have to fend off any amorous advances from gentlemen—*if* there were any—if she lived and worked alone.

Maybe she would go through with it. It could be a good plan.

Danna's thoughts were interrupted by a shout from down the street. She looked up to see a lone figure trotting down the end of Main Street toward the open prairie that stretched for a ways before the mountains rose behind it.

"…he stole my horse!" came a second shout from a man now running down the boardwalk in the same direction as the first had gone.

Without a thought, Danna kicked her mare and took off after the thief. The rider looked over his shoulder once, and when he caught sight of her in pursuit, spurred the stolen horse to a gallop.

She heard another yell as she raced past a group of

people on the boardwalk, their faces a blur. It sounded an awful lot like "You get him, Marshal!" but that couldn't be right, because her badge had been rescinded.

As she passed the edge of town, she urged her mare for more speed and they gained on the stolen horse and its rider. A cold wind ate through Danna's long coat and the sweater she'd added beneath it.

Drawing abreast of the rider, she was astonished to see Sam Castlerock at the reins. Why would the boy steal a horse, when his father was rich enough to buy him as many as he wanted?

The younger Castlerock looked over at her and she saw his face pale.

"Stop!" she shouted, but the boy hunched forward in the saddle and used the end of the reins to try and whip the horse to move faster.

She considered launching herself onto the other horse, but at their speed, one or both of them might break something when they hit the ground. And she still had to catch Lewis's gang, so that wasn't an option for her.

Instead, she slipped a length of rope from atop her saddle horn and fashioned a lasso. Sam saw what she was doing and tried to steer his horse away, but she watched the movements of his torso and guessed his next move. She drew closer to horse and rider and with a quick flick of her wrist, tossed the lariat over the other horse's head. She began to slow, and so did the horse, even though the young Castlerock continued to kick its flanks. The horse's lather and tossing head told enough of the story. It wasn't used to running like this, nor did it appreciate the boy's treatment.

"Your little jaunt is over," she cried so he would hear over the hooves pounding on the prairie grass. "Stop!"

When it became apparent his horse was no longer obeying his commands, Sam threw himself out of the saddle and began racing away on foot.

Danna growled low in her throat. The boy was causing her an unneeded delay. She hopped off her mare long enough to picket the stolen animal, then re-mounted and took off after the boy. She fashioned a second lariat from another length of rope out of her saddlebag and within minutes had looped it around the boy's shoulders. In no time, she had him trussed like a turkey and slumped over the saddle in front of her. They returned to the stolen horse at a slower pace, and she tried to talk some sense into the young man.

"I don't think you're going to get away with this, Sam. Horse thievin' is a hanging offense." And with the number of witnesses on Main Street, there was little chance of his father buying his way out of this. "Why'd you do it?"

"You wouldn't understand, Marshal." He spat the title in a mocking voice and didn't say another word as they neared the picketed horse. In the distance, she could see riders heading toward them.

She made the boy dismount from her horse and was helping him get on the stolen horse—he nearly lost his balance with his hands tied the way they were—when several men from town rode up.

"I thought he'd get away for sure," said one, and she recognized the blacksmith, Dodie Bennett. "You sure didn't waste any time, M— uh, Miz Marshal. Thank ye."

She ignored him when she should have corrected him. She wasn't marshal any longer.

"Too bad the town council wadn't here to see this."

Undertaker Burr McCoy almost sounded...impressed? But that couldn't be right.

"Yep, maybe they'da changed their minds about firin' ya."

Danna frowned. "I didn't run him down for any recognition." She removed the lariat from around the horse's neck.

"Why'd she do it then?" another voice asked.

She rolled the rope into a small coil and draped it over her own saddle horn before mounting up and wheeling her mare toward the mountains, now in plain view after the race across the plains. She'd reach the foothills in less than an hour.

"She did it because it was the right thing to do, ya goose."

Again, she chose to remain silent. Let them think what they wanted of her motivations.

"Danna, where you headed? Town's the other way."

She didn't respond to the question from behind her.

"A storm's comin' in," a second voice cried.

"I've got a couple more gents to bring in," she called back to the group.

"I wish we could help ya!" someone yelled out. "I really do!"

She pondered the last exchange as her mare galloped over the grassy plain. It almost sounded like he'd meant something—or someone—stopped the men from giving her aid. She remembered Chas's suggestion from days ago that perhaps someone in a position of authority was keeping the men in town from being deputies. But was it O'Rourke, or someone else?

In less time than she'd thought, the prairie gave way to small conifers, and she was crossing the foothills. Before the disastrous ride up here with her deputy, she hadn't been closer than viewing distance to the mountains. She hadn't had any desire to return to the place where she'd broken her brother's trust, where her happy life as a little sister on his ranch had ended. She wasn't superstitious, not really, but ever since that night, she'd been on edge in the mountains.

But returning now, even with a cold wind shaking the tree limbs and making them creak, and with all her failures hanging over her head, she felt like she was coming home.

Her knowledge of these mountains would determine if she won or lost against Lewis's gang.

She guided her mare around an outcropping of rock, content for now with the horse's surefootedness on the changing terrain. As far as she remembered, the cave was less than three miles away, as the crow flies. She glanced up at the sky. Almost the same color as the steel of her rifle barrel, it was certainly menacing. But she thought she could make it to the outlaws' hideout before the worst of it hit.

She was still working on her plan to take down the group of outlaws.

She could handle being outnumbered, if she was careful. She and Fred had talked strategy often enough. She ought to be able to handle four or five armed men. Hopefully.

The sharp crack of a pistol's hammer broke her concentration on her route, and the mare faltered.

"Hands up," a thin, menacing voice snapped. A familiar voice.

Heart hammering, Danna turned in her saddle to find herself staring down the barrel of a mean-looking Colt .45, not a handful of yards away. Even a bad shot wasn't likely to miss from such a short distance. Her gaze followed the pistol's barrel back to a craggy face. O'Rourke.

"Do it, or I'll shoot."

His voice brooked no argument, but she considered reaching for her own pistol anyway, until she saw the second man a few paces behind O'Rourke. Pale and trembling, it was the injured outlaw. He, too, had a gun trained on her, a rifle that lay across his horse's shoulders, balanced against the saddle horn.

With two weapons aimed at her, she had no choice but to release the reins and push her hands above her head. So much for sneaking up on the outlaw camp.

Chapter Nineteen

Standing on the Calvin train platform alone, Chas waited for the locomotive to arrive and take him away from here. Trying to keep his mind off Danna and everything he was leaving behind, he dug through his saddlebags, looking for the letter with the name of his contact at the WSGA in Cheyenne.

Instead, his hand closed over a smooth leather item, and he drew it out so he could see it. Fred Carpenter's journal. How had it ended up in Chas's things?

In all the chaos of the previous night and this morning, the journal must have been tucked into his saddlebag by mistake.

He snorted his self-derision. Mistake, or subconscious desire to be close to Danna in any way that he could?

Well, it wouldn't work. He could return the diary when he brought the annulment papers, after all the trouble with Lewis died down.

Idly, he flipped open the book to a spot near the middle. *Anything* to help pass the time.

Danna and I spent the day picnicking and then

several hours of target practice. It was a nice break from our normal routine. We watched the sunset down by Pa's Crik and she started to open up to me…

It's been years since she's revealed her inner thoughts, and that she felt comfortable to do so today meant the world to me—

Chas closed the book with a snap of his palm. He didn't want to read about Danna and Fred Carpenter's relationship after all. The man had obviously never meant for this to fall into the hands of Danna's second husband.

Morbid curiosity had him flipping the book open again, searching for that same entry. He had to know what happened next. Spying a familiar name on a different page stopped him cold.

O'Rourke in town again. I wish I had firm proof he was behind the rustling, or just proof of his involvement, but in the six months since Stevenson saw him settling a sale of cattle at the Cheyenne train station, he's proven more wily than I thought.

Perhaps he has help?

Reaching the end of the entry, Chas stared down at the page and let the words blur out of focus. Carpenter had suspected *O'Rourke?*

Chas knew lawmen weren't above reproach—he'd taken down a marshal near Houston, Texas, who'd murdered several men in a gambling den and had almost gotten away with it.

From all he'd gathered, Danna's first husband

had excelled at his job, so if he suspected O'Rourke, chances were the sheriff was dirty.

In the distance, the train whistled. Chas was running out of time.

He flipped through the book rapidly, looking for more entries that mentioned the sheriff or suspicious activity. Several entries mentioned suspicions of a gang of rustlers, most likely very the same ones Chas was hunting. Carpenter didn't know identities, but had found the prairie cabin. On the last page, Chas came upon an underlined entry.

O'Rourke's involvement confirmed. Meeting tomorrow at 3:00 p.m. Will follow O'Rourke to cattle holding location then return for backup.

There were no further entries.

Fred Carpenter must have been spotted as he tried to take down the gang. Danna had said he'd been murdered in cold blood, but nothing about his suspicions.

Because he hadn't told her, Chas realized. And she couldn't read his journal for herself.

The train platform shook as the locomotive shuddered to a stop, chugging and hissing. Time was up.

He couldn't go to Cheyenne. Not with O'Rourke out there and possibly thinking Danna knew too much. She needed him, even if she wouldn't admit it.

He turned to leave the platform, ignoring the stare from the curious ticket-taker who hung off the side of the train. As he approached the stairs down to street level, a man he recognized as the town doctor ran up to him, huffing and panting.

"I'm awful glad to see you haven't left yet," the older

man huffed, out of breath. "She's gone after the bank robbers."

"What?"

The man's words didn't make sense, and then, all of a sudden, they did.

The doc frowned. "I have reason to believe the sheriff may be a part of the outlaw gang. He came and got the outlaw that was shot up—but hasn't been seen around town since."

This was new information. Was there a possibility the bank robbers and rustlers were the same group?

Chas's heart started thumping harder, but he wasn't ready to get too worried yet. "But she doesn't know where they're holed up, does she? She'll have to head to town before the storm gets here."

The rigid set of the older man's mouth did not reassure him.

"I'm afraid she *did* have a clue about the gang's whereabouts. I told her about a cave the shot outlaw mentioned... She seemed to know where it was...." The doc's voice faded out.

The implications made Chas's knees go weak, and he fell onto the bench. Panic clogged his throat and threatened to overtake his senses. He couldn't think straight.

Danna had ridden into the face of Hank Lewis's gang. Alone.

"So she is as good as dead." Despair made the words a whisper when he pushed them through frozen lips. What was he thinking when he'd let her go? This was all his fault. Again.

"I wouldn't say that." The doc laid a hand on Chas's shoulder, but it offered no comfort.

"Why not?" Chas rubbed his hands over his face,

trying to find some hint of hope that he hadn't thought of. There was none. "Even if she doesn't find the outlaws, she could freeze to death or get injured. If she does find them, she's *completely* outnumbered."

"Don't give up on the marshal so easy." The older man sounded so confident. All Chase felt was empty.

"She's a tough one. And clever. Why, I remember when she rounded up those three fellas that hoodwinked half the town into buyin' them fake medicine tablets."

Chas shook his head, helplessness drowning him.

"And an incident where she single-handedly stopped a train robbery while it was in progress.

"If you're gonna go, you don't have much time."

As if to punctuate the doctor's words, several snowflakes swirled down out of the iron-gray sky.

Chas couldn't let it end like this. Not for Julia, and not for Danna. Urgency rising, he told the doc, "Gather every able man you can find. We'll meet here in half an hour. Be ready to ride."

After the allotted time had passed, Chas had drawn a curious crowd, but no one seemed to be willing to chase after Danna and the outlaw gang. Chas's horse was the only one saddled and ready to go.

Chas was getting more and more desperate as the minutes ticked on. Finally, he could stay silent no longer.

"I know that several of you men have worked with Danna when her first husband was still alive. You know her abilities."

The crowd murmured, but no voices rose in either agreement or disagreement.

"Danna has given years of her life serving the

residents of this town. You should be ashamed of your-selves."

"A woman shouldn't be marshal."

"She cain't handle the job!"

That had gotten a rise out of them. Unfortunately, it didn't seem to be the response Chas wanted.

A familiar voice called out, gaining volume above the noise of the gathered crowd. "The marshal can do just as good a job as any man. She caught Sam Cas-tlerock riding out of town with your horse today. And last week she broke up two fights at the saloon before things could get out of hand and someone got hurt. This town *needs* the marshal."

Chas looked over the heads of the crowd and spot-ted the speaker, the young man he recognized from the livery. The young man stood slightly apart from the crowd, face set.

One boy was better than nothing, but Chas's hopes, small as they had been, began to dim.

The crowd continued to make noise, but no further voices called out with any willingness to help. Several men in front refused to meet Chas's eyes, and his sus-picions mounted.

"Is there some other reason you won't ride with Danna?" he called out, desperate now. "Is someone paying you not to help her?"

Heads lowered, but no one said a word.

"Would you sacrifice the marshal's *life,* just so you can keep your secrets?"

No answer.

Well, *he* couldn't give up on Danna, not yet. Not if there was a chance he could save her, no matter how small.

As Chas was turning to mount his borrowed animal,

the sound of multiple horses approaching at a gallop drowned out the crowd's murmurings, and even Chas's own heart that beat for Danna.

A group of rough-looking men on horseback—six or eight by Chas's count, although the ones in the rear shifted and he couldn't get an accurate count—rode right up to the gathering.

The man out front pushed his stained Stetson off his brow, allowing Chas a good look at his face. Dark stubble covered his cheeks and chin, while a full mustache hid the man's mouth. His coffee-brown eyes reminded Chas of someone, but he couldn't place the man. Those eyes shifted across each face in the crowd, as if searching for someone in particular. He didn't seem to find them, his dark eyes growing narrower as the moments ticked by.

Finally, he spoke in a gruff voice that sounded as if it hadn't been used in a while. "I'm looking for the marshal."

Chas bristled. He didn't like the looks of these ruffians one whit. "Who's asking?" he demanded.

The man's dark gaze honed in on Chas, and his expression made it clear he had no intention of being the first to divulge any information. Chas refused to look away. He didn't trust this newcomer and wasn't going to be the first to break. Silence stretched out between them, taut and deadly.

Someone else spoke, breaking the tension. "Ain't got no marshal no more."

The man on horseback looked away from Chas to the speaker, face going white beneath his tan. "Whaddya mean?" His tone indicated that, if he didn't like the answer he received there would be consequences.

"She resigned."

"She was forced to resign," corrected Chas, losing the tight rein he was holding on his temper. "After you all lost your faith in her. Fred trusted her enough to be a deputy, and I'd be willing to bet she was better than any of the men he hired." Chas pushed his way through the edge of the crowd to his borrowed horse, preparing to ride. "You may not think much of your lady marshal— my wife—but I do. I'm going to find her and help her bring those outlaws in."

With that, he swung up on his mount and turned the horse toward the mountains visible over the roofs of the town buildings. He didn't make it far before the sound of hoofbeats joined those from his own horse. The stranger with dark hair came abreast of him.

"We'll ride with you," the stranger said, and made it sound like a command, not a request.

"Thank you, but I don't know you—"

"I'm her brother." The man's terse words were offset by the jumping muscle in his jaw. "Rob Creighton. Sounds like we're family now."

Chas knew his expression betrayed his shock, but the kernel of hope growing inside him was making it hard to maintain his composure. So this was the brother who'd pushed Danna to marry so young? What was he doing here now?

Creighton motioned to the six men following. "These are a few of my hands. One of my men heard about Danna's troubles while calling on a lady friend who lives in these parts. I came when I could, but it sounds like it wasn't soon enough. So Danna's taken off to chase a group of outlaws on her own?" Creighton didn't sound surprised.

"It's worse than that," Chas told him, itching to move faster, to get out of town, but knowing it would be impossible to talk once they let the horses go. "We think the sheriff is involved. Fred wrote in his journal that he was close to being able to prove O'Rourke was guilty. I think O'Rourke was behind Fred's murder. Danna doesn't know about the last part, though."

With a glance to the rapidly darkening sky and the snowflakes swirling around them, the set of the cowboy's mouth turned even grimmer. "We don't have much time. If they catch her before we do…"

Chas knew. He was trying not to think about what could happen to a woman alone. "Apparently, Danna knew the location of this cave in the mountains. I believe you might know it, as well?"

"She went back there? Alone?" The rising alarm in the other's man voice was not comforting to Chas in the least.

"I know she was injured near there, years ago," Chas said. "But she's a good rider. We just need to catch up to her. Can you find the cave?"

"Probably. But it's been years."

"Or I could take you right to it," a female voice called out. Creighton reined in to allow the young woman running down the boardwalk to catch up. Chas gritted his teeth in an effort to keep his impatience inside.

Then he recognized the girl. Katy.

She shied from Creighton when his horse sidestepped toward her. Approached Chas instead. Because he'd been kind to her before?

"I can take ya right to the cave."

"How do you know it? Who are you?" Rob demanded.

"We can trust her," Chas put in. She might've run away, but he knew she liked Danna.

When Katy spoke, it was to Chas. "My pa...used to run with that awful Jed Hester. Then a few months ago, that lyin', no good snake shot him in the back. Tried to come after me, too, but Pa had taught me how to disappear in the woods."

So she'd been on her own for months, probably near to starving when Chas had caught her outside the grocery. No wonder she'd eaten as if his eggs and bacon had been her last meal.

"Anyways, I want that no-account varmint dead, and I guess hangin's the next best thing to shootin' 'im when you lot catch up to them."

Even though he was used to Danna and her trousers and her being marshal, the violence spewing from this girl surprised him. He supposed she was only expressing the same thing he felt about Hank Lewis.

"I'm coming, too," a second voice rang out, this one accompanied by hoofbeats. Chas turned in the seat of his saddle to see the livery stablehand, Will, gallop right up to the girl before reining his mount in. The girl didn't flinch away from him as she had from Creighton. "Katy and I both want to help the marshal."

He knew Katy?

Winded, the boy must've run all the way across town to the livery, but he didn't complain, just swung the girl up in the saddle behind him.

Chas didn't particularly want the young man involved, but perhaps he could watch over the girl if they got into a troublesome situation.

Now could they get going?

Danna's mind whirled as the three horses neared the crude campsite spilling out of the mouth of the yawning black hole that marked the cave. With her hands bound in front of her, it had been all she could do to cling to the saddle horn and not topple as her horse followed O'Rourke's mount, traversing the difficult terrain in the foothills of the Laramie Mountains. Never mind reaching a weapon to help her escape or to overpower O'Rourke.

She looked over her shoulder again, seeing the kid who'd been shot wasn't doing well. His complexion about matched the color of the snow now swirling around them. If she could somehow get close to him, maybe she could get his weapon loose. And if his injury was getting worse, maybe she could convince O'Rourke to let her help him.

It was a risky plan, relying on an awful lot of maybes. But it was all she had.

O'Rourke reined in outside of the camp and dismounted. He hauled her off her horse, none too gently. Her ankle jarred when she landed on the ground, but he didn't give her time to even catch her breath before he shoved her in the direction of the cave.

"O'Rourke—"

"No talking," he ordered. "I've got a job for you. Now move it."

She didn't argue. He unholstered his gun in an obvious silent threat. She ducked through the mouth of the cave, carefully stepping over a man laid out on the ground, snoring, and had to start breathing through her mouth at the overpowering stench of unwashed flesh.

O'Rourke kicked the sleeping man, who roused with a disoriented huff.

"You're supposed to be on watch, Wilson. If I catch you sleeping again, I'll put a bullet in you."

The man didn't respond, but Danna read anger in the set of his mouth before he spit a stream of tobacco juice against the cave wall. He stood up and moved outside the cave.

O'Rourke motioned her farther inside with his pistol. She walked around the small fire in the center of the cave, noting how little warmth it exuded, and moved toward a man with a distinctive handlebar mustache squatting next to a bundle of rags. Jed Hester.

"He any worse?" O'Rourke asked, and the man looked up, his face grave.

"No change."

That's when she realized the bundle of rags was a man. One who was seriously injured. Between the flickering firelight and shadows, his pant leg appeared nearly black with slick blood, coming from a wound in his upper thigh.

Well, that answered her question of why O'Rourke hadn't killed her outright.

The sheriff glared at her through narrowed eyes. "Fix him up. No funny business or yore dead."

"I can't—I'm no doctor," she stalled. The injured man already appeared close to death. He was so pale, she didn't know if there was anything she could do for him.

"I know you ain't a doctor, girl. But you saved yer Freddie-poo when he got shot up a coupla years ago, an I 'spect you to do the same for my boy here."

She knelt next to the injured man, wobbling as her tied hands put her off balance. She pushed aside the ripped shirt used to bind the wound, and blood immediately poured from the leg. Hastily, she re-covered the wound as best she could.

"You're going to have to untie me. There's a few medical supplies in my saddlebag. And we'll need some clean cloths. How long has he been like this?"

"Stu! Get the woman's saddlebags." O'Rourke nodded to the other outlaw. "Take off his gun belt. Then untie her."

He didn't answer her question of how long the man had been injured, but she could guess. He must've been shot last night, during the melee in town. She didn't want to feel the guilt surging through her, so she focused on the best way to tend his wound.

Once her hands were freed she shook them, and pinpricks like needles of ice ushered the return of feeling to her fingers. Holding her emotions in check, she rummaged in the saddlebag that was thrust in her face. It was hard to think with the gun barrel mere feet away, focused directly on her. Was there anything in her bag she could use to affect an escape?

Even if there was, could she leave the man to die?

"Hurry up," a voice from behind her warned. She wasn't sure who spoke, but she knew she was out of time. She would have to dig for the bullet and then stitch him up.

And then maybe she could figure out a way to get out of here.

"What's your name?" she asked softly, as she removed the blood-soaked cloth from the wound.

He didn't respond, instead focusing his pain-glazed eyes above her head.

"'Is name's Hank," grunted the man who now squatted near the fire, gun in hand. Danna glanced around the small cavern, but O'Rourke was nowhere to be seen.

Every single one of Danna's muscles tensed as she returned her gaze to the man beneath her hands. So this was the man who'd killed Chas's sister-in-law, the woman he loved. The outlaw's breathing was irregular, his face translucent. He was obviously in a lot of pain, and if Danna couldn't remove the bullet, there was a strong possibility he would bleed out.

It wouldn't take much to let nature take his course. To let him die.

Chas thought he deserved to die. She was inclined to agree.

But if she let him die, would God forgive her? Would Chas forgive her if she let him live?

And whether Hank ended up dead or alive, she knew O'Rourke would kill her once she was no use to him anymore.

Chapter Twenty

Bitter wind cut through Chas's coat and all the layers he wore, but his soul felt frozen from more than the cold weather. If they didn't rescue Danna—if she died—he would be responsible. He'd hurt her by not standing up for her. Then he'd left. And she'd gone after Hank Lewis's gang alone.

He chafed at the delay, but the storm had worsened, and Creighton had insisted their party stop until the blizzard waned or morning light, whichever came first.

The torches they'd lit upon nightfall had been used to light a large campfire, and the horses staked in a tight group not far away. Creighton's men, along with the stablehand and the teen girl, had huddled under whatever blankets or bedrolls they could find, and dozed off.

But Chas couldn't sleep. He was too worried for Danna, sick with the desire to reverse time and change the events leading up to this moment. He had an awful feeling something was wrong, that Danna had been overtaken by Lewis or O'Rourke, or both. And he was stuck here, waiting for morning.

Sitting so near the fire reminded him of sharing another fire with Danna, and how she'd trusted him with her past, with feelings she hadn't even shared with her first husband. And he'd thrown that trust in her face when she needed him most.

He loved her. And he'd failed her.

"So you're married to my sister."

The quiet statement shook Chas from his despondent musings. He hadn't realized the other man was still awake, but with a shift of his head, he saw Rob Creighton's eyes shining in the light from the campfire, though the man didn't look at him directly.

Chas didn't know what information the man was fishing for. So he went with a simple answer. "Yes. For a few days."

"She's a special woman."

No argument there. "She is."

"And a lot to handle."

Chas couldn't contain a rueful quirk of his lips. "I don't think there is any such thing as 'handling' your sister. She makes her own way."

"You're probably right." Creighton shifted under his horse blanket. "Is that why she went off after this gang alone?"

Chas's shame made him unable to look at the other man. "I'm not good with women. I was heading to Cheyenne while she was going after Hank Lewis's men."

"I ain't real good with them myself. She tell you I was the reason she left home?"

Chas nodded, but the words didn't make him feel any better.

"I didn't know what to do with a kid sister. It wasn't that I didn't want her around. She was a pretty good kid. Hardheaded, but then so am I. I didn't know nothin' about raising a girl."

Creighton's voice grew softer as he got nostalgic. "She scared the life out of me when she went off into the mountains by herself. I knew what could happen to a grown man alone, and she was just a girl. And then she *did* get hurt. It terrified me. But I never would have sent her away."

Chas had guessed as much after reading Fred Carpenter's journal entries. Creighton went on talking.

"Fred loved her so much. Even then. I remember him telling me he wanted to marry her. I lost my temper and told him he could have her and good luck. She was a handful at sixteen. I couldn't imagine what she'd do at eighteen.

"Then, the next morning, she just marches out of her room—as much as she could with a broken leg—and announces she's ready to go marry Fred—right then." He shook his head, a sad smile on his lips. "I had a time convincing her to wait a couple of weeks while her leg healed. She was determined. Never did know what the rush was."

"She overheard you and her first husband talking the night you rescued her. She took it to mean you didn't want her around anymore."

"She tell you that?"

Chas nodded and the other man was silent for a long time. "Things weren't the same after she married Fred. Didn't see her much at all, and then they moved away. I stayed away because she didn't seem to want me around. It makes sense now, if she thought I wanted to get rid of her.

"Fred wrote once a month and kept me up-to-date

on how she was doing. But he never said she asked about me."

It was obvious the man cared about Danna, even if he didn't know how to show it. Chas had a strong urge to give him some kind of comfort.

"One thing I know about your sister, is that she hides the most important things close to her heart. She misses you. I'm sure of it."

Rob Creighton stared into the fire. "I hope you're right. I feel like I've lost too much time with her already."

"Well, let's find her and you can tell her."

Creighton grunted in response, but Chas was only half joking. The waiting was killing him. His feeling that Danna was in danger intensified by the minute. But the snow continued falling, and he knew he wouldn't convince the others to leave until it let up.

His inner turmoil was compounded by Creighton's presence. On one hand, he was grateful the man was here to help him find and rescue Danna. On the other, Rob's presence meant that Danna had someone to take her in once all this craziness was over. If the town wouldn't return her badge, it sure sounded like her brother wanted her to come back to the ranch with him.

Which would be great for her, once Chas got the annulment and they'd gone their separate ways.

So why did the thought leave him empty inside?

Danna shifted on the frozen ground, brought her knees up in front of her as she tried to conserve her body heat in any way possible. Her hands had been tied again, this time behind her back. Around a tree. Tightly.

She was going to freeze to death if she couldn't get loose.

Hank Lewis's wound had been deep, and with her every move being scrutinized by the outlaw O'Rourke had left behind, it had been nearly impossible to snitch anything that might help her escape.

But she'd done it. She had a small knife slipped up her sleeve, and O'Rourke hadn't found it when he'd brought her out here—well away from the cave—and tied her up, leaving her to freeze.

She was surprised he hadn't just shot her, now that his purpose for her had been fulfilled. But whatever had made him tie her up—she thought it was God's hand—was enough for now. She was alive and she'd get out of here.

She'd done her best to save Hank Lewis's life, but there was no guarantee that he'd live. Not in the crude surroundings—a cave filled with empty food tins and some trash. Even Doc, in his sterile environment, would be hard-pressed to save the man.

But she'd done her best.

And she'd spotted a flash of gold under some blankets piled on a crate in the rear of the cave. She'd bet anything it was the stolen money from the bank.

If she could get out of this pickle—alive—she had a chance of bringing back Castlerock's gold. Not that she expected it to get her her job back, but at least she'd have done her duty.

Only problem was, by her head count, there was another outlaw out there somewhere. After the robbery, there had been four sets of tracks, but one man—the kid—had been injured. So that was probably three men on horses and one horse with no rider. That accounted for Jed, Hank Lewis, Earl Wilson. O'Rourke had gone back to the cave. But what about the fourth man who'd been involved in the bank robbery? Where was *he?*

Hours later, Danna hadn't managed to free the knife from her shirtsleeve, no matter what she tried.

Settled in a small dip at the base of the tree, snow had been piling up against her left side, providing insulation against the colder night air, but it wasn't enough.

She was getting sleepy.

She knew better. How many times had Fred told her that, once a person dozed off, hypothermia would set in and then they were a goner? Probably dozens.

Even the panic building in her throat didn't seem so important anymore.

She was going to fail. She was going to die. She didn't want to, not with all the unfinished business between her and Chas, and not without bringing to justice the man or men who'd killed Fred. But it looked like her time was almost up.

It was a shame she'd rushed out of town alone. And been so careless that she'd allowed herself to get captured.

She hoped Chas remembered her with less pain than he remembered Julia. She didn't want him carrying around another load of guilt for something that wasn't his fault.

She wished she could see him one more time. If she saw him, she'd tell him she loved him. She'd never told Fred, and even though her first love felt more like a comfortable friendship, she regretted that Fred hadn't known before he died.

She also regretted that no one had ever told her the same. All these years, she'd thought she didn't need the softer things in life, didn't need love. But she'd been wrong.

She wanted it.

And if by some miracle she got out of this mess, she was going to find it. Even if she had to make herself into the most ladylike woman in the West. Wear dresses. Learn to read.

She might not have all her toes by then, but she'd make do. Danna kicked both feet against the ground in turn to keep the blood flowing, keep them from going numb. It wasn't working.

She would try one more time. She bent her wrist to a nearly impossible angle, biting back on the cry of pain that wanted to slip past her lips. There! Somehow, she'd managed to wedge the knife into her palm. Now if she could just angle it this way...

The tip of the knife slipped off the frozen rope and she almost dropped it. Her numb fingers weren't working right. The ties were so tight that her circulation was nearly cut off—she couldn't operate the knife like she needed to.

She wouldn't give up!

Knowing this might be her last chance to do something, she began to sing. Loudly. All the hymns she could remember. The effort it took to sing sent blood pumping through her veins and made her feel more awake.

And she remembered the last time she'd been trapped on a mountain, this mountain. Back then, she'd believed the words to the hymns. Believed God was faithful, that He would take care of her. Maybe it had been naive. Had she been blind in her faith?

Was Chas right, thinking God didn't really care about individuals?

Just like she couldn't give up, she couldn't believe that, either.

Hadn't He kept her from freezing on this mountain once before? He'd brought Rob to her in time, and her leg had healed from the fracture. She hadn't suffered any lasting effects from her near-disaster getting tossed from her horse. And marrying Fred had been a blessing in her life, even if she hadn't seen it as such in the beginning. Fred had taught her about being a lawman, about being a wife, even though she hadn't been a conventional one.

But what about all of the bad things that had happened to her lately? Fred's death, getting fired from her job?

All of a sudden, a sharp whine broke through the silent blackness and shook her from her thoughts. Danna sang louder, determined not to get eaten by a wolf while she was out here, either.

The sound of a branch breaking nearby had her craning her neck to try and see where the intruder was coming from. A shape took form, a shadow darker than all the others. It grew bigger as it neared, and she prepared to kick out with her feet.

It came even nearer, and the whine turned into a yelping bark. One she recognized.

"Wrong Tree?" Her incredulous question must not have offended the dog, because it came nearer, right up next to Danna, and snuggled into her side, offering the warmth of another body, albeit a furry one.

"Good boy," she cooed, and for the first time since Fred had brought the mutt home, she meant it. "You're so good! How did you find me? Did you bring someone with you?"

The dog whined again, a pitiful sound.

And the hope that had sprouted when she'd recognized the dog waned as precious minutes ticked by.

"Okay," she said, when it was obvious no one else was coming to her rescue. "Well, I guess you're better than nothing."

The dog barked, as if he agreed with her. He moved away, the loss of warmth instantaneous, then turned back a few feet away, as if beckoning her to follow.

"I can't, boy. I'm stuck here." She pulled against her bonds, shaking her head that she'd fallen so far as to talk to Fred's dog.

Wrong Tree tipped his head, looking at her with a quizzical, lopsided doggy grin.

"Come on over here, boy," she urged, shivering as another gust of wind sliced through her clothing and made her insides quake.

For once, the dog listened to her, scooting up real close to her midsection, all his weight leaned against her.

"What a good boy," she cooed. "You'll keep me alive."

Thank you, Father.

She now had a speck of hope she could survive the night.

She'd never been more thankful for the smell of damp dog, but he was *warm*. She nuzzled her face into the ruff of fur on his neck. *God, please don't let him leave again.*

The warmth covering her from chin to thigh shifted, and cold blasted through the layers of Danna's clothing, jarring her into wakefulness.

The dog grunted and moved away, leaving only freezing air to take his place.

Had she fallen asleep? She'd been sawing against the frozen ropes binding her hands for what seemed like forever—hours, at least.

The first fingers of light showed slate-gray against the horizon. She'd survived the night. And it had stopped snowing.

She had to get away quickly. If O'Rourke returned and found her alive, he'd probably kill her.

She shifted the knife in her numb hands, trying for a better grip, straining to get even one coil of the rope to break.

A limb snapped behind her, cracking like a gun-shot in the early morning stillness. Wrong Tree turned, hackles rising.

"Danna?"

Chapter Twenty-One

At first, Danna thought she must be imagining the voice—Chas's voice. But the shock of heat when his hands touched hers, as he untied her, was real.

And then she was free. Time seemed to suspend itself as she stared into his impossibly blue eyes, and all she could think was, *He came for me!*

"What—how did you find me?" she asked in a hushed voice, afraid to disturb the silence that surrounded them. Afraid he was an apparition she'd conjured with the strength of her wish to see him again.

Chas nodded to the side, toward a figure that hadn't even registered while she was fixated on Chas.

"Rob?"

Chas watched Danna's brother rush to her and swing her up in a hug, and *still* he couldn't make his feet move.

Danna was alive.

She hadn't been hurt or killed.

The rush of relief left him light-headed.

Danna's dog jumped and danced around the pair still embracing, and then he started to bark. Both Danna and Rob shushed him.

Danna nodded over her shoulder. "O'Rourke has set up a camp just there." The pair of them started moving toward Chas. Rob held her tightly to his side, supporting her weight, and Chas knew a sudden fear that maybe she *was* hurt. He turned and hustled to where he and Rob had left their horses, just over the top of the hill.

He pulled his bedroll from where it was tied behind the saddle, knowing Danna would need its warmth if she'd been out in the cold for any length of time. He was still facing his horse, trying to school his rioting emotions into submission, when he sensed her approach.

"I can't believe you came." The soft-spoken words from behind him threatened his composure *again,* and he spun to face her, needing to see for himself she was all right.

Tears sparkled in her brown eyes, and it prompted him to swing the blanket around her shoulders and clasp her to his chest. One hand clung to her waist while the other cupped the back of her head, his fingers threading through her hair.

"I never left," he admitted.

In his arms, she felt fragile, but he knew it was an illusion. She was strong and capable. She'd managed to nearly get herself loose and was on her way out of there, all without help. She didn't need him or anyone else.

So what was he going to do, now that he knew *he* needed *her?*

"We should head out and meet the others," Rob said. Chas looked up to find the other man already mounted up, with a small smile quirking the corners of his lips.

Rob's assessing gaze made Chas uncomfortable, and he shifted away from Danna.

Her head came up. "Others?" She wiped her face with the corner of the blanket and stepped away from Chas. The emptiness of not having her in his arms had him sliding into his own saddle, lest she see his emotions written on his face.

Rob answered her, speaking quietly. "Yeah, there's ten of us crazy enough to come out here after you. We got halfway up the mountain last night and had to stop because of the snow. Your husband refused to wait until morning, though. He dragged me away from a warm fire and my bedroll to get to you sooner."

Danna's upturned face revealed her surprise, and was that joy in her eyes? When Chas reached for her, she came easily into his arms and used his boot in the stirrup to boost herself into the saddle in front of him.

Chas wrapped his arms around her, unable to keep from noticing how perfectly she fit there. He didn't ever want to let her go. Careful not to bump her, he guided his horse to follow Creighton's down the same way they'd come. Danna's dog followed a little off to the side, silent, but with his tongue lolling out of his mouth.

"Men from town?" Danna murmured over her shoulder, giving Chas a good look at her profile. She didn't have a single bruise on her face.

"I'm afraid not. Your brother brought several hands from his ranch. And your stablehand friend brought a little gal who happened to know where this cave was located—Katy."

He read her disappointment in the tightening of her lips before she nodded and turned her face forward again. Until he mentioned Katy, and then her face lit up. "You found her?"

"She found us. Just before we left town. Said her pa used to run with Lewis's gang until Hester killed him. She ran away from them. I think she's been afraid all this time that they'd track her down and kill her, too."

His thoughts jumped from the outlaw gang killing Katy to what he'd feared the most since yesterday afternoon—them killing Danna. He hated riding away. He'd never been closer to enacting his revenge on Hank Lewis than right now.

"How'd you know where I'd gone, though?"

Danna's question broke through his thoughts. "The doctor found me right after you rode out of town. And I'd...well, I found a passage in Fred's journal that implicated Sheriff O'Rourke as part of the rustling ring."

"You read the journal? That's why you came after me?"

He couldn't tell if that made her angry. He had invaded her privacy.

"I couldn't...let you face the danger alone, not if these men were ones who killed your first husband. I couldn't leave you to die!"

He knew he'd said something wrong when she frowned and turned her face into the blanket. Her breathing changed and he thought she might be crying. Maybe he shouldn't have brought up Fred Carpenter. He knew she loved the man, and it must hurt to know who had murdered him.

She stayed that way for the short time it took them to reach the site where they'd camped. The other men were up and about, as were the stablehand and girl. The scent of coffee welcomed them when they pulled up near where the other horses were tied off.

Chas hopped to the ground and reached up for Danna, then released her as soon as her feet touched the ground.

His head spun with confusion. She'd been happy to see him, he knew she had. Why was she pulling away?

Embarrassed by her teary breakdown, Danna kept her eyes averted from Chas's face as he set her down off his horse.

It was exhaustion and relief that had caused her to cry like a little girl. Not Chas's admission that the only reason he'd come for her was because he felt *responsible* for her.

Not because he loved her.

What had she expected? Their marriage was temporary. They'd agreed on the coming annulment.

Her feelings hadn't changed since she'd first fallen in love with him, but she held on to hope.

Chas propelled her over to the blazing fire and pushed her down to sit on a conveniently placed log.

"Let's get some coffee into her," he called out, and men jumped to do his bidding.

He pulled off her gloves, and she saw her hands were chapped, but not discolored like she'd expected them to be, with little blood flow in the freezing conditions. She might not lose any fingers after all. Chas chafed her hands between his, and the warm that infused her was more than just from the fire and his hands.

It felt like he cared.

No matter how much she told herself not to feel too much for Chas, her love for him continued to grow.

Wrong Tree butted his head under Chas's arm, looking for attention from the man he'd liked from the beginning. Chas gave the mutt a playful push out of the way and settled close to Danna's side.

"All right. So what's the plan?" Rob squatted down next to Danna's other side. He handed her a tin cup, steam rising from its rim. The rest of the cowpokes stood near enough to listen without intruding on their conversation.

"The plan?" she echoed.

"You mean to tell me you weren't working on a way to round up those bank robbers while you were tied up?" Rob's voice held both a teasing quality and a note of seriousness.

"I'm sorry." She shook her head, feeling as if it was stuffed with cotton. "I'm not thinking real clearly yet." She drank a big gulp of the coffee, hoping it would help.

"You didn't think we came all the way up here just to save your hide, did you? We're going to help you bring in those outlaws."

She risked a glance at Chas, who was staring hard into the fire, his jaw tight. Had that been his intention? She couldn't tell. But she had a job to do, even if she didn't have the official title, and if these cowboys were willing to help, she'd be foolish not to take them up on it.

"I saw four men in the cave last night, plus O'Rourke. Two are injured. By my count, there should be another man, but I never saw him."

"Who are the two injured?"

She couldn't look at Chas when she told them. "Hank Lewis and the man who was shot during the robbery."

"How bad is Lewis?" Chas asked, his voice low and angry.

She shrugged. "He'd lost a lot of blood. The gunshot was in his upper thigh. He was alive when I got done patching him up, but I don't know if he made it through the night."

"You *patched him up?*" Chas spat the words and vaulted to his feet so she had to look up at him. His face and neck had gone red, making his light freckles disappear. "After what he's done? He murdered my—" He cut himself off, but she could still hear the words, as if he'd said them aloud. *He murdered my love.* The reminder burned a hole in her gut.

"He killed my brother and his wife," Chas said in a slightly more controlled voice. She could still hear the undercurrents of anger in his tone. "He doesn't deserve to live."

She'd known his temper would blow when he found out she'd helped Lewis, but she'd been hoping he'd be a mite more rational.

"I'm not a judge," she replied. "I can't make the decision whether he should live or die. Plus, they had a gun on me. If I refused to treat him, O'Rourke would have shot me."

Chas's face paled, all the red seeping out of his cheeks, but he still stared at her as if he didn't know who she was, couldn't believe she'd done what she had.

Slowly, he shook his head, then ran a hand from forehead to chin. The action wiped all the expression from his face, leaving only a hard-set jaw and empty eyes behind. "So what do we do now?"

Rob shifted in his crouch, clearly uncomfortable to have witnessed their conversation. "We can assume they've figured out Danna's disappeared. The question is, what'll they do about it?"

"If they saw our tracks, they'll know she's not

alone," Chas put in. "They could follow us pretty easy in all that snow." He shared a secret smile with Danna, warming her down to her toes. "I think even I could track in these conditions."

Danna didn't like the way her stomach swooped to think that O'Rourke and his men might be heading this way right now. Their group was out in the open and would be easy targets for a rifle. She glanced around the craggy, snowy scene around them, but didn't see any sinister shadows lurking behind the trees.

"Or they might decide to hole up in the cave, to see if we come after them," Rob offered. That thought wasn't particularly comforting either, as they'd be much too vulnerable if they tried to approach the cave with the scant cover the landscape around it offered.

"They might make a run for it." She knew that alternative was the least likely, due to the injured men. Or maybe they'd leave the hurt kid and Lewis behind to shoot it out, and the rest of them would try to run.

After a moment of tense silence, Rob said what was on all their minds. "If O'Rourke knows he's been caught out, he's going to want us dead."

Rob's hands all murmured their agreement. They all looked to her, and their gazes were like a weight on her chest. She'd *wanted* this responsibility?

Chas turned to her from where he'd stood with his back to the group, one hand massaging his neck. "So tell us what to do, boss lady. You wanted deputies. Now you've got 'em."

In the end, everything fell into place beautifully. Danna took command of the situation, like Chas had known she could. She sent four of Rob's men out scouting for anyone who might have left the camp after the snow had stopped, with instructions to fire a sequence of shots if they caught the men or needed help. She ordered the stablehand and the girl to stay put and to keep her ornery dog tied up with them. That left five of them to figure out a way to approach the outlaw's campsite without getting shot.

"We came in from the south last night, and there wasn't much cover at all." Danna seemed to have regained her equilibrium. She paced a tight ring around the fire, alternately clasping her hands in front of her and waving them around when she spoke. She was adorable.

"Is there another way into the cave?" Rob asked, as he checked his weapon.

Danna shook her head. "The inside walls are solid rock. I couldn't see any other way in or out, and believe me, I looked."

"From what I could tell, we'd have the most cover approaching from the east."

"Or we could hang a rope and someone could shimmy down to get to the cave."

It was risky. He hadn't gotten much of a glimpse of the cave through the trees this morning, as Danna had been tied pretty far from the entrance, but he'd seen enough to know it was a sheer drop of thirty feet.

"Danna could do it. She likes to climb things. Like roofs." For the second time, he gave her a smile that said they both shared a secret. She flushed under his gaze and looked away.

"I guess you never grow out of some things," said Rob, shattering the moment.

Danna kept her face averted, but then her gaze cleared and she turned to Chas. "Do you have Fred's journal with you? And a pencil?"

He'd thought she would be angry that he'd violated her husband's memory by reading the journal, but she'd done what she always seemed to do when faced with a situation that needed to be handled—put aside her personal emotions in order to work.

He retrieved the book from his saddlebag, along with a stub of a pencil he had to dig for, and brought them to Danna. She flipped to a blank page near the end of the book and completed a quick sketch of the area around the cave, including trees, rocks, larger impressions in the hills. Her memory was impressive.

She tapped a corner of the page. "If your two hands come from this direction, and I slip down from above the cave, you—" she nodded to Rob "—and Chas can approach from here." She indicated a thick stand of trees. She shook her head as if she wasn't terribly happy with the plan, but said, "I think this is the best we can do. Ya'll ready?"

She didn't wait for an answer as she strode to her horse and swung up into the saddle. Confident they'd follow. And they did, Chas hopping up behind Danna.

It didn't take long to retrace their route to where they'd found Danna in the woods. The storm clouds had dissipated after sunrise, and now the sunlight sparkled off every surface, almost blinding in its intensity.

Shortly before they reached the place where Danna had been tied, Rob and Chas broke away from the other two men to circle around the other side of the little valley.

Letting Danna down from his horse and watching her slip away into the snowy mountain was hard for him. Especially after she'd come so close to death the night before. Chas clamped his teeth together to keep from calling her back.

He had to remember how capable she was. And at least she wasn't unarmed, as she'd been able to take an extra pistol her brother had provided.

Chas and Rob moved quietly into place, hobbling the horses a fair piece away, in case gunfire erupted. They snuck through the winter-white landscape together.

Not as comfortable as Rob was at sneaking, Chas followed the other man and tried to stay behind barren trees, outcroppings of rocks, or even getting down on hands and knees in the snow, so as not to be seen.

When the mouth of the cave was in sight, Rob began to move even more cautiously. Rob found a spot he liked and pointed out a covering of brush not far away, mouthing instructions for Chas to go over there and wait.

Lying there with his belly wet and cold wasn't Chas's idea of a good time, but he did as he was told. He wouldn't endanger Danna as he had the other night. Sighting his rifle, he drew a bead on the cave, black against the white landscape.

In minutes, a length of rope unfurled down the ledge above the cave. He saw Danna's dark head at the top of the cliff, and then her backside as she began to lower herself hand over hand, right down the wall of rock.

Chas's heart drummed in his temples at her being so exposed. If any of the other outlaws were out in the woods, they'd have an easy shot at her. He sent up a desperate prayer that no one with nefarious intentions was near enough to do her harm.

For a moment, his breath cut off and he thought he was going to get caught up in a memory of those few moments before Julia and Joseph died, but instead of the images he expected, all he could see was Danna hanging off that dangling rope, her life in the balance.

After she was out in the open so long he was beginning to feel sick to his stomach, she braced her legs
against the rock wall and raised one hand in a prear-
ranged signal.

"O'Rourke!" Rob roared, and Chas jumped, even
though he'd been expecting the shout. "We've got you
surrounded! Toss your weapons outside the cave and
walk out with your hands up!"

No sound emerged from the cave. The woods themselves were eerily quiet, without the normal sounds of
birds and small animals moving about, as if even they
knew something was happening. The snow muffled everything, but Chas knew it could be hiding death and
danger.

Danna fisted her hand and pumped it once in the
air—the signal they waited for—and a voice from
across the clearing called out this time. "We know
you're in there, and we're not leaving. We've got
enough ammunition to wait you out!"

Still no answer from the cave, no movement. Had
the men left after they'd discovered Danna was missing earlier in the morning?

Chas watched with bated breath as Danna dug in her
heels and leaned to the side until she was nearly hori-
zontal. Her braid hung down like a pendulum, as she
lowered her head enough to peer into the recesses of
the cave. A shot rang out and she scrambled a few feet
up the rope.

So there was at least one man in the cave.

Chas squinted, cursing the bright sun glinting off
every surface, as he tried to determine if she'd been
hit. He couldn't see any blood on her face or neck. That
was a good sign, right?

"Stop worrying so much," came Rob's voice, this

time so quiet, Chas knew it was meant for his ears alone. "She knows what she's doing."

That was debatable. Danna was taking an incredible risk right this second. Chas knew how quickly a life could be snuffed out, and Danna was putting herself in danger. And did so every single day. Chas's jaw was so tight, he didn't know if he'd ever be able to unclench it, so he didn't try to answer Danna's brother.

"You have to let it go," Rob said. "Her life is in the Lord's hands. If He wants to take her home today, He will, and nothing we can do will stop it."

But I need her, Chas wanted to cry out, and he would've, if he could've wrenched his mouth open.

If only Danna had a safer job. Of course, just living out here in the West was a bit more dangerous than his parents' home in Boston. But he couldn't picture her living in his parents' world, with their society parties and boring lives. If she sat down to tea with his mother, Danna would likely send the older woman into a swoon.

He loved her the way she was.

The realization shocked him into silent stillness. It felt right.

He loved the marshal.

He just didn't know if he could handle her dangerous job. He was so afraid of watching her die, like he had Julia. And although Julia's death had devastated him, Danna's death would rip him to shreds. Because he loved her. Not the love of a childhood friend, but the deep, abiding love of the woman he wanted to spend his life growing old with.

Fear held him immobile while Rob crept toward the cave. Chas watched as the other two cowhands came into sight on the far side of the clearing. All three men advanced on the cave, now in plain sight of anybody inside.

A volley of shots rang out. The men darted for cover. A figure ran out of the cave, straight toward Chas, but he doubted the man even saw him.

Rob jumped onto the man's back and took him facedown in the snow. The two hands joined him and helped hog-tie the man before Chas had time to blink.

"How many more are there?" Rob demanded, his knee in the outlaw's ribs.

"Just the two hurt ones."

And Chas went a little crazy.

He had to know if Hank Lewis was inside.

Not caring if he got shot himself, Chas slipped in to the cool darkness, keeping close to the wall, and let his eyes adjust. The kid sat against the farthest wall, unconscious, though a gun lay near his thigh.

Lewis was there, too. Unarmed, from the looks of it, lying prone and flat on the ground.

Which meant there was nothing stopping Chas from killing him. Chas stood over the man who'd taken so much from him, and pointed his pistol right at Lewis's heart.

Danna dropped to the ground as Chas ran into the cave. She rushed in after him, foolishly not taking the time to determine if it was even safe to go inside. She had to stop Chas before he did something he'd regret his entire life.

The instant her eyes got used to the dimness inside the cave, she saw Chas standing over the prostrate Lewis, with his pistol trained on the outlaw. His hand shook, but the tension in his shoulders told her everything she needed to know.

He was ready to shoot the man that had killed two people he loved.

Heart in her throat, she knew she'd never get to her husband in time to stop him. She couldn't call out, but she started toward her husband.

"You deserve to die," Chas said, and she knew a moment of fear that he would shoot. She'd have to arrest him if he did.

Lewis didn't respond. She was nearly there, but from this distance she couldn't tell if Lewis was even conscious.

As she drew near, she saw that Chas's whole body was trembling.

"Chas."

He turned his head, and even from the side view of his face, she could tell he struggled with himself.

Please, God, don't let him do this.

Slowly, feeling as if she was swimming through molasses, she reached out and touched Chas's arm.

And he let her push it down until his weapon pointed at the floor.

Chapter Twenty-Two

~

They rode into town to a hero's welcome, with the three surviving outlaws strapped to the saddles of three horses.

Rob's men had made all the difference. They were experienced operators, and had caught up to and captured O'Rourke and Big Tim, who'd made a run for it, with no trouble. If Danna had had men like them to help her, she wouldn't have lost her job in the first place.

And the best part was, Rob's cowhands had agreed to go with her to track down the last outlaw, the one the kid had admitted was probably guarding the rustled cattle. The kid had wanted to talk—apparently tired of a life of crime—and had even given them the location. Before they could go after the cattle, they had to get the outlaws they'd already captured locked up in the jail.

The kid had also mentioned that the outlaws had taken it upon themselves to get rid of the marshal when they'd seen her riding alone in the ravines outside of Calvin. They'd scared the cattle with whoops and gunshots and caused the stampede that had nearly killed Chas and Danna.

The worst moment for Danna earlier in the day had been realizing that O'Rourke's horse created a crescent-shaped hoofmark. She'd been riding behind the animal when she'd noticed it. Her husband had been killed by a man who'd sworn to uphold the law. She would do her best to prove it to the judge when he came to town, and to see O'Rourke receive what he was due—the noose.

To her surprise, people lined the streets and clapped as they walked their mounts through town to the jail. Several people called out to her, and one child even cheered for "the marshal."

It sounded like they respected her, or at least the job she'd done, bringing down the bank robbers. Was there a chance they would give her badge back?

Castlerock waited with Albert Hyer, one of the other town council members, on the steps of the jailhouse.

"Where's my money?" he demanded, even before she'd reined in.

She wanted to tell him off. So badly that she had to grit her teeth to keep the words inside.

"The marshal's brother has custody of it," Chas said, pulling his mount to a halt next to her and jerking his head to indicate Rob, who rode midway in the pack of riders. "Kindly thank the marshal, and you can take your cash right over to your bank." His voice brooked no argument.

Why did he keep calling her that? She hadn't gone after the robbers to reclaim her job, and it wasn't likely the council would agree to give it back to her. She hadn't been able to do the job alone, after all.

Castlerock looked a mite green, but he uttered the

words, though it was obvious by his demeanor he didn't want to. "Thank you, Miz Carpenter."

His words were a sharp reminder that her marriage was about over. They'd survived the chase, captured the rustlers and robbers—who'd turned out to be the same men—and Chas's job was over. He'd be leaving soon. They'd get an annulment.

And she would be alone again.

But not totally alone. She waved over to Katy, in the back of the pack of riders, pointed to her—their rooms above the jail. Danna had offered to let the girl stay with her as long as such an arrangement was needed. She remembered the girl's questions the one night they'd shared her rooms before. Danna also remembered how Fred had taken care of a similar teen who was lost and alone…and she determined that she would make Katy her family, like a little sister.

Rob rode up and tied off his mount at the hitching post across the street from the jail. She needed to talk to him, as well—find out why he'd come for her. Maybe she'd get her brother back, too.

But she wanted a husband…a particular one: Chas O'Grady.

Will joined their group in front of the jail, but he ignored the group of businessmen. She warmed at his loyalty. "I'll take your mounts over to the livery, Marshal."

She dismounted and handed the reins over to him, but didn't let him leave without an impulsive hug. Without his help, Chas and Rob might not have reached her in time.

Hyer cleared his throat and stepped forward to the edge of the boardwalk. "Mrs. O'Grady, we'd like to reinstate you as marshal. We made a mistake in firing you."

Her heart began to thud in her ears. It seemed too good to be true.

"Where's Parrott? And Shipley? Did they agree to this, too?"

Hyer shook his head. Castlerock looked away. It was Hyer who spoke.

"After yer husband made such a passionate plea for deputies, several people came forward and admitted they'd been threatened not to help ya do your job. Parrott and Shipley ran outta town pretty quick. A coupla fellas went after 'em. We didn't have no part of their plan, and we want ya back as marshal."

She looked to Castlerock, who nodded his agreement with the mayor's statement. He still looked green, but his mouth was set and he didn't argue.

"You've got some loyal friends. They made quite a case for you yesterday evening," said Hyer.

She shot a look to Chas and mouthed *they?* But he shook his head like he didn't know either.

"We've got three men who've agreed to work as your deputies—" he named off three of the men who'd previously worked for Fred "—and a possible fourth, as well. We've agreed to pay them a salary—not much, mind you—and they'll answer to you."

That was new. And it would make her life a whole lot easier. She wouldn't have to be in charge of the whole town, all day and all night. She'd have some help, men she knew she could trust.

Chas touched her shoulder, moved next to her, forming a wall of solidarity. "You should take the job back," he said quietly. "You deserve it. You'll do a good job."

She looked up at him, her hat brim shading her eyes

and hopefully hiding them from the watchful gazes of her bosses. She could read the truth on his face, that he wanted her to take the job, but that he also couldn't stay.

Not with a wife who had such a dangerous job.

They needed to have a serious conversation, but this wasn't the place or the time. She looked at the men who made up the town council and nodded her consent. "Calvin is my home, and I'm proud to protect it."

She shook the men's hands in turn, and they left. Rob's men were already untying the outlaws. She went to the jail to get their cells ready, leaving her temporary husband behind.

Chas meandered down the boardwalk, vaguely heading toward the hotel, his saddlebags over one shoulder.

He'd tried to follow Danna into the jail and help as she locked up the three healthy outlaws plus Hank Lewis. She wasn't willing to take the chance of putting Lewis at the doc's office, not after what had happened with O'Rourke springing the kid—but she hadn't needed him, not with her new deputies jumping at her beck and call, and the other men who seemed anxious to make things up to her by helping out.

Plus, she'd looked exhausted. He hadn't wanted to add to her strain by trying to have a serious discussion when she hadn't slept and had been working all day.

So he'd slipped back out of the jail, figuring she wouldn't even notice he was missing.

What was he supposed to do now?

When he'd become a deputy, the arrangement had been beneficial to both himself and Danna. He'd needed her help conquering the Wyoming terrain; she'd needed his support.

Now that she had all these other men to help her out, and now that his case was wrapping up, he was free to go.

But he didn't want to.

The realization hit him hard in the stomach, almost worse than when he'd realized he loved Danna last night. But it couldn't be. He enjoyed larger cities like St. Louis, even Chicago....

Shaking his head, he knew there was no way to deny what was in his heart. He loved his wife, and he didn't want to leave Calvin.

But how to convince Danna not to go through with the annulment? He knew she'd fancied him at one time. And when they'd kissed before, there had been a certain spark....

All of a sudden, he remembered her face as she'd held Corrine's baby boy the day after his arrival. Danna wanted a family.

But...could she even love someone who wasn't reconciled to the God she loved so much, trusted so much?

He'd settled things in his mind with Hank Lewis in that cave. He'd given up on taking his revenge, even though he could have killed the man.

Perhaps it was time to settle things with his Lord?

"You did a good job today, Miss Marshal," Rob said, borrowing Chas's nickname for his sister. He finished the last of his coffee and placed the mug back on the table.

Danna waved off his compliment, but he touched her hand, his face serious. "I was proud to ride with you."

"I wish you could stay longer," Danna told her brother, startled to realize that it was true. Rob was leaving at first light, headed back to his ranch.

Rob leaned back in Fred's old chair, his lean form stretched out, legs turned toward the center of the room, instead of the small kitchen table in the corner.

"That's saying something, coming from someone who didn't want to see me for years."

A flush stole up her cheeks, embarrassment flaring. "I wanted to see you. I just…I thought…"

"That I'd gotten so mad I stopped loving my own sister?"

She looked down at her hands clasped on the table. "I heard you and Fred that night—I think you must've thought I was out from the pain or exposure, I don't know. You said…"

"I said that Fred could have you and good luck. I didn't mean it."

"No?"

"No. And the only reason I *let* you marry him was because I knew how crazy he was about you."

Her face hot once again, Danna scratched at a scar in the tabletop. "I miss him, but…"

"But you've fallen in love with your deputy."

She nodded miserably. "The marriage was only to appease the town council—we'd already planned to have it annulled on the grounds that we were coerced into it. He's…he's still in love with someone else."

"You sure about that? The man was sure fired up to come to *your* rescue."

She closed her eyes briefly, so he wouldn't see the hope that unfurled in her heart. "There's something else I wanted to ask you. Chas said Fred had made notes about O'Rourke's involvement in his journal. Would you read it to me? I want to know if there are any more clues as to why Parrott and Shipley would pay off the men in town."

* * *

Late into the night, Rob closed the journal and placed it on the table. Danna wiped tears from her eyes, knowing Fred had given his life for this little town she loved so much.

Rob stood to go and surprised her with an embrace.

"We won't go so long without seeing each other again," he said. "You and that one." He nodded to Katy, asleep in Danna's bed and softly snoring. "Come for Christmas. You've got enough help now to take a few days off." He paused for a moment, his eyes scrutinizing her face. "And bring your husband, too."

Chapter Twenty-Three

The timid knock came soon after Danna had descended from her rooms to the jail, leaving a sleeping Katy upstairs. Braced to face her husband, Danna was surprised when the door swung open to admit several women.

"Well...good morning, Mrs. Kendrick. Mrs. Stoll, how are you? And Anna! What are you doing in town so early?"

"It's Martha, dear."

"Marianne."

Several more women crowded into the jail behind the others, although all of them stayed a careful distance away from the cells and the rough-looking outlaws within.

"What—what are you all doing here?"

"We brought you some breakfast." One of the women held up a cloth-covered basket.

"And jam." Someone else pressed two jars of ruby-red preserves into Danna's hands.

Their smiles surrounded her, warming her. But... "Why?"

Martha Stoll stepped forward. "Young lady, I know I've complained about your dog, but you've done a fine job as marshal, and you should know it."

"We want to thank you, Marshal," came a voice from the back. "For sticking with the job, even when our men weren't a bit of help to you."

"Umm…" Danna didn't know what to say. This was unexpected—she'd thought the women had never liked her, but this outpouring of goodwill said just the opposite.

A second soft knock came and the door opened to reveal Corrine, who froze in the open portal, a bundle of baby in her arms. The women closest to her turned their heads away; one even went so far as to sniff and put her nose in the air.

"Oh," Corrine said quietly, her eyes widening and a flush creeping into her cheeks. "I'll go—"

"Corrine!" Danna moved through the throng of women and grasped her friend's forearm, pulling her aside. "I was going to come see you this morning. I found out—you'll never believe it, but Brent was working with Fred on the rustler case. Actually, Chas found out. It was all in the journal."

A whisper rustled through the women, Danna winced. She had kept her voice down when sharing Corrine's private news, but maybe it was best that they'd all heard. She couldn't bear for her friend to be slighted, when her husband had actually done something good for a change.

Corrine's eyes filled with tears. "Was?"

Putting an arm around her friend's shoulders, Danna led her to the desk chair. "Yes. I'm so sorry, Corrine. The kid—one of the outlaws—told us he'd been killed.

Helping Fred. Two of my new deputies went out to recover his body early this morning."

Corrine began to sniffle, but not the sobs Danna had expected when she planned to give her friend the news of Brent's death. A hand pushed a lacy handkerchief at Corrine and she accepted it without looking up.

"Honey." A buttercup-yellow skirt swished around Danna's desk, and Mrs. Burnett, the preacher's wife, put a comforting arm around Corrine's shoulder. "That man tried his best for you. He really did." Danna wasn't so sure about that, but the other woman was still talking. "You should be proud he died helping Marshal Fred."

Corrine nodded, still pressing the handkerchief to her eyes with one hand, while cradling the baby with the other. Suddenly she looked up with her teary eyes, right at Danna. "Danna—I forgot! I came in here to tell you that I saw your deputy—er—your husband at the train station, buying a ticket."

Danna's face flamed. "We're not—not really married. It was all a show for the town council. We're getting an annulment."

"But you love him, don't you?" one of the women—Danna thought it was Marianne—asked.

"Yes," she said, because she couldn't deny it anymore. Not to herself or anyone else.

"Then you should fight for him," Corrine put in, her hand on Danna's arm. "Do whatever you have to—make him want to stay married to you."

Danna looked around at the expectant faces around her. She took a deep breath. "I'm going to need your help."

"All of us?"

"All of you."

* * *

Shaking with nerves, the skirts of her mama's blue dress swirling around her feet, Danna made her way down the boardwalk.

She felt foolish with this dress on, and her hair put up, as if she were attending a fancy ball. Was it too late to run back to her room above the jail?

"Miss Marshal, Miss Marshal!" Young Cody Billings ran up to her on the boardwalk, waving both arms. "Them depities brought back those dirty council members. They're comin' to th' jail now."

She moved down the street to meet them, grateful for any reprieve from having to face Chas like this. She wanted to convince him to stay in Calvin, and trying to be feminine had seemed like a good idea, until she'd seen the stranger in the looking glass. But with a roomful of expectant women behind her, she couldn't back out of the plan.

Now, walking down the boardwalk, she was getting lots of stares.

The lead deputy reined in his horse, eyes wide as if he didn't recognize her. He tipped his hat to her, then seemed to change his mind and took it off. "M-Miss Marshal. We got 'em." He waved to Shipley and Parrott, riding with bound hands between two other deputies.

"Good job. I've taken to carrying the jail keys with me, but I'll turn it over to you for a bit." She took a deep breath. "I have to go over to the train station and settle some business."

She'd stepped around his horse and was headed across the street, when Shipley dropped down and his bound hands came around her in a chokehold.

They scrabbled as she tried to break free, but with

the element of surprise, his wrists were already around her neck, cutting off her air.

The deputies jumped from their horses, pistols coming out, but she couldn't breathe.

Danna swung her elbow back, catching Shipley in the midsection. She heard the distinct sound of fabric ripping.

Chas's heart raced as he hopped off the train station platform and headed toward the jail and a much-needed talk with his wife.

He stopped a moment to breathe deeply of the crisp Wyoming air. He did love it here.

Loved the weathered buildings. The bustling activity on the streets. Even the crooked boardwalk that took him over to the jailhouse.

Except, there *was* something different about Calvin since he'd headed into the mountains yesterday. There was a peace in the air, a sense that the town was safe, wholesome.

He was halfway to the jail when he came upon the scuffle. And a woman in a pretty blue gown was right in the middle of it. Danna!

He moved to help, not surprised she was holding her own in a struggle against the larger man, even wearing a dress.

Before Chas reached the melee, the one remaining man on horseback—Parrott—pulled something from his boot.

A derringer. The man had a gun and was using his rope-bound hands to point it straight at Danna.

This time Chas didn't freeze. He reacted, drawing and firing his pistol before he even blinked.

Parrott screamed in anger as Chas's bullet struck his hands. His weapon dropped to the ground harmlessly.

Chas approached on shaking legs to find Danna with one pretty knee in Shipley's back.

"Why?" she asked, still panting from exertion. "Why did you do all this? Have Fred killed? Did you hate us so much?"

The man beneath her remained silent.

"You've ruined it all," Parrott spat, as one of the other deputies took him roughly off his horse. "Your husband was eliminated because he started asking too many nosy questions. You were only appointed because you weren't supposed to figure any of it out."

Danna flinched, and Chas moved to her side, taking her arm when one of the deputies hauled Shipley to his feet. The man looked beaten, defeated.

"But, I don't understand..."

"We had a plan," Shipley said, voice nearly a monotone.

"Shipley..." Parrott warned. "Don't say another word."

"Parrott thought he could run many of the smaller ranchers out of the area if they lost enough cattle. He brought in a gang and had a few unsavory cowhands of his own."

"Shipley!" Parrott lunged for his fellow town council member, but the deputy who had hold of his arm was made of muscle and wouldn't be moved.

"C'mon, you. Let's go get Doc to patch up your hands, and then you're going to jail with the rest of 'em."

The other man continued as if Parrott hadn't spoken at all, staring off into the distance. "It was unfortunate that Marshal Fred and Brent Jackson had to die, but they started asking questions of the wrong people. They got too close to our operation.

"With O'Rourke on our side, we planned to start extorting money from the businesses in town. We've heard of other...*businessmen* making good money that way.

"The only problem was Castlerock. He may be a selfish lout, but he's arrow straight."

"So you set up the robbery, thinking his bank would fold if the money was never recovered," Danna whispered. Chas noticed she was shaking.

"It would've been best if he'd left town, yes."

Chas couldn't believe the man spoke so calmly of the criminal enterprise they had masterminded.

"And the payoffs?" Chas asked. "So the men wouldn't help Danna?"

"At first no one wanted to work with a woman. They were glad to take the money. After that, we could threaten to reveal they'd been bribed—ruin their standing in town—and that's how we kept them quiet."

"Marshal, I'm going to take him in now." The deputy stepped forward

"See if he'll write out his testimony first," she murmured. "For the judge when he gets to town."

With the mess sorted, Chas took Danna's arm and swung her up onto the boardwalk and out of the dusty street.

She looked up at him, her dark eyes questioning. She was something else, with her dark curls falling out of the updo they'd been pinned into, dirt smudged across her chin, one sleeve missing and a rip in the hem of her gown. He'd never seen anything so beautiful.

He wanted to sweep her up in his arms, but he wasn't sure about his welcome.

"Hello," he said instead. "I was coming to talk to you."

Danna looked down at herself, and when she looked up again he could see the distress on her face.

Was she still upset about the crooked town council members? Personally, Chas was relieved to know the motivation behind the men's actions, outrageous as it was.

"You all right?" he asked, wondering if she was shaken up. "He didn't hurt you, did he?"

"No, that's not it," she said, shaking her head.

With a tiny sigh, she tried to smooth away the wrinkles and dirt from her skirt. Then she seemed to realize her sleeve was torn, and her hand fisted. "I guess I'm just not meant to be a lady."

Her words confused him, and so did the sudden tears that sprang to her eyes.

She looked down again, fingered her dusty skirt.

"I had this grand plan," she whispered, "to show you I could be a lady as fine as your friends back in Boston. I put on this dress, let them put perfume on me—"

"You do smell nice."

"—I let Marianne Kendrick do my hair," her voice turned into a wail, as she reached up and realized her hair was falling down around her ears. "And Merritt Harding promised she'd teach me to read. I thought I could *impress* you."

"You did all that for me?"

"Yes." She swallowed hard, and for a moment he was afraid she might start crying. "Only…"

"Only, you had to do your job," he said, busting with pride.

Tired of looking at the crown of her head, he chucked her on the chin, waited until her luminous eyes met his gaze. "I won't complain if you want to wear a dress, but I like you fine in your trousers and vest."

Murmurs from nearby interrupted everything else he wanted to say. He looked around to find several townspeople on the streets, watching his interaction with Danna and not bothering to hide their curiosity.

"Can we talk?"

She nodded. "Katy went home with Corrine for the day, to help her take care of Ellie, so the room should be empty for now."

He tucked her hand into the crook of his arm so he could escort her home. *Home.* He liked the sound of that.

And he was dying to kiss her, but he didn't want to do it in front of the whole town.

She was unusually quiet, until they rounded the staircase leading up to the marshal's private room. She hopped up on the first step and whirled to face him, pressing both palms against his chest to halt his progress. "Are you leaving town or not?"

They were out of sight of the main thoroughfare, so he did what he'd wanted to do since he'd caught sight of her on the street…

The extra height of that first stair put her face a few inches above him, but it was easy enough to grab her waist and draw her in for a kiss. A sweet, deep kiss, to tell her everything he wanted to say—and that he *wasn't* leaving.

And from the way she kissed him back, it sure seemed like she returned his sentiments.

With a last, lingering touch of his lips, he joined her on that first step and pressed her close, her cheek against his shoulder. "I'm not leaving," he said, voice husky.

"Hmm," she hummed, seemingly content to stay resting against him. He couldn't get enough of having her close like this.

Then, abruptly, she pushed away from him, eyes a little wild.

She took a step backward, moving up another step. Putting distance between them. His hands felt empty, so he braced them on both sides of the stair railing. Plus, that blocked her from brushing past him, as well.

"But you were at the train depot—Corrine saw you at the ticket window."

He groaned. "Are there really no secrets in this town?"

Danna crossed her arms in front of her chest, as if she was protecting herself. From him? She looked so vulnerable, with her mussed hair and clothing, and her eyes shining like they were filled with tears, but he knew that couldn't be right. She never cried.

But she seemed awfully weepy today.

"Darlin'." He purposely lengthened out the endearment, his voice a soft drawl. "I'm here to stay."

She blinked, looking a bit like a sleepy owl. "To stay," she repeated. "But…"

"I bought a *pair* of train tickets," Chas said slowly. "So I could take *my wife* to Boston. I thought we might go on a honeymoon trip."

Her eyes softened and she blinked. "You're going home?"

He nodded. "If you go with me."

"To make peace with your parents?"

"It's past time, wouldn't you say?"

Then she frowned. "But the annulment... We agreed—"

He couldn't help the grin that quirked his lips. "Maybe you misunderstood my kiss. I thought it was pretty clear I'd changed my mind, but perhaps it wasn't..."

Her eyes widened as he followed her up the steps, until they were even again. "Chas..."

He kissed her again. And again, trying to show her everything he'd felt since he'd realized she had gone after the outlaws alone, everything he wanted to share with her now. When they parted, he spoke into that crown of beautiful hair. "Just so there's no misunderstanding... I love you. I want you to stay my wife."

"I love you, too," she whispered. "I'm glad I got the chance to tell you."

She squeezed his middle, burrowed her face into his chest. "I almost hate to ask, but...will you mind terribly if I'm still the marshal?"

"I won't mind. I'm going to talk to the town council—or what's left of it—and see if they'll let you keep me on as deputy. I think we work pretty well together."

"You won't mind me having a dangerous job? Getting into trouble sometimes?"

"Not as long as I'm there to help get you out of it." He paused, but this seemed like the right moment. "And in the future, if we want to...maybe buy a homestead. You can teach me to ranch."

Epilogue

"**S**top! Thief!"

Reacting on instinct, Danna stepped in front of the teen boy running out of Hyer's General Store, taking hold of his arm to stop him.

Then she leaned over the edge of the boardwalk and got sick right there in the street.

"Missus Marshal? You okay?" Hyer came out of the store as she braced her free hand—the one not holding on to the thief—on her knee and straightened.

"Mmm." She hoped he would take her hum for agreement, as she didn't want a scene out here on the street, but she didn't feel okay.

"Danna, darling?"

Oh. Her husband had seen that lovely display. Chas came up behind her and took her arm, letting her release the teen. Hyer was griping, but it didn't seem the boy had stolen more than a handful of candy, so Danna allowed herself to be led off by her concerned husband.

Head spinning, she leaned against her husband's broad shoulder. In the three months they'd been married, she'd become more used to him pampering her.

Right this moment, she didn't mind his arm supporting her one bit.

"Are you still feeling under the weather?" Chas's tone conveyed his worry. "Perhaps you should go see the doctor."

"Just been there," she said, keeping her voice low. Even though the town accepted her now—liked her—she still didn't want everyone knowing her business. "I just need to lie down for a bit."

"But, Danna…"

She pushed away from him, walking toward the jail and their room above it, leaving him no choice but to follow. In a few long strides, he caught up to her and wrapped an arm around her waist. That was nice. She leaned her head against his shoulder again, the queasiness still gripping her.

"You've been ill off and on since we visited your brother at Christmas. Did the doctor know what's wrong?"

"Mmm-hmm. Said I'm much too happy with my new husband and adopted sister, Katy. And that I've had it too easy around here lately."

At the foot of the stairs, Chas swung her around to face him, one eyebrow raised expectantly. "Oh, really? I have to admit, it *has* been quiet around Calvin since you put all those ornery coots in jail."

"Since *we* put them in jail, with Judge Allen's help," she corrected, smoothing the collar of his chambray shirt. He dressed more like a cowboy now, though he still wore his black suit for fancy occasions.

He was right. Other than a few drunken brawls, there hadn't been a hint of trouble in Calvin in the last three months. She'd almost been…bored.

Chas touched her chin, turning her face up to meet

his intense gaze. She could still see the worry behind his expression and wanted to erase it.

"Danna?" he asked.

Suddenly shy, she lowered her eyes to stare at her hand on his chest. "How would you feel about…oh, in about seven and a half months…meeting Baby Marshal?"

His stunned silence said more than any words could. Worried, she looked up, just in time to see a humongous smile split his face.

"We're in the family way?" he asked. Then, not waiting for an answer, he whooped loud enough that she was sure they heard it all the way across town. So much for everyone not knowing her news yet. But she couldn't be happier.

* * * * *

Dear Reader,

Thank you for reading my first novel! From the moment I "met" Danna, I knew I had to tell the story that this courageous, stubborn woman whispered in my ear. And with God's help, I have. I hope you enjoyed the adventure as much as I have.

To find out about book news, read short stories, and be a part of giveaways, please visit my website: www.lacywilliams.net.

Lacy Williams

QUESTIONS FOR DISCUSSION

1. Chas has never met anyone like Danna. What things make her different from the other women he has met before?

2. Have you ever met anyone who was so different from yourself that you weren't sure how to relate to them? What things made that person different from you?

3. Chas and Danna were able to find common ground and work together. Give an example of a time when you've had to find common ground with someone else, and how it changed your relationship.

4. In the beginning of this book, Chas is consumed by guilt for things that happened in his past. Have you or someone you know felt this way? What event caused this guilt?

5. Have you been able to accept God's forgiveness for your past? Why or why not?

6. Danna has a hard time fitting in with other women because of her clothes and her job. Give an example of a time when you felt you didn't fit in.

7. How did you overcome the barriers of not fitting in?

8. Until Chas came along, Danna accepted the way others saw her as reality (for example, she didn't

believe she was pretty because no one ever told her so, and because she did not dress in a womanly fashion). Has there been a person in your life who challenged your perceptions about yourself? Tell about that person.

9. Throughout the book, Danna works hard to try to take care of everything by herself. Tell about a time when you realized you couldn't complete a task or get through something on your own. Did you have to rely on someone else to finish?

10. There are several things in the book that allowed Chas to confront his past and begin to heal. What were they?

11. Can you think of other things that might have helped?

12. Throughout the book, Danna wants to have a family. Were there other characters in the book that took on family-type roles in her life (e.g. big sister, little brother)?

13. Name some people in your life who have been like family, but who weren't blood relations.

14. What made these relationships so special?

15. Do you think Danna and Chas will live happily ever after? Why or why not?

INSPIRATIONAL

Inspirational romances to warm your heart & soul.

Love Inspired.
HISTORICAL

TITLES AVAILABLE NEXT MONTH

Available September 13, 2011

COURTING THE ENEMY
Renee Ryan

ROCKY MOUNTAIN HOMECOMING
Pamela Nissen

THE RELUCTANT OUTLAW
Smoky Mountain Matches
Karen Kirst

THE ARISTOCRAT'S LADY
Mary Moore

LIHCNM0811

REQUEST YOUR FREE BOOKS!

2 FREE INSPIRATIONAL NOVELS
PLUS 2
FREE
MYSTERY GIFTS

Love Inspired
HISTORICAL
INSPIRATIONAL HISTORICAL ROMANCE

YES! Please send me 2 FREE Love Inspired® Historical novels and my 2 FREE mystery gifts (gifts are worth about $10). After receiving them, if I don't wish to receive any more books, I can return the shipping statement marked "cancel". If I don't cancel, I will receive 4 brand-new novels every month and be billed just $4.49 per book in the U.S. or $4.99 per book in Canada. That's a saving of at least 22% off the cover price. It's quite a bargain! Shipping and handling is just 50¢ per book in the U.S. and 75¢ per book in Canada.* I understand that accepting the 2 free books and gifts places me under no obligation to buy anything. I can always return a shipment and cancel at any time. Even if I never buy another book, the two free books and gifts are mine to keep forever.

102/302 IDN FEHF

Name _____ (PLEASE PRINT) _____

Address _____ Apt. # _____

City _____ State/Prov. _____ Zip/Postal Code _____

Signature (if under 18, a parent or guardian must sign)

Mail to the Reader Service:
IN U.S.A.: P.O. Box 1867, Buffalo, NY 14240-1867
IN CANADA: P.O. Box 609, Fort Erie, Ontario L2A 5X3
Not valid for current subscribers to Love Inspired Historical books.

Want to try two free books from another series?
Call 1-800-873-8635 or visit www.ReaderService.com.

* Terms and prices subject to change without notice. Prices do not include applicable taxes. Sales tax applicable in N.Y. Canadian residents will be charged applicable taxes. Offer not valid in Quebec. This offer is limited to one order per household. All orders subject to credit approval. Credit or debit balances in a customer's account(s) may be offset by any other outstanding balance owed by or to the customer. Please allow 4 to 6 weeks for delivery. Offer available while quantities last.

Your Privacy—The Reader Service is committed to protecting your privacy. Our Privacy Policy is available online at www.ReaderService.com or upon request from the Reader Service.

We make a portion of our mailing list available to reputable third parties that offer products we believe may interest you. If you prefer that we not exchange your name with third parties, or if you wish to clarify or modify your communication preferences, please visit us at www.ReaderService.com/consumerchoice or write to us at Reader Service Preference Service, P.O. Box 9062, Buffalo, NY 14269. Include your complete name and address.

LIH11B

When private eye Skylar Grady is kidnapped and abandoned in the Arizona desert, she knows her investigation has someone scared enough to kill. Tracker Jonas Sampson finds her—but can he keep her safe? Read on for a sneak preview of LONE DEFENDER by Shirlee McCoy, from her HEROES FOR HIRE series.

"The storm isn't the only thing I'm worried about." He didn't slow, and she had no choice but to try to keep up.

"What do you mean?"

"I've seen camp fires the past couple of nights. You said someone drove you out here and left you—"

"I'm not just saying it. It happened."

"A person who goes to that kind of effort probably isn't going to sit around hoping that you're dead."

"You think a killer is on our trail?"

"I think there's a possibility. Conserve your energy. You may need it before the night is over."

"I still think—"

"Shh." He slid his palm up her arm, the warning in his touch doing more than words to keep her silent. She waited, ears straining for some sign that they weren't alone.

Nothing but dead quiet, and a stillness that filled Skylar with dread.

A soft click broke the silence.

She was on the ground before she could think, Jonas right beside her.

She turned her head, met his eyes.

"That was a gun safety."

He pressed a finger to her lips, pulled something from beneath his jacket.

A Glock.

They weren't completely helpless, then.

He wasn't, at least.

She felt a second of relief, and then Jonas was gone, and she was alone again.

Alone, cowering on the desert floor, waiting to be picked off by an assassin's bullet.

No way. There was absolutely no way she was going to die without a fight.

A soft shuffle came from her left, and she stilled as a shadow crept toward her. She launched herself toward him, realizing her weakness as she barreled into the man's chest, bounced backward, landed hard. She barely managed to dive to the left as the man aimed a pistol, pulled the trigger. The bullet slammed into the ground a foot from where she'd been, and she was up again.

Fight or die.

It was as simple as that.

Don't miss LONE DEFENDER by Shirlee McCoy, available September 2011 from Love Inspired Suspense.